CRUEL LEGACY

CRUEL LEGACY

CRUEL BOOK THREE

K.A. LINDE

Visit my website at
www.kalinde.com

Join my newsletter for free books and exclusive content!
www.kalinde.com/subscribe

Cover Designer: Sarah Hansen, Okay Creations,
www.okaycreations.com
Photography: Sara Eirew Photography,
www.saraeirew.com
Editor: Jovana Shirley, Unforeseen Editing,
www.unforeseenediting.com

This book is a work of fiction. Names, characters, places, and incidents
either are products of the author's imagination or are used fictitiously.
Any resemblance to actual persons, living or dead, events, or locales is
entirely coincidental.

ISBN-13: 978-1948427265

To 'The Count of Monte Cristo'
Revenge never looked so good.

PART I
IT ALL STARTED AT A
MASQUERADE IN
MANHATTAN

CHAPTER 1

NATALIE

Elizabeth,

We met last month at Trinity for Jane Devney's club opening in Midtown. I was wearing a one-of-a-kind Cunningham Couture piece, and I'm reaching out to you today at your insistence. I will be attending Jane's New Year's Eve Masquerade and want something to blow everyone away. Something no one else has seen. And you're the only one I'd go to for this.

I'll be back to the city for a fitting the day of, but you already have my measurements. Have your assistant reach out if you need anything.

Best,

Natalie

"*I*'m still shocked you had the balls to send that," Amy muttered. "You sound like an entitled brat."

"Reality check, Ames. That's the level of confidence and bravado she's used to dealing with."

K.A. LINDE

"Don't get me wrong, I'm impressed. You didn't even give her an option to say no."

I chewed on my bottom lip. No, I hadn't. I'd rewritten the email about a hundred times before I got the tone right. The self-righteous, take-no-bullshit attitude that demanded and didn't request. While also including enough flattery that Elizabeth would give me a chance.

A chance was all I needed anyway. Because without Elizabeth's business card, I wouldn't have a dress. Unless I asked Jane, and I wasn't ready for that yet.

"Well, it worked at least," I said to Amy.

"Fuck yes, it did."

I'd been afraid it wouldn't. Either Elizabeth's assistant hadn't bothered to check with her before agreeing to the dress or, as I'd suspected, she and Katherine Van Pelt weren't as close as family just because they were now both married to Percy men.

I didn't care which it was. Either was good for me right now.

We took the elevator to Elizabeth's studio and strode through the glass door as if I owned the place. I'd thought that it would be a disaster zone, as it had been backstage for the fashion show at Trinity. But without the models, the studio was a well-oiled machine. Elizabeth's assistant barked out orders like a drill sergeant. Sewing machines hummed. Fabric covered the space. Final details were being sewed onto mannequins. Row after row of purple Cunningham Couture garment bags hung on racks, and a half-dozen sumptuous gowns were still waiting for final approval.

I cleared my throat. "Excuse me."

4

Amy shot me a look and mumbled under her breath, "One more time with feeling."

Jesus, she was right. I couldn't half-ass this first encounter. I had to make them believe it. But this came about as naturally to me as it did Hermione pretending to be Bellatrix Lestrange when they infiltrated Gringotts.

"I'm here for my fitting. Let's get this over with. I have a busy day ahead of me," I snapped.

Elizabeth's assistant jerked his attention toward us. His look of annoyance immediately shifted to a welcoming mask. "Miss Bishop, you made it." He strode across the busy room and took my hand. "Pleasure to meet you again." He shook Amy's hand next. "I'm Pierre, executive assistant to Elizabeth Cunningham. Come right this way. We secured a private room for you to check your dress before the event tonight."

"Perfect," I said.

We entered a brightly lit dressing room.

"Make yourselves comfortable. I'm going to bring the dress in. Elizabeth picked out an exquisite piece for you."

Amy and I exchanged a look. So, Elizabeth *did* know. Interesting.

Pierre exited back to the main room, leaving us alone to investigate. Champagne chilled in an ice bucket on a table filled with finger food and tiny French pastries. Amy helped herself. In a second, I had a mimosa in hand. I left her to the indulgent treats that I probably needed to forego if I wanted to fit into this dress. A full week of nothing but cake frosting straight from the container was probably not going to help my figure. Though it had helped my mental state.

I held my glass aloft as I stepped onto a pedestal before

a trifold mirror. The figure looking back at me showed my thin face, baby-blue eyes, and pink lips, the Cupid's bow as prominent as ever. My silvery-white locks flowed down over my shoulders, covering my breasts in the plain white T-shirt and black jeans I'd donned for the occasion. Amy had done research and decided that was what models wore to these sorts of things.

And while I saw myself looking back, I didn't *feel* like myself.

A week ago, I'd been dating Lewis Warren, hoping against hope that we had some sort of future in this messed up Upper East Side world. Instead, it turned out that he'd kept a file on me that revealed how he'd manipulated me into dating him and then stalked me. He'd photographed me back home in Charleston, purchased my building here in New York, watched video surveillance of my apartment, and most demoralizing, gone behind my back to read my manuscripts. Something I found beyond unforgivable. When we'd broken up, he'd gone even further and ruined any chance of my dream career as an author. I was blacklisted.

Between that and Katherine revealing my pen name, my world had shattered. And I was being pieced back together out of order. Into a deep, dark, vengeful version of the Natalie I had been. The one that said I was ready to burn this city to the ground, and nothing would stop me.

"So, what are you going to do about Penn?"

I sighed out heavily. "I'll handle it."

Amy stared at me in a way that said exactly what she thought about that. Before she could voice her concerns, Pierre reappeared then with a purple garment bag. He

6

unzipped it to reveal a long, flowing gown that made my eyes widen with both excitement and alarm.

"Whoa," Amy whispered from across the room.

"That's...wow."

"You did say you wanted to blow everyone away."

I nodded mutely.

There was a twinkle in Pierre's eye as if he had been waiting for someone this daring. "Well, this is the dress."

I scanned it, admiring the simplicity coupled with its inherent boldness. A statement number that said I wasn't slinking away into the shadows and letting the Upper East Side chew me up and spit me out. I was here to play.

"Let's do it."

A FEW HOURS LATER, I pulled up to Trinity in a limo. Nerves quaked through my body, but I refused to let it show. Not for this crowd.

Flashes went off at the first glimpse of my Louboutin heel and continued as they took in my daring Elizabeth Cunningham gown. The mostly sheer material fell down my body in a form-fitting sheath, giving it the appearance of artful lingerie. Black accents covered my full breasts and ran down the middle of my body. They crawled up from my feet as if I stood in a ring of black flames. It was fitting, as I was rising up from the ashes.

My fingers moved to the edge of my black lace mask that obscured the upper half of my face, and I checked to make sure it was secure. I hastily dropped my hand and stepped into the spotlight.

Alone.

Alone for the very first time.

Every time I'd ever made this sort of appearance in the past, I'd had an Upper East Sider crutch to help me through it. First, Katherine, then Penn, and then Lewis or Jane. But now, it was just me. Just me taking on the world. And I wasn't going to cower.

I raised my chin, put a devilish smirk on my cherry-red-painted lips, and stepped into the spotlight.

Despite the fact that I hadn't been born into this life and had no real money of my own, my name was on their lips. The scandal from last week had given me a sense of notoriety. If I hadn't returned, perhaps I would have floated away into obscurity, but since I was here, now I was someone. All on my own.

The crew had given me that. Penn had given me that by drawing me into this world with a bet. Katherine had given me that by making me a pet project and then a household name. Lewis had given me that simply by putting me on the arm of a Warren. Even Jane had given me a piece of it by including me, befriending me.

And she was the one who had told me to fake it. I intended to heed her advice.

I posed for a few carefully positioned pictures, slowly making my way up the red carpet. Giving everyone a view of the dress, of me.

Take your fill, boys.

I shot them one more devious smile and then stepped across the threshold into Trinity. It was bustling with partygoers. I had no idea who would be here tonight. Which Upper East Siders I would run into during this. But I wasn't here for them. I was here to be seen and photographed and gossiped about. *Mission accomplished.*

A passing waiter offered me a glass of champagne,

which I took with relish. I could do this. I could see through the glossy shine of this world. The rhinestone society polished to look like diamonds.

Money couldn't hide the sewage, and when I was done with them, money wouldn't save them from it either.

Now for the real fun.

I withdrew my phone from the matching black clutch and read the waiting text from Penn.

I'm here. You didn't really give me specifics. Where should I meet you?

My lips curled in excitement as I sent my reply.

Do you want to play a game?

I'm listening...

If you can find me, you can have me.

CHAPTER 2

NATALIE

*T*his was the moment that would determine it all.

Would Penn play the game? Would he chase me here, as I suspected he would? He'd said that he wanted this. That he would wait for me. But a week of radio silence as I'd figured out my next move meant anything could happen.

Especially considering what had happened to me.

I wasn't the same person I'd been when we had sex in that hotel suite at The Plaza. I wasn't the same person who had turned him away because I wasn't ready for a relationship. I was someone...something else entirely.

I didn't know where that left me.

Let alone us.

But I dared to find out.

I had to.

My eyes skimmed the crowd as I sipped my glass of champagne. My dress drew looks like a moth to a flame. People whispering behind their hands. I was sure they were explaining who I was. The risk I'd taken in showing up tonight. And I just tilted my chin up and let them look, let them talk. With luck, it'd get back to the people I wanted it to. It would snowball from there.

I smiled viciously at the thought of Katherine's face when she found out that I was back in the city. But that wasn't here or now.

I couldn't predict how Katherine would react. But I was making my own way now. No longer waiting with the ball in her court.

Right now, I needed to focus on Penn.

My phone buzzed, and I glanced down at the message that had come in from him.

Fuck.

I laughed despite myself.

Yes, that's the idea.

What are you wearing?

That's cheating.

Any hints?

I took another sip and tried to reel in the giddy feeling at the center of my chest. Penn was dangerous in every way to my heart. But I figured I should give him something.

I flipped to the camera and took a picture of the crown necklace dangling at my throat. The crown that he had given me a year ago. The crown that I'd thrown at his feet when I found out about the goddamn bet. The crown that he'd returned to me when he decided to pursue me again.

Even though my heart still skipped when I was near him, I'd been certain that I'd never go back to him. Never allow myself to fall into his trap again. And yet, here I was, in his necklace. Maybe I'd catch him in my trap this time.

I approve.

The pad of my finger traced his comment before I returned the phone to my clutch. He'd find me. I was sure of it. Not that I intended to make it easy for him.

I went looking for him in hopes of drawing out our game and the anticipation. But I found Jane first.

Jane Devney was a force of nature. Shoulder-length ash-blonde hair and hazel eyes with a small stature that might make you overlook her. But she had stepped into the Upper East Side and claimed it as her own. She'd opened Trinity with sheer willpower and the enormity of her connections.

Tonight she looked stunning in a rose-gold dress as she clutched on to the arm of Court Kensington. Penn's brother looked so much like him that it was sometimes jarring. While they were similar in looks, they were opposites in personality. Even if he wasn't as bad as Penn had always made him out to be...or at least to me.

I evaded Jane. I wasn't ready to see her yet. Or to hear her excitement at me being back and how she was right that it had all blown over. When I was certain that it hadn't.

I escaped into a crowd of people and came out on the other side to find Penn standing there with none other than Harmony Cunningham, the daughter of the designer whose dress I wore currently.

My smile disappeared. I knew that Penn and Harmony had history. He'd used her to make Katherine jealous—or so Lewis had said. Right now, I didn't know what to think of them. She was standing awfully close with her hand on his arm. Not that he looked pleased by it.

I hated the jealousy that settled in my stomach. It was an emotion I wanted to snuff out.

I retrieved my phone, snapped a picture of them standing together, and sent it to Penn with one line attached.

Wrong girl.

Then I creeped deeper into the crowd, keeping my eye on him as Harmony left his side and he checked the message. I reveled in the smile that lit up his features. He looked as sexy and alluring as James Bond. Dark hair artfully styled, blue eyes wide and bold, tuxedo crisp and tailored to his incredible build. But it went beyond that. To the casual confidence that had been bred into him. From living in this world with its expectations and scandal and silver spoons.

He was an enigma. It was what had drawn me to him in the first place. The Manhattan royalty playboy who wanted a different life. Who was so much more than what he portrayed to the world. The morality that he so fiercely tried to cultivate. The duality of his character that strove against his upbringing for a better life.

13

We all stumbled. We didn't all get back up.

I circled Penn like a lioness stalking her prey.

He might be coming for me. But I was keeping him in my sights. Drawing it out until he got closer.

I turned away for a second to grab another glass of champagne, but when I looked for him again, he was gone.

My eyes widened in surprise and then scanned the room. Where the hell had he gone?

I walked carefully around the perimeter of the club, trying to figure out where I'd lost him. Every guy was in a tuxedo. Everyone was in a mask. That was the point. That was the fun. But I'd thought I had this figured out.

Then I felt strong hands brace my hips, a hot body press into my back, the flush of a breath against my neck. My body tensed at the first brush of his lips against the most sensitive spot behind my ear.

"Found you," he breathed.

I relaxed back into him. "How did you know it was me?"

"I'd recognize you anywhere."

"Even with my hair up?" I teased.

My sheet of silvery-white hair was my most telling feature. And I'd purposely had Amy pin it up so that only a few tendrils fell down around my face and over my shoulder. Otherwise I'd have stood out like a spotlight on a dark night.

"I know the way you move," he said, our hips swaying to the tempo of the music. "My hands know every inch of your body. They long ago memorized your gentle curves." He slid his hands forward over my hips. "I know the shape of you, the sensuous way you walk, the confidence in every step."

Something got stuck in my throat at his words. I tried to push it down. Down and away. "Oh?"

"Oh, yes. With your shoulders back, chin up, eyes steady." His lips trailed down my neck, capturing me completely. "You might not have been born into this world, but you carry yourself as if you belong in every situation. Even when you're terrified."

"I'm not terrified," I said hoarsely.

"Of course not." He sounded disbelieving.

Maybe he wasn't a hundred percent wrong. I was afraid of this world, of failing. But I wouldn't fail. I couldn't.

I turned in his arms and wrapped mine around his neck, staring up into his dark mask. I wanted nothing more than to peel it from his face and look up into his perfect features. But I wouldn't. Not yet.

"Well, you found me. I guess that means that you can have me."

"I guess it does."

"How exactly do you want me?" I purred seductively.

"In every way," he said seriously.

"Shh," I said, pressing a finger to his lips. "Don't complicate things."

"Is this all it is then?"

I stared up into those big blue eyes, willing him to see the truth. "Would you be mad if it was?"

He pursed his lips. "This doesn't feel like you."

I laughed at his words and ran my hands up into his hair. "Doesn't it?"

A muscle flickered in his jaw at my nonanswer. Because of course, this wasn't me. I wasn't *me* anymore. That was what this world did to people. It changed them. He was the one who had taught me that. And he'd been right.

"I thought you said that you wanted me," I told him.

"I do."

"Just not like this?"

His hands roamed from their position at my hips, up, up, up until his thumbs ran under my breasts. "I want you like this."

"This is what I want," I told him. "You said you'd wait for me. However I was."

"I knew that you'd still be hurt after what happened, but this isn't exactly..."

I stepped back, aching with the absence of his hands. But Penn was already pulling me back into him.

"You don't have to play games with me."

"Who said I was playing games?" My lips coyly curved upward.

"You forget who I am. I know it when I see it."

"I'm offering myself up, Penn." I spread my arms wide. "Here I am. Take me."

"You're just offering sex," he corrected.

I lowered my arms with a sigh. "Is it ever just sex with you, Penn?"

His voice turned low and gravelly as he dragged me tight against him. "Not with you."

Then his lips were against mine. And I forgot about how I had planned to keep him at a distance. I forgot about Amy's warning that there was no way I could handle Penn Kensington. No one could handle him. It wasn't possible. I forgot everything.

There was a reason that I'd fallen for him seven years ago on one blissful night in Paris. Why he'd won me over in the Hamptons a year ago. Why I'd never been able to get him out of my system for the next year. Not even while I was dating someone else.

Penn Kensington had ruined me for all other men.

And this one kiss proved that all over again.

CHAPTER 3

NATALIE

*P*enn's fingers reached for the satin ribbon of my mask, but I held him back.

"Not yet," I breathed.

A question lingered on his lips. I wanted to answer that question. The one that said we didn't need to wait. He'd already found me.

But there was a sensuality...and anonymity to the mask. It made me daring. It brought me back to the giddy feeling I'd had when I was young and innocent and sitting on top of the world. I needed that tonight. I needed it now and every night after if I hoped to survive the Upper East Side.

"Later," I assured him.

"Now," he said, stealing another kiss.

I indulged in the sweet taste of him. "Make it worth my while."

His hand slipped into mine. Our fingers laced together.

"Then let's get out of here."

I didn't have to nod. He could read the answer in my eyes.

Yes.

We glided out of the party as quickly as I'd come. I had no concept of time. Only that the city was packed with New Year's Eve revelers, spanning out from Times Square and filling the already-crowded streets. Penn flagged down a cab. If I'd been in anything other than a one-of-a-kind Elizabeth Cunningham and Christian Louboutin heels, then I would have said we could brave the walk to his place on the Upper East Side. But it seemed pretty impossible at this point.

The cab crawled inch by inch through the traffic and away from the mayhem. Away from the center of the Big Apple and the ball that would drop in front of the entire world. For years as a girl, I'd stay up late with my sister, Melanie, and later Amy to watch the musical talent and celebrities grace the stage. Now, I was in New York City for the spectacle, and I had no interest in being surrounded by a mass of people in the freezing cold.

Everything looked more glamorous through a lens. The reality was much more lackluster. Like finding out your idol was just a person after all. Making all the same mistakes you'd always made.

"Finally," Penn muttered once the cab stopped in front of his apartment.

He paid the outrageous fare and then helped me out of the cab. My nerve wavered for a split second. The last time I'd been at his place, I'd found myself there after an argument with Lewis. It should have been one of the many clues that Penn and I couldn't escape each other. Even when we hadn't been expressly sexual, I'd still gone to him. He'd provided a means of safety. A circle of trust. Or at least, a semblance of it.

But I couldn't stop now. And, frankly, I didn't want to.

There was a reason I'd come here that night. There was a reason I was here now. I wasn't a hundred percent sure where all of this was heading. I wasn't sure if I was even ready to make the next move. But I'd be lying to him and myself if I said that I didn't want something. Despite the anger and pain...I still wanted to find out what that was.

We took the elevator up to his penthouse suite overlooking Central Park. Penn immediately stepped in front of me when it dinged on the top floor.

"Totle!" he called.

And then a ten-pound gray Italian greyhound puppy bounded toward us across the living room. He was all long limbs and awkward proportions. His tail whipped back and forth, and his eyes lit up at the sight of us together.

"I'm going to try to save you from him. He'll ruin that dress," he said, snatching up the puppy before he could jump onto me. Penn cradled Totle like an overexcited baby.

"Hey, buddy." I scratched his head and gave him a big kiss. "You're just so cute, aren't you? Is your dad taking good care of you? Or are you deeply neglected and need some time with me?"

Totle answered by licking my face. I laughed and scratched his floppy ears.

"I'm going to take him out real quick. Make yourself at home."

I nodded and stepped into the apartment while he

grabbed Totle's leash and descended with the puppy. Penn's place was how I remembered it. Though slightly less messy than the time I had unexpectedly turned up. His worn leather notebook rested on the wooden coffee table next to a fountain pen. His philosophy journal articles had been straightened into a neat pile on the other corner. Nothing was out of place. Which was crazy since he was inherently messy when he was working. He liked to leave coffee cups and whiskey glasses all over the place. Loose paper lying haphazardly across his desk. Books strewn in some order that only his brain could comprehend. Because that brilliant brain of his worked best in a cluttered environment.

For it to be this meticulous, he must have been anticipating taking me home. I'd let him know to meet me at Trinity. A smile quirked on my lips that he'd been so presumptuous. But what could I say? He wasn't wrong.

I stepped over to the liquor cabinet and retrieved two whiskey glasses. My fingers trailed over the various bottles and decanters before selecting the prettiest bottle and pouring each of us a glass. Liquid courage never hurt anyone.

I carried the drinks back to the neatly arranged coffee table when Penn returned with Totle. My gaze scanned over his features that had been carefully hidden by the mask, which now dangled from his hand. It wasn't a particularly large mask, but somehow seeing those high cheekbones and bright blue eyes unobstructed was so much more satisfying.

"No mask?" I breathed.

"I got weird looks," he said as he scooped up the little dog and carried him over to me.

"Fair."

"I see you took 'make yourself at home' literally," he said, nodding toward the alcohol.

"Can't blame me." I scratched behind Totle's ears, and he nuzzled his head into my hand. "God, he's so cute."

"Me or the dog?"

I grinned up at him. "The dog. Obviously."

"Obviously," Penn repeated.

He set the puppy down on the couch where he promptly curled up into a tiny ball on top of a blanket. His big, dark eyes staring up at us, saying, *Love me.*

"And now yours," he said.

His hands moved to the ribbons holding on my own mask, and I let him pull the string, releasing it. He caught the edges of the mask and removed it from my face. And with it, that last line of defense was stripped away. I was bare before him, even still in clothes that adorned my body like armor.

"That's better."

"Ah, the physical mask," I purred as I passed him the glass of bourbon. "So much less potent than the mental ones."

He arched an eyebrow. "Since when do you wear a mask for anyone?"

"You just took mine off."

"Hmm," he murmured, unconvinced.

"Yours comes and goes though." I took a sip of the bourbon and felt the liquid forge a pathway for the flame.

"Not with you."

"Ha!" I said with an exaggerated laugh. "When it's convenient for you."

"I don't have one on right now."

"Good," I told him, slipping an inch closer and staring up into the face of the man who had tricked me so completely. Who I fought to hate ... and forgive ... and decide. The face of someone eternally torn between right and wrong.

"Tell me about the last week, Natalie." His voice was strained.

"What's to tell?" I asked. I downed another swallow of the liquid.

"Don't bullshit me. We both know that you went home, messed up from that thing with Katherine. Then I didn't hear from you until this."

"So?"

He sighed and set his glass down, untouched. "How are you?"

"As well as expected. How are you?"

I wanted to confide in him about what had happened the last week. What Lewis had done to light my career on fire. The place I'd sunk into to deal with it. And the way I was pulling myself up, hand over hand, to escape it. But I didn't. I wasn't ready. Not yet.

"Nat…"

"What do you want me to say?"

"Just talk to me."

"Or," I breathed, running my hand up the front of his tuxedo, "we could *not* talk."

He chuckled softly. "You're determined to keep me at a distance."

"No, I'm not." And I wasn't. But I couldn't do this right now. "It's New Year's Eve, Penn. You want to talk feelings. And I want to enjoy the evening."

"We can't talk and then enjoy the evening?"

"You got me back to your place. Hasn't anyone told you not to play with your food?" I said dramatically but with a hint of a smile.

His powerful hands came to my arms. Those long fingers trailed their way up to my shoulders. The pads digging gently into my sensitive skin as he moved to my neck. My throat bobbed as his thumbs dragged from the hollow of my throat up to my chin. He commanded me in that moment, tilting my chin upward and then to the side, exposing my throat to him. I looked at him out of the corner of my eye as my pulse jumped in excitement. His thumb lingered along my jawline as he took his time to examine every inch of me before sliding back down the side of my neck.

He dropped one featherlight kiss to the space on my neck he'd just caressed. "Are you saying that I should eat you?"

"Devour me whole," I breathed, still trapped in his heated gaze.

He didn't respond, just slipped his hands into his pockets, as he'd done so many times before, and strode in a slow circle around me. I stayed perfectly still. I was no longer the apex predator in the room. And he watched me with complete confidence and all the control.

I'd surrendered it to him when I entered his apartment.

Penn stopped at my back. I didn't move. Hardly even breathed. Was he going to undress me? Take me right here, right now in my Cunningham dress? Or do nothing?

Sometimes, it amazed me that I knew Penn so well and still couldn't predict what he was going to do. He kept me on my toes. And while I wanted to give in, a part of me coiled, waiting for the rug-pull. Waiting for this to be a trick, too.

It was the waiting that nearly did me in. I couldn't relax with someone at my back. I'd had one too many knives stabbed through it.

But then I felt Penn's hands in my mass of silvery-white hair. My eyes fluttered closed at the feel of him touching me. Something eased in my chest. I breathed out in relief before I realized what he was doing.

A pin pinged on the floor. Then another.

The pins that Amy had carefully put my hair up with earlier that day fell to the ground. And as Penn removed more and more, he loosened the strands of my hair until it fell down to the middle of my back like a waterfall whose dam had been broken. His fingers slid up into the strands, checking to make sure he'd gotten them all. When he was satisfied he slowly massaged my scalp until I was practically swaying with sleep from the relaxation.

He collected all of my hair in one hand and then put it over one of my shoulders. Then he pressed one more kiss into my neck.

"I like it better down."

My heart thrummed in response. "I don't wear it up often."

But he wasn't finished. He found the zipper on the Cunningham dress and tugged it all the way down. I slid the straps off of my shoulders and let the priceless material fall down my narrow hips to pool at my feet.

"Shoes," he demanded.

The Louboutins followed. I faced him then in nothing but nude underwear and his crown necklace.

"Better," he said, his eyes traveling down my naked

body. "You don't need any of that adornment." He tipped my chin up. "You should always be unbridled with a flair of wildfire. Fearless, all-consuming, and so bright that you burn."

My throat bobbed at his words. At the way he cut straight through me.

I was consumed by rage, and I wanted to burn the city to the ground. I was fearless in my desire to make the people pay for what they'd done to me. Finally free and wild.

But not in the way he was talking about. He was seeing me as he had seen me before. The Natalie who had let herself get run over, manipulated, used, and crushed under a stiletto heel. I wouldn't let that happen again.

He must have seen some of that flair in my eyes because his widened. But I didn't back down. I didn't douse the spark that had grown to flames in my eyes. I let him see a part of the person I was now. Let him get his fill.

Then I stepped forward and captured his lips with my own. The tension sizzled between us, flames building, steam rising. The world ceased to exist around us as we set it on fire in that one searing kiss.

CHAPTER 4

NATALIE

$\mathcal{I}$t was all I could do not to rip his tuxedo off. My hands were making quick work of the buttons. Hastily tugging them out of each individual loop. The restraint I'd felt evaporated.

Then Penn's hands grasped each of my bare wrists. My arms were pushed up over my head. The grip tightened until he was once again in complete control.

My breaths came out in hot pants as I stared into his impossibly blue eyes. Dark lashes framing those midnight-ocean orbs that only got wider and wider as his pupils dilated and his gaze shifted down my naked form.

"Tell me this isn't like last time," he instructed.

"It isn't like last time," I said on instinct. At his command. The words were out before I thought of what he was asking.

Last time. When I'd found out about Lewis and we'd fucked like animals. He said yes to me when I confessed I'd always wanted him. But it didn't make it any better. It was pure and primal need. Anger mixed with lust that fed

27

into carnal bliss. Nothing more. I hadn't been able to give anything more then. And he'd accepted it.

The look in his dominating eyes said he wouldn't this time.

"Natalie."

I huffed out a short breath and released the tension in my body. Turning into water against his hard touch. Was it different? This had nothing to do with Lewis. Nothing to do with what came next. I didn't have to do this to reel Penn in. He wanted to talk first and foremost. But I wanted this. And I was tired of holding back. Tired of hating him so much. Of pretending that I didn't want him when I did.

"It's different," I assured him.

He read my own eyes as if he could see all my secrets laid bare before him. He must have approved of what he saw in me because he nodded once. "Then we have all the time in the world."

He stepped forward, releasing my arms, and scooped me up into his. I felt weightless in his grasp as he carried me out of the living room, down the darkened hallway, and into his bedroom.

The space was enchanting in how closely it reflected the professor, whose body was pressed tight to mine. The bookcases filled with tomes and skinny philosophy texts and a row of leather journals. The navy-blue comforter that beckoned as he laid me out like a feast. The glass window that opened onto a balcony overlooking the park, fireworks already bursting in the distance even though it wasn't yet midnight.

I propped myself up on my elbows, so I could get a better view of him. Something had shifted in his features at my acceptance. At whatever he'd seen on my face before he picked me up. Now, he was the Penn Kensington that I'd fallen hopelessly head over heels for. He was all male. Standing taller with those wide shoulders that fell down to his narrow hips. The bulge straining at the front of his slacks. My fingers itched to remove his length and feel that hardness against my skin, in my mouth, but one look from him held me in my place.

He was in control here. We might push and pull, fight, argue, and debate outside of the bedroom. But here, I was his.

No, this wasn't some midnight romp to expunge my anger. This was finally taking back what I wanted despite the costs.

Penn untied the bow tie at his throat and let it hang loose around his neck. Then, he finished where I'd started, unbuttoning his shirt and tugging it from his pants to bare his defined chest before me. I wanted to run my fingers down his chest, lick my way down his abdominal muscles. Feel each ridge under my tongue. Watching and not touching was torture.

And maybe he knew that because one corner of his mouth lifted at my response.

"Tease," I murmured.

"You have no idea," he said with that same heady grin.

"I think I do."

"We'll test your theory."

The heat in his look went straight to my core. "Okay, Professor."

He dropped his shirt off of his shoulders at my comment. He snapped open his slacks and dragged the zipper down, revealing the erection hidden beneath.

"Let's see if you can pass the exam."

"Oh dear," I said, playing along. My body ached all over at his playful words. "I didn't study."

"Who knew that you were such a bad student?" he said. "Let's see how fast you can learn."

"I'm definitely a fast learner," I breathed.

He smirked. "We'll see."

He stepped forward, his erection still straining against his boxer briefs, but he was attentive to me. His fingers hooked into the soft material of my thong, and then he slid it down my body, effortlessly tossing it away. His strong hands came down on my inner thighs, spreading me wide open before his face.

My pussy pulsed with anticipation and need. He leisurely stroked one finger down my core, and I trembled with the desire for more. More, more, more. I couldn't stop the need. Then he was spreading my lips apart, slicking through my wetness, hitting every nerve ending, and making my back arch off of the bed.

How could one finger make me this fucking needy?

"Don't move," he said, withdrawing.

I pushed toward him and felt a slight smack against my pussy. I yelped at the same time fire struck me with desire.

"I said, don't move."

I froze in place. Torn between wanting to move while demanding more than the little he was giving me, the torture I was enduring, and following directions so that I could get more. My eyes tracked him across the room to where the sound system was located.

Because, of course.

Penn liked his music. I'd almost forgotten. Indie music,

as unknown as possible, was his preference. Though I knew he also liked some mainstream stuff if he was pushed for it.

The melody picked up, and my smile grew as I forgot all about my needs. "Is this obscure enough for you?"

"It felt poignant. I do have a taste for timing," he said with a hint of the pain he'd felt in the last year touching his eyes.

"I love it," I breathed as "This Year's Love" by David Gray filled the room through surround sound speakers.

When he returned to me, the pain was gone, but I could feel the tension in the room. The tension of a year of separation. A year of fractured trust. A year of other people who never quite satisfied.

And I wished that I could wipe the slate clean. Start over. Fresh and shiny new, but I couldn't. It wasn't possible to erase the pain we'd caused each other. There was no do-over. This wasn't a video game. We didn't have unlimited lives. Just this one. So while it hurt, it had also somehow brought us to this moment. While it was far from perfect, it was still perfection. Perfection to imagine that I could trust him enough for sex after what he'd done. Perfection to imagine that he could trust me enough to be intimate and vulnerable after what I'd done.

Penn slipped out of his pants. I admired the strong lines of his thighs. The pure strength and control from a methodical obsession with running. He wasn't overly bulky but so defined. The very shape of him aroused me in a way that I had never understood about myself until him. Everything about our connection made me want to be adventurous. Break all my boundaries. Lay myself bare.

"Where's your head?" he asked softly.

"I was cramming for the exam."

He chuckled. Then his hands came down on my thighs, and he yanked my body toward him until my ass nearly fell off the bed. A gasp escaped my mouth, and then he was between my legs. No gentle coaxing or teasing, just tongue straight to my clit. Another gasp followed, but this one was of a wholly different nature.

This one had all to do with the motion of his tongue swirling around my most sensitive area. The flick against that nub. The sucking and gentle, unexpected nibble that had my eyes rolling into the back of my head and wetness pooling in the exact place his fingers were stroking to life.

I could feel my orgasm right on the verge, close enough that I could reach out and grab it. But as if Penn knew that, he slowed his strokes, pressed a kiss to my clit, and then glanced up at me with a devilish look on his princely features. How could someone that good-looking be so very bad?

"Not yet," he told me.

As if I had an option.

"Please," I asked him because I wasn't above begging here.

This was nothing compared to my finger or a vibrator. This was prolonged need that shook me to my core and made me incapable of functioning beyond the precise thing that he was doing to me. And right now, that was circling my pussy opening like he was about to finger-fuck it at any moment. And the wonder of *when* made it all the more intense.

But he didn't stop. He continued on as if he could do this all day. Bring me to the edge and then pull me back and then bring me forward again and again. My body protested, and yet I'd give anything for more of this. Whatever he was giving.

"Are you ready to come for me?" he asked, flicking his tongue against my clit again.

I nearly jumped off the bed at the unexpected motion.

"Yes, yes, yes," I murmured.

"And do you want my fingers?"

"Please, Penn," I panted.

"Tell me where."

My eyes snapped open, and they locked on his. He stared back just as hotly, waiting for my answer. I could see he was holding on to control like a whip, waiting to wield it with a crack.

"Inside me."

"What was that, love?" he purred.

"In my pussy," I gasped out.

At my words, he entered me. One finger delving into my heat, getting the feel for me again. My walls contracted around him, and I whimpered.

"So greedy," he said with a laugh before giving me what my body had not-so-subtly asked for.

A second finger went into me, stretching me but not filling me. I knew what I wanted for that. I knew at this point of the warm-up that I'd give anything for it.

He dipped his head back down to my clit and sucked on me with his fingers buried deep inside me. My body bucked, as the edge I'd been hanging on to came closer and closer.

Then another finger swirled through my wetness. I groaned at the feel, but then he was moving, going lower and lower. I tensed for all of a second in surprise as he pressed the liquid to the pucker of my asshole. But then he gently rubbed me in slow circles, drawing out my orgasm even deeper. Something I hadn't thought possible.

He dipped barely a digit into my back door, and I shattered into pieces. Just the feel of that much stimulation rocked through me like a tidal wave. I had been so close as it was that, by the time he went further, there was no chance I wouldn't come on the spot.

It took a few seconds before I realized the cries of pleasure were coming from me. I tapered off as I came down from my high. I lay back on the bed, my chest heaving, as Penn straightened with a satisfied smile.

"If I'd known that you'd respond that well to anal, I would have started a long time ago."

My cheeks flushed at the comment. "Well, you learn something new every day, Professor."

"I suppose that means, you passed."

I slid off the bed and landed on shaky legs. "Thank god. Wouldn't want a mark on my transcript."

"You're enjoying this," he said, stepping into my space. His hand came to the back of my neck, taking hold of my mass of hair in a way that said he was in control and also like I was going to come again at any moment.

"I am," I gasped out as I tilted my head up to look him in the eye.

"Open your mouth."

I did as I had been told without thinking about it. He inserted the two fingers that had been in my pussy into my waiting mouth. I tasted my own hot desire as I licked his fingers clean of my arousal. His nostrils flared at my easy acceptance and the feel of my lips going to work on him, just like I intended to do to his cock.

My hands reached for the hem of his shorts. He was so

aroused that the tip was jutting out of the top of his boxer briefs. The pad of my finger skimmed the head, glistening with pre-cum. I licked my lips, anxious to get on my knees for him.

"You're going to have to wait for that," he told me with a ragged, barely constrained tone.

"I don't want to wait," I said impishly.

"One touch of your hot mouth, and I'd come all over you."

My smile ticked up at the power of that statement. "What's wrong with that?"

"I'm going to fuck that smart mouth later," he said confidently. "But I need to get inside of you."

My heart skipped a beat at the coarse words that had left his mouth. The sophisticated professor devolving into the sex-god playboy who owned the Upper East Side. It shouldn't have turned me on as much as it did. But fuck, I understood how he ruled his own kingdom. I saw why everyone fell to their feet for him when he growled commands at me and made me eat my own cum off of his fingers. I'd crawl for him. And he knew it.

"I'm yours," I breathed, running my thumb across the tip of his dick one more time before he freed himself entirely, dropping his boxer briefs to the floor.

The song switched to something even I didn't recognize. But the rhythm was hypnotic. The bass rocked through us. The words flowed like silk, driving us together. There was just us, the music, and the clock ticking down to the New Year.

"Mine," he said roughly.

He twisted me in place and then folded me in half at

the waist. My hands reached out to grip the comforter as he temptingly pressed his cock against my opening.

I was primed for him, and still, he teased, pushing the head in and then out, back and forth against my clit until I thought I would burst with waiting for him to take me. But he didn't make me wait long. His hand braced himself against the small of my back as the other gripped my hip before he drove his cock home.

My body shifted forward with the force of his motion, but it wasn't painful. A moan escaped me at the sweet feel of surrender. The pleasurable stretch of being completely full. Then he started moving, and my moan turned into gasps. Out and then fast in. Out and then faster in, slamming into me. Taking my body. Owning my body. Slicing through any last hesitation I'd had that he wouldn't fit.

Penn Kensington had been my first.

Seven years later, still, no one compared to him.

Penn's voice became incoherent as he thrust deep into my pussy and took his pleasure, coupled with my own. Something coiled in my belly, low and urgent. Something begging to get out, to be released. I tensed all over as I felt the first hints of it strike my body.

I clenched down on the comforter hard as he penetrated me one more time, and then I loosed my scream into the bed as it burst forth. I came to new heights, seeing stars in the night sky. I saw the planets and galaxy and even beyond that. I saw heaven in my den of sin.

Penn groaned and grunted loudly as he finished right after me. I felt the sheer force of his orgasm and sighed with pleasure.

It was a minute before he could move again, and my core immediately begged for him to return. A small mewl left my lips in protest, and he chuckled softly, rubbing my back again.

"There's time for round two."

I uneasily stood up and looked at his naked form, his cock still erect, jutting out between us. "There'd better be."

Fireworks exploding noisily behind us kept him from a reply. We both watched the night sky light up with fervor out the window.

Penn stepped back into me with a tender smile. He pulled my mouth to his. A chaste kiss compared to what we'd just shared. But somehow, it fit perfectly. "Happy New Year, Natalie."

"A new year for a new us," I breathed against him.

He grinned at my choice in words. "To a new us."

Then he kissed me again, and we lost the rest of the night to that toast.

CHAPTER 5

NATALIE

I stretched like a cat as I woke to a brand-new world. A distinctly delicious male figure slept soundly on the other side of the bed. And between us was the smallest and yet *largest* ten-pound dog in existence.

I rubbed Totle's belly and planted a kiss on his head. "You're so lucky that you're cute."

Pulling Totle's sleeping body closer to me, I rolled over him and onto Penn's side. Then I wrapped my arms around his waist like I was the big spoon and sighed in pleasure. This felt right. Unbelievably right.

Like maybe I could live in this life right here, right now. Maybe I didn't need anything else but this. Especially after the night that we'd had.

But this wasn't the real world. Penn's room was like a magical fortress that no one could possibly access. They'd have to slay a fire-breathing dragon to get inside. And there were no white knights in this city. Only dark sorcerers and evil witches set to ruin a princess's life.

As soon as we left this sanctuary, we'd have to deal with that world out there again. Which I knew and hated and wished weren't true. But Penn had told me time and time again that, once you were in on the Upper East Side, there was no out. He was proof of that. And while Katherine was trying to drag me *out* of the Upper East Side by my silvery-white hair, I wasn't here to play nice. I was here to make sure she never hurt anyone ever again.

That meant...the real world had to come into this perfect place earlier than I would have liked.

"I could get used to this," Penn muttered groggily. A yawn broke on the last word, and he rolled over to get a look at me. "Morning."

Despite my dark thoughts, a smile broke across my features at his sleepy greeting. "Good morning."

His hands slipped around my waist, pulling me flush with him. "Last night wasn't a dream."

"That would have been quite a vivid dream."

"They've been vivid before," he confessed.

"Oh?"

"Not like last night, but usually, I'm fucking some sense into you."

I laughed and shook my head. "I don't think it works that way."

"Think it did last night."

I made a disbelieving sound. Men!

He pressed a kiss into my hair. "Don't move. I'm going to take Totle out, and when I get back, I want to return to this discussion."

"You are unbelievable."

He hopped out of bed, revealing the taut contours of

his impressive ass. I bit down on my lip at the sight. God, that body.

"I think you told me that last night, too, but in a slightly different context." He winked at me and then patted the bed near Totle's head. "Come on, Aristotle. Get up, you lazy beast. I have plans for the sex fiend in my bed and want to hurry back."

I snorted as Totle's little head popped up out of the covers, and he trotted toward Penn, who was tugging on clothes to brave the January chill.

"Ten minutes," he assured before disappearing from the room.

I flopped back on the bed.

January. A new year. A new me. A new us.

So absolutely optimistic.

I was going to have to tell him. I'd put it off long enough. And I wasn't looking forward to what was to come. Because I had plans, and I didn't know how he was going to respond. But he was the linchpin. So much of this rested on his shoulders. I could do it without him. I could. The means would be uglier, more volatile.

And then there was the matter of trust. Trusting him with my body. Trusting him with my safety. Those were different than simply trusting him. Believing that, in the end, he wouldn't fuck me over. Just because we could fuck didn't prove anything.

My phone buzzed on the nightstand, bringing me out of my thoughts. I checked the text from Amy.

Ready to head to the apartment whenever you are. How did last night go?

I'll text when I'm leaving Penn's place.

> *I take that to mean...very well? ;)*

Oh, yeah!

> *How'd he take the news?*

Pray for me. I'm about to tell him.

> *Fuck. You need more than prayers.*

I laughed and set the phone back down on the nightstand. She wasn't wrong.

With a sigh, I pushed myself to my feet. My body was sore in all the best ways. I stretched my arms overhead and then stole a pair of sweats and a gray-and-blue Columbia T-shirt from Penn's drawers before heading into the bathroom. I was just pulling the tee on when Penn came back into the bedroom. I could hear Totle eating in the other room.

"This was not what I told you. Those are clothes." He wrapped his arms around my waist. "And you should not be in them."

"Busy day, Dr. Kensington. I'm going to need to borrow these."

"And where exactly are you going?"

I took a deep breath and then slowly released it. "I have to empty out my apartment."

His jaw tightened. "Because of Lewis? Did he force you out?"

"No, but I don't feel comfortable, let alone safe, there any longer. I don't like the idea that he can see when I get to my apartment. That he knows my every move." I shuddered as real fear licked down my spine. "I haven't even been back. I've been staying with Amy at Enzo's place. She's meeting me there to help."

"I can go, too," he said quickly.

"All right. I'm just glad that I got out of my lease. Who knew that threatening to expose the security footage would be enough for a broken lease?"

"Jesus, Nat. You didn't have to do this on your own. Why didn't you let me deal with Lewis?"

I closed my eyes and shook my head before looking back up at him. "I don't know. I just…had to do all of this. I was still so *mad* after what happened. Mad at Lewis and Katherine and this world…" I bit my lip again before admitting, "You."

"Me?" he asked softly. "But I was trying to help."

I nodded. "This time." *I think.* Though I didn't say it.

I didn't say that Lewis's words had gotten in my head. That I didn't know Penn's true motivations behind getting that file that had revealed Lewis's actions. I didn't know if he'd manufactured any of it. And I *hated* having those feelings, but the truth was that Penn had brought me into this world. He'd put the bet on me. He'd tried to break up my relationship with Lewis, no matter what I'd said. Those pesky trust issues couldn't just disintegrate.

"Nat, you do know that I was trying to help, right?"

"Look, we have history, Penn. While I want to think you had all the best intentions, the truth is…no one in this society has perfectly pure intentions. And I didn't know who to believe or what to think. So, it wasn't even

42

possible for me to accept help. Not from you. Not from anyone."

"Okay," he said after a minute. His hands were still balled into fists at his sides. "While that's all true, I want you to know that you are not alone. And you should not have to single-handedly deal with your stalker."

"Yeah," I muttered, "about that."

"What?" His blue eyes searched mine in earnest as if he could see the deep lines of hurt inside me. "What did he do?"

And the fact that he'd automatically known that Lewis had done something worse, something else to destroy me, only made my vehemence solidify. These people. These fucking mongrels ruling from their gilded thrones. I would pull them down piece by piece, so they could never hurt me or anyone else. Ever again.

"Because it always escalates, doesn't it?" I muttered with my jaw clenched.

"Unfortunately."

"He put his weight behind Warren Publishing. They rejected my manuscript and in so many words said I was blacklisted. Because, even though BET ON IT has been selling like hotcakes since my name was revealed in the paper, the tell-all looks bad for them. Oh, and my literary fiction is fucked because I'm a whore, thanks to Katherine."

"Jesus Christ, Natalie. When did this happen?" Penn looked like he was on the verge of marching down to Lewis's apartment and finishing what he'd started the night of Katherine's wedding.

"Thursday," I whispered hoarsely.

Penn paced away from me, cursing violently under his breath. "I'm going to murder him."

"I don't think even *you* can get away with that."

"He's fucking with your *life*, Natalie. How are you so calm?"

I laughed a soft, brittle thing. "You think this is calm? This is the reason I didn't want to talk last night, because I knew how you'd react. That you'd storm out of here and beat the shit out of Lewis. Not to say that he doesn't deserve it. But it'll hurt *you* and not him. So, it's kind of pointless."

His beautiful features were contorted in pain and anger when he looked back at me again. "He shouldn't get away with this."

"But he has."

"Fuck," he spat.

"They all get away with it. All of you," I said pointedly. "You always have. You always will. It's how it fucking works."

"Natalie, this is *not* how it's supposed to work."

"Tell me about it," I said bitterly.

"Let me talk to him. Maybe I can make him see his error."

I rolled my eyes. "Talking doesn't work. And he's not going to listen to you after we fucked in his hotel room. That's seared into his mind. You might be linked by history and secrets, but I don't think that applies here."

"It might." I could see him scheming. "If I get the crew together…"

"Penn, that's not going to be enough. The only way it'll be enough is if there are consequences to actions," I told

44

him flatly. "If the people that the Upper East Side stomps on don't scurry into the shadows and disappear."

His gaze shifted back to mine, clarity forming there. "That's why you're back."

"Lewis once told me that, if I walked away every time Katherine wanted me to, then she won. How is this any different?"

"You're *choosing* this."

"What I'm choosing is to stop running. I want the people of the Upper East Side to stop hurting others," I told him. "And I want you to help me. You helped build this world. You helped create the rules. And you said that you'd help me learn them."

Penn looked skeptical. "You can't want to actually *be* in this world."

"It's too late, Penn. I'm already in." I kept my eyes leveled on him. My head held aloft. "You dragged me in it, and then Lewis dragged me back."

Penn's face only darkened further at the mention of Lewis. Or maybe at what he'd done. "This isn't what I meant with that offer to help you."

I huffed. "What exactly *did* you mean when you said you'd help me survive this world if you could?"

Penn didn't respond immediately. He just walked toward the balcony and looked over the world he'd ruled for so long. The one he claimed he wanted to escape and yet never let their hooks out of him. The city that owned him.

"It was different then. When I thought...you and Lewis..."

"It's not different. If I leave, they win. Again. Just like everyone else they've hurt and discarded."

His words were pained when he finally answered, "I don't want to see you on this path."

I sighed in frustration and disgust. "It was *you* who put me on it," I snapped at him. "And you're still living it. No matter how many times you claim that you're going to get out."

"I am trying to get out."

"And how is that working out?"

A muscle flickered in his jaw as he faced me once more. "Poorly."

"So, you're in this life. I'm in this life. Help me. Teach me."

"I *can't*. I can't do that."

I shook my head and reached for my phone. Real anger suffused me. I'd thought that, once he saw my point, he'd agree. That he'd see the damage that they'd done and that I needed his help and he'd give in. But he was being adamant.

"Katherine ruined our relationship. She toyed with me. Lewis kept us apart. He stalked me. They've both destroyed my career. And they show no remorse. I can't even imagine what they've done to *you* over the years. Let alone to everyone else in their warpath," I said with barely contained fury. "And you just want to let them win. Again. I guess that tells me everything that I need to know."

I stormed to the elevator, jamming my finger down on the button. Penn was hot on my heels, reaching out to stop me.

"Don't go," he begged. "Not like this. Not after last night."

"You want me but only the parts of me that you can control. You don't want the Natalie who fits into your world. I'm not that doe-eyed young girl anymore. You wrecked her. You slayed her innocence. I won't be half of *anything* anymore."

Then I wrenched my arm out of his grip and stepped into the elevator.

CHAPTER 6

*T*he elevator closed in my face.

"Fuck," I growled into my now-empty apartment.

I fisted my hands into my hair and tugged on the strands in frustration. Goddamn it! That hadn't been how that conversation was supposed to go. That hadn't been how this fucking morning was supposed to go. Not after last night. How fucking incredible last night had been.

Just … where had this Natalie come from?

This vengeful angel set out to prove herself.

When she had first messaged me to let me know that she was coming back into the city for New Year's Eve, I'd been surprised that she wanted to meet at a party of all places. After what Katherine and Lewis had done, I'd thought she'd still be broken. Still beaten down, eating straight out of a tub of icing. Not in the city, looking like an exotic, sensual phoenix rising up out of the ashes.

After finding out the extent of what had gone down this week, I *understood* where she was coming from. We

48

had fucked with her life and won. We always won. It was the way a world filled with unending wealth and privilege worked.

But she was coming out swinging.

On one hand, she hadn't deserved to get kicked to the curb. But that didn't mean that learning to be more like the enemy was the answer to all of this. She was too *good*. Too kind and honest and...everything. This world would rip that right out of her if she stayed in it.

I knew first-fucking-hand.

It was a dangerous road she was walking on.

And while I wanted her in *my* life, I wanted a way for us to be together *without* the Upper East Side bullshit between us. That was what I should have done all along.

I still thought there was a chance for us. I just...had to convince her of that.

Totle trotted out of the back bedroom with his head cocked to the side, as if to say, *Where'd she go?*

"Excellent question, buddy. I have to get her back."

I pressed the elevator button and then dashed around my apartment, pulling on shoes, grabbing my jacket, and then realizing in horror that Natalie had left my house in nothing but a T-shirt. I grabbed a second jacket just as the elevator doors opened.

My foot tapped impatiently on the short ride to the bottom floor. She might have taken a cab and then had no need for the jacket. But knowing Natalie, her anger would have fueled her straight into Central Park. Especially since her apartment was nearly directly across the park from mine. And without another book contract, she probably wouldn't want to spend the money.

I jogged across Fifth Avenue and into the park, taking

the direct route. My eyes scanned the park, looking for the only person insane enough to be out in a T-shirt this time of year.

I knew that she wouldn't have let me say anything else when she was that upset. But that didn't mean I was comfortable with her going out in the cold like this. Let alone going back to her apartment when there was a chance that Lewis could be watching the surveillance footage. There was no fucking way I was letting him near her ever again. No fucking way.

She might be pissed at me for telling her no, but I'd put her safety first. We could figure out the rest.

A breath of relief escaped me, puffing a cloud of white in front of my face, as I saw Natalie's shivering form stumbling across the park.

"Natalie!" I called out to her.

She turned around with a look of surprise on her beautiful face. Her lips were already leaning more toward blue than pink, and she ran her hands up and down her arms. But a small smile touched her features as I approached her.

I held the jacket up and swung it around her shoulders.

"Hey," she muttered.

"You ran out too fast," I said softly. "I couldn't let you walk outside in just a T-shirt."

"Thanks. I can't feel my fingers now," she said, stuffing her hands into the oversize pockets of my jacket. "And...I shouldn't have stormed out."

I shot her a lopsided grin, flashing my dimples. It was good to hear her admit that. The cold must have knocked some of the oomph out of her fire.

"I'm glad that I caught up to you. At first, I didn't know if you'd grabbed a cab."

"Nah. Didn't even think about it until I started to freeze." Her eyes dropped to the ground and then came back to mine. "I should have controlled my temper. I took my problems out on you when you aren't even the crux of them."

"You don't have to apologize," I told her.

She just nodded, as if accepting that we were past her anger. "I'm guessing the dash out here didn't change your mind?"

I shook my head once. We were going to figure out what the best way was to be in each other's lives. But I couldn't see how helping her learn the games us Upper East Siders had been playing since birth would be the right answer.

"No, but I don't want you to go to your apartment alone. Even if Amy is there, it doesn't feel safe to me. Especially since you just told me what Lewis did. I wouldn't put it past him to do something worse."

"Great," she grumbled as we fell into step toward her apartment.

I thought she might tell me not to come with her if I didn't agree with her, but the thought that Lewis might do something else must have been enough incentive to let me tag along. I'd be happy when she was finally out of that fucking apartment. Natalie might not want me to say anything to Lewis, but he had it coming.

"I wish you'd told me what he'd done."

She shrugged helplessly. "I was overwhelmed. I could barely tell Amy the truth, and she's my best friend. I thought, if I didn't talk about it, then maybe the end of my career wasn't real."

"It's not the end of your career," I assured her.

She gave me a disbelieving look. "You should have heard my agent."

"It'll blow over."

"No, it won't. It would blow over for someone with the wealth, status, and family connections to control what happened to them and make this sort of thing go away. It won't blow over for a nobody who they deem a jilted ex, fraud, and whore."

I had a million fucking things to say to that. But the crumpled look on her face said that those opinions wouldn't be welcome right now. She didn't need someone to tell her she was wrong and that everything would be all right when it felt like the sky was falling.

We walked the rest of the way across Central Park in the dewy morning light.

Natalie broke the silence as we approached her apartment. "I hate that I have to move."

"I hate that he ever made you feel like you weren't safe."

She sighed. "Yeah. It was my refuge in this big city. I'd thought that this was my new start. My first solo apartment, my first book deal...everything seemed right," she said wistfully. Her gaze was lifted to the line of windows on the apartment complex off of Amsterdam. "I just didn't see the forces working against me in the background. The lies that ran off of lips as easy as breathing. The manipulations that had gotten me to this place. The machinations that wreaked havoc in the picturesque life I'd dreamed that I'd made for myself. How wrong I'd been."

And I had no response to that. I'd been as much a part of that as Lewis. I wanted to say that I'd lied, so we could be together, but wasn't that Lewis's rationale, too? I shuddered to think I was like him at all.

"It's *about* time," Amy said, hopping from one foot to another to try to stay warm in the entrance to Natalie's apartment building.

Natalie must have texted her when she left.

"Sorry. It took me longer to get here than I thought." She nodded to me by way of greeting.

"Hey, Amy," I said.

Amy suspiciously eyed me. "Let's get inside where it's warm. Enzo dropped me off, like, an hour ago."

Natalie rolled her eyes. "So, like, five minutes ago."

"Not even," Amy said. "But damn, it's cold."

Natalie opened the door, and I took it out of her hand and held it open for them.

Amy shot me a wary look as she passed. "You and I need to have a talk."

"Looking forward to that," I said with a lazy smirk.

"It's not going to be pleasant."

"I expect nothing less."

Natalie rolled her eyes at us and then took the stairs first. I noticed her checking the hallways, searching all the nooks and crannies. And then I realized what she was doing, and my anger resurfaced. She was searching for hidden cameras.

Fuck Lewis.

"I'd hide that look until we're done with this," Amy said.

"What look?"

"Like you're going to fucking murder someone." Amy's eyes flickered up to Natalie. "She's not okay right now."

"I know," I said, my blank mask falling into place with ease. "I've noticed that."

"And look, I'll only say this once, but if you hurt her, I will find you, chop off your balls, and feed them to you," she said with such pointed vehemence that I had to laugh. "I am not joking."

"I know," I said delicately. "That's why I laughed. You're actually giving me the best-friend talk."

"How would you know? Your best friends are all shitheads."

My lips tipped into a frown. "Perhaps."

"So don't fuck this up. The fact that she's even talking to you is a mystery to me. And I will end your life before I see her sink back into that place she was after you."

Natalie had just reached the third-floor landing and opened the door to her apartment. She glanced back at us, whispering secretly in the hallway. Amy's smile beamed out of her as if we hadn't been talking about Natalie at all. Mine must have been convincing, too, because she continued inside.

"I won't do that to her again," I told Amy.

"Good. Because I won't be here to watch over her, and she needs you."

I nodded once, surprised by her vehemence. The fact that she was even asking me about this shit meant that she was that concerned about Natalie. Which was extra troubling, especially considering the conversation that Natalie and I had just had.

Amy crossed the threshold into Natalie's apartment, but I froze in place before stepping inside.

The last time that I'd been here, ready to come into her apartment, she had turned me away. She said she wasn't ready for a relationship. That she wasn't ready for my first impression of her place to be her breaking down. Admittedly, I was fucking frustrated after that. After I left, I was certain I'd made a mistake by walking away. She'd asked for her space, but what if I gave it and then she never came back? What if I was an idiot and she'd just fucked with me? I'd fucking hated having those feelings, but after dealing with her with Lewis, it had been hard not to listen to my shattered trust and instead to the logical side of my brain.

But all of that aside, I couldn't enter her place yet.

"What are you waiting for?" Amy asked.

Natalie whipped around and found me standing on the threshold.

"You said that you weren't ready for me to come inside," I reminded her. "I thought it appropriate to ask if it was okay for me to come in now."

I watched her melt at my words. A small smile just for me and then a nod.

"Yes," she said softly. "Please come in."

"So dramatic," Amy muttered and then strode directly to the heater to warm up.

I stepped into Natalie's apartment for the first time. I understood immediately why she'd liked the place. It felt like her. Quaint and cozy with exposed brick and sparse belongings. A desk shoved up to the window, so she could stare out at the city streets below as she daydreamed and wrote out her magnificent stories.

I gritted my teeth to keep from commenting on how

fucking awful Lewis was for making her lose this. "Where are you moving anyway?"

Natalie chewed on her bottom lip. "I don't know if this place is...being recorded." She nervously glanced around the room, paranoia setting in. And I hardly blamed her. "So, how about I just show you when we get there? It's not far."

"Fair enough. Where should I start?"

Natalie pointed me to the closet and passed me a few boxes. "Label it *Closet*, and I'll figure it out from there. I don't have much stuff. Should be quick with three of us."

"I remember the two suitcases you carried your whole life in."

"I'm kind of regretting having more than that right now. It'd be a lot easier to load those suitcases up and go."

"I like that you're putting down some roots though."

"Something like that," she muttered. Then she was about to walk away but stopped. "Hey, thanks for your help. I feel...a lot safer with you here."

My hand came up to cup her cheek on reflex. "That's all I want for you."

Amy noisily cleared her throat. "Let's get to work, people. Lots to do here."

We broke apart sheepishly and returned to the large project in front of us. I got to work. I had no experience in packing, but how hard could it be?

After an hour of stuffing shit into boxes, I was wishing that I'd played a little bit more Tetris, growing up. Nothing fit how it was supposed to, but at least I was trying. Together, we were making it work.

I closed up one more box and then stood and stretched my arms overhead. My back ached a little from being hunched over the boxes. Who knew packing boxes could make a person feel so out of shape?

There was a knock on the door, and Amy groaned from the other room. "Finally! I never thought the pizza would get here."

"I'll get it," I said, reaching for my wallet. I opened the door and simultaneously pulled out a twenty. "How much do I owe you?"

"A lot more than twenty, Kensington," Lewis said crisply from the doorway.

CHAPTER 7

NATALIE

*T*hat voice.

Oh god. I knew that voice.

I dashed out of the bedroom, dropping the shirt I'd been about to fold. Lewis was here. He was *here*. My mouth dried up, and my stomach clenched.

I was shocked to find that my anger didn't surface at the first glimpse of his beautiful face. The perfect brown skin, high cheekbones, and molten dark eyes that I'd grown to adore over the time we were together. I'd always admired his good looks, but it was his easy smile, his quickness to laugh and joke, the poise of his powerful body that knew himself so completely, and the way he could draw me out of my protective shell that had won me over.

There had been something so good about Lewis. But it was a mask. An Upper East Side mask that I'd let myself be glamoured by. If he had ever been that carefree boy who loved to read and play baseball, then I had never met him.

58

My heart ached, cracked as his eyes slid to my features. As the mask tilted, I saw the truth of his own pain from our breakup. Or maybe I was just seeing what he wanted me to see. It was so complicated. He had ruined my life out of spite. Pure spite. I didn't want to be conflicted. We would never be together again. Never. And I wanted to destroy the sympathetic side of my personality that said he was hurting and I should care.

"What are you doing here?" I demanded.

Lewis's gaze swept from mine back to Penn, who looked ready to punch him again. "Checking in."

"You're not wanted here," Penn said.

Lewis just smirked. "Never stopped you."

"Cut it out," I snapped. "Both of you. I am not going to deal with this right now." I stepped around Penn and glared at Lewis. "How did you even know I was home?"

"Checking your security footage again?" Penn taunted at my side.

"I have no idea what you're talking about," Lewis said smoothly. "And I guessed you'd be here because of this."

He produced his phone and passed it to me. I warily took it in my hands and saw he had it open to *Page Six*. He scrolled about a quarter of the way down the page, and there, in a small photo amid other celebrities, was *me*. I read the caption in shock and excitement. This was... exactly what I'd wanted.

Sightings: Inside New York City Elite's Decadent New Year's Eve Celebrations

I read through the list of names that I recognized and

many more that I didn't. But there, at the bottom, near my picture, was my name.

Natalie Bishop wearing a stunning Cunningham Couture original at the Trinity club event.

My heart skipped a beat in wonder. I forgot for a second that Lewis was standing in front of me. That I was holding his phone.

I had come to be noticed at that event. I had known that my picture would be taken. That I might end up being circulated for the dress even if they never used my name. But this was more than I could have wanted. They had listed *me* as a part of the New York elite. Me…without a Warren or Kensington in sight.

My insides coiled in joy. I sure hoped Katherine saw this. It would be pretty fucking brilliant. Though only a start.

"Convenient," Penn muttered under his breath. "Natalie, give him the phone back, so he can leave."

I pushed it back into his hands, careful not to touch him. "You should go."

"Listening to everything he says again I see," Lewis said. He sighed. "I just wanted to talk."

"That's not happening," I said at the same time Penn barked, "No."

"I can handle this," I told Penn. I wanted him at my side, not answering for me.

"Give me five minutes to explain," Lewis said. "Please."

I narrowed my eyes at him. "Explain. *Explain?* You want to explain why you blacklisted me? Why you made it so that I couldn't get another book deal? Why you *ruined* my career? Sure, go ahead. But don't think that I'm going to believe a word of your bullshit anymore. And I sure as hell am not going to be alone with you again."

"That was a mistake," he said with earnest. He glanced between me and Penn as if he really hadn't known that he'd be there. As if he'd thought all along that he could corner me.

"A mistake," I said in a huff of disbelief.

"Yes. I can fix it."

I looked at him in disgust. Of course. Just fix it. A snap of his fingers, and he could be Mary Poppins and set everything to right, too. That was how it worked on the Upper East Side.

"Don't insult her," Penn growled.

"I've texted you about a hundred times since you left. Surely, you got at least one of them to read what I'd sent you. How sorry I was about how I'd reacted. That I wanted you back." Lewis took a step forward into the apartment, and Penn straightened at my side. "Please, we can fix this."

"You know, I didn't get any texts actually," I told him, standing my ground, even as my heartbeat pulsed wildly against my throat. "I blocked your number after what you put me through. We can't fix this. And you can't fix my career and think that we're going to suddenly be okay again. Believe it or not, Lewis, there are consequences to your actions. You've never had one before, I know. This is one. *Me*. So, fucking get used to it."

I grabbed the door and went to slam it in his face. But Lewis slapped his hand on it before it could even get close. His mask had completely fallen. All of a sudden, he looked like he might attack us at the provocation.

"You have no idea what you're doing," he said.

"I think I finally do. I'm not a pawn anymore, Lewis," I told him. "I'm the queen on the board."

Lewis looked as if he were about to do something very, very stupid. And then, Amy appeared at my side, flanking me like Penn was.

"If you don't get the fuck out of here, I am going to call the police. You'll get off easy because you're a Warren. They probably won't even give you a slap on the wrist. But we have enough evidence of your stalking behavior, coupled with a call for your disturbance, then it'll start to look like a case. Maybe you'll get that slap...or worse, maybe it'll all catch up to you."

"I'll put my weight behind it, too," Penn spoke up.

We all knew how much the weight a Kensington carried, especially since his mother was the mayor.

Lewis glared at us, at the solidarity between the three of us standing against him. "I'm not doing anything wrong. I just wanted to talk to Natalie."

"I don't want to talk to you. So...go."

"Fine," he spat. "When you wake up and stop acting like I'm the bad guy, call me, so we can figure this out."

My eyes rounded in shock at his words. He was beyond delusional. I might have doubts about Penn's involvement in all of this, but I had none about Lewis. The fact that he'd responded by blacklisting me said everything I needed to know.

Lewis jutted his chin out one more time and then left the doorway. I shut the door the rest of the way. My hands were trembling. The indignation that I'd held together in the confrontation evaporated. It was just me again. The woman who had to deal with this all. Who had flown home to Charleston and cried on Amy's couch while eating frosting all week.

My strength disappeared, and the weakness returned. I put my back to the door and slid down it, dropping my head into my knees.

"Oh my god," I gasped out.

A sob shook my shoulders. I'd been trying to keep it all together since I got into the city. Since I decided that I was going to make everyone pay for what they'd done to me. But there was a difference between the vengeance that fueled my heart and the brittle reality of dealing with the man I'd been falling for. Seeing him for what he really was and knowing that even he didn't see it as wrong. On some level, I was just that same obsession for him. The thing that he wanted. And now that he couldn't have me, he was getting desperate. Acting out to hurt me and then trying to rectify things to make up for it. It was...delusional and insane and made me ache all over.

Penn sank to his feet in front of me. His hand slid over top of mine and squeezed. "Hey."

I didn't move. I hated feeling this way. Even more than I hated the deep, dark pit that I'd fallen headfirst into when I found out about Lewis's file. The yawning darkness that had beckoned when Katherine revealed my pen name. The inky black that had suffused me and called me home after I lost my writing career.

This was vulnerability.

Much, much, much worse than rage.

"Natalie, look at me."

I shook my head.

His fingers brushed back through the loose strands of my silver hair before lifting my chin. This was nothing like his commanding touch as he'd assessed me last night before he fucked me. This was almost painfully gentle, achingly tender. A different man than the sex god he was in the bedroom.

"He doesn't deserve your tears," he said. Then he swiped the traitorous, wet streaks from under my eyes.

"They're not for him," I finally muttered. "Not really."

He angled his head, those liquid blue eyes asking the question he never voiced.

"I hate dealing with him. I hate that he manipulated me into feeling something for him, and then it all turned out to be a lie. That it wasn't the first time," I said pointedly. "And yet, I fell for it again anyway. I thought defiantly, naively, *stupidly* that I could have one foot in both worlds. That I could be the bohemian, wild, daydreamer Natalie while stumbling aimlessly into this Upper East Side world with big doe eyes. I thought I'd seen the worst of this world. I thought I knew all it could do to me. And that, somehow, I could be both people. But you were right. I can't."

Penn frowned. "I don't enjoy being right in this."

"Yes, well, but you were. Those two things don't go together. They might as well exist in separate universes. And once I truly realized it, once all the walls came tumbling down, I saw the truth. I couldn't play by my rules. There are only the rules of the Upper East Side."

His gaze was steady on mine as the tears ran black rivers down my cheeks. As I mourned that loss right before his eyes.

"So, you see, the tears aren't for Lewis. They're for the person I was before all of this. They're mourning the loss of a part of me so that I could gain the strength I needed to stand up to him. To live in this world."

"Why would you want to live in it?" he asked in earnest. Not the same question he had asked me earlier. The other one had been disbelief. That I was insane for wanting it. Now, it was curiosity. Like he was seeing the truth in my eyes for the first time. And not just my anger.

"My whole life, I've only ever really had one friend, and she's standing in this room. I never really felt like I belonged anywhere. I needed to jump from place to place to place to find what I was looking for. I was just beginning to feel like I belonged here for the first time in my life." I swiped at my eyes and cleared my throat. This was the first time I was admitting this, even to myself. "I won't let Katherine or Lewis or anyone take that away from me."

Penn sighed heavily, as if coming to some conclusion. "Okay."

"Okay?" I asked in confusion.

"I'll help you."

My eyes rounded in surprise. "Lewis changed your mind."

"I'd be lying if I said it didn't help. I want to keep you safe. I want us to spend more time together. I can make this world easier for you. As easy as this world will allow it to be for anything. So if this is where you think you belong, then you'll belong here with me."

PART II
TRICKS OF THE TRADE

CHAPTER 8

NATALIE

"This is not how I thought we would start the training," I told Penn.

My freshly manicured hands brushed down the front of the dark blue dress that had been delivered earlier that morning. It was simple and elegant. A sharp contrast to the jaw-dropper I'd worn only last week for New Year's Eve.

"Well, this is where we will begin. You're under my tutelage now, and I believe in a hands-on approach."

I raised my eyebrows at him. "*That* I did know."

The tilt of his lips said he was amused by me, but he didn't let it show otherwise. He was fully in control tonight as we took a sleek black car to a charity dinner for the children's art foundation. It felt too soon for me to be out in public. I'd thought that he'd want to show me the ropes or give me a PowerPoint slide lecture or something equally professorial. But he'd insisted this was the best way to learn. Since it was how they had all learned.

It made me unbelievably nervous. I'd been to any

number of events for the Upper East Side, but I hadn't been trying to *be* one of them. I'd just been me and thought that was enough. But, for me to pull all of this off, I had to be *more* than me. I had to belong.

"I can tell you how to act and think and feel. I can walk you through it. Observe and critique as if I were in a classroom, but it would be for nothing. Think of this as an immersive language experience. Instead of learning French in school, you're being dropped into Southern France with a family who speaks broken English. You have to find a way to fit, and you have to do it pretty quick."

"You make it sound terrifying," I told him.

His eyes flicked to mine. "Now, you're getting it."

"Thank you," I said softly. "For helping me even though you don't want to be in this world and you hate stuffy dinners and galas."

"I'm thinking that, if I fuck you at all of these stuffy dinners and galas, I might find them more tolerable," he deadpanned.

My cheeks flushed, and heat flooded my body. "You're not serious."

"Do I look like I'm joking?"

No. No, he did not.

"I do have one rule," he said carefully, sidestepping right over the fact that he intended to have sex with me in public places as part of my training.

A fact that I was...very interested in hearing more about.

"Oh? I'm surprised you only have one."

"It's an important one." He looked tense as he said it. "I reserve the right to add more as we go though."

I chuckled. "Fine. What's the main one?"

"This is going to be...uncomfortable for me. This training is unorthodox and goes against the man that I was trying to become. I realize that I was only half as successful as I wanted to be. And only tried about a quarter as hard as I should have to get there. So the Upper East Side is home, and I guess it's where I'm to stay, but that doesn't make me okay with that fact."

I nodded in response. I had known that he was conflicted on helping me. That he was only doing it after he saw my breakdown about Lewis. About this damn seductive world that had pulled me in like Alice falling down the rabbit hole.

"I'm not always going to be the Penn that you know. I will have to be the Penn Kensington who owns Manhattan. The dark beast within that paces through my mind and threatens to unleash himself upon the world. The beast that I've leashed ever since my asshole father died of an overdose and left me to realize what the fuck I was doing with my life. You won't always like what I do, what I say, or who I am. Are you okay with that?"

I swallowed before nodding. I'd seen his mask before. I knew what he was capable of. And I was the one unleashing him on the world.

He blew out a breath before regaining composure. "You say that now. We'll see later. But the only thing that I ask from you, the only rule I want us *both* to follow, is, no masks in private." He stared deep into my eyes as if he could convey the importance of that rule in just one look. "No matter who we are or what we do or how we act in public, you're still my Natalie in private, and I'm still your Penn in private. Can you do that?"

"Yes," I told him.

I didn't want him to be fake with me either. Not if I was going to be able to see past the man who had bet on me and back to the one I'd fallen in love with. Those two people were already blurred in my mind. But I could see when the mask came up. I was sure that he'd be able to see me, too.

"You're sure? No hiding from me."

I nodded. "This is who I am."

"After tonight, this will just be one side of who you are. Are you ready?"

My stomach coiled into a knot. "You're sure Katherine won't be here?"

"As far as I know, she is still on her honeymoon. I have no idea how she could stomach a month alone with Camden Percy. But there are so many things I don't understand about Katherine."

"Well, that's good for us at least," I said as the car rolled to a stop. I took a deep breath and then released it. "I'm ready."

I KNEW THIS PART. How to make an appearance. Katherine had inadvertently taught me how to survive this a year earlier when she brought me to my first ever Upper East Side event. I could walk a red carpet with a coy smile on my face. I knew which way to stand that flattered me best. There had been proof of that on *Page Six*.

That was the easy part.

It was everything that came afterward that I always second-guessed. Even when I'd been brought in with the entire crew, I hadn't felt entirely with the crowd. It was easier on the arm of a Warren or a Kensington, but I was still small-town Natalie whose father had moved us all around the country with the military. I still had the moral compass that said right and wrong were black-and-white issues. I didn't see their strategies or straight-out lies. I had been ill-prepared for what I witnessed, but Penn was in his element.

It was crazy to think that someone who *hated* this world so much could fit in so seamlessly. As if he had never left. As if he had been born for this role. And I supposed that he had, in fact, been born for this. He just rejected it on base principle.

Yet he was here for me.

The charity function was held in a stunning domed banquet hall fit for royalty. It was bedecked in navy-blue and gold with large, circular tables facing a small stage. A row of items was on display along one side of the room for the silent auction. I wondered what outrageous big ticket items the uber wealthy would bid on.

Penn effortlessly guided me away from the tables.

"We won't look until later. No one wants to look eager," he told me.

"Oh," I said softly. "But there are people over there."

"What do you think that says about them?"

"That they're bored?"

"No, there's an array of people at this event. It's one of the reasons that I decided to choose this one. I thought it would be beneficial for you to observe people. Everyone here has money. But not everyone is Upper East Side. There's a difference, and it's very obvious to people who know what to look for. So tell me, the people at the auction before dinner are…" he prodded.

"Not Upper East Side," I guessed.

"Correct. No one would outbid us, and if there were something we had an eye on, we would have been informed about it ahead of time by the organizers. So, there's no point in going to browse. We're here to mingle. The auction is secondary."

"I see." Though it sounded ridiculous to me. But that was the point. I never would have noticed that.

"Look around. Tell me who is the wealthiest person in the room." Penn's arm was warm on my elbow as he stopped us in our tracks. He snapped his finger at a passing waiter, and the man scurried over, eager to please. He plucked a glass of champagne off of the tray and passed it to me. "I'll have a bourbon, neat. Make it a double."

The man nodded quickly and then disappeared into the crowd to get Penn his drink.

I shook my head in surprise. "You're good at this."

"Yes," he said in dismay. "Now, focus. Did you select a person?"

My eyes traveled the room. I felt, at some level, like this must be a trick question. Penn was incredibly wealthy, but it probably wasn't him. My eyes skittered around the massive space as I tried to figure out how the hell I should answer this.

"I don't know. Everyone's rich. Maybe…that woman?" I said with a hitch, making my statement an uncertain question. I gestured to an elderly woman a couple of rows over in a mink coat and diamonds.

"Hollywood," Penn said grimly. "That's Henrietta Groves, a very successful fifties film star. Charming but handsy. She probably has less than half the net worth of that couple."

My eyes followed to where he was pointing out a man in a tailored black suit with a trim, graying beard and a woman, who I guessed was his wife, in a loose black dress. Her hair was pulled severely off of her face. They both looked disguised but nothing out of the norm.

"George and Alessandra Moretti. George's family owned half the utilities in the country. Alessandra brought five chains of motels that crisscross middle America to the marriage. Together, they have money from generations and generations in America and Italy. You'd never know it, except that, once you see it, you can't *not* see it."

"What is it?" I asked, observing Alessandra.

She was sharply dressed and by all accounts sophisticated and in charge. But there was nothing to suggest they were as wealthy as Penn had claimed.

"Do you remember when you first came to this world? How did people treat you? Who did they think you were?"

I shrugged. "Camden thought I was some kind of California model. Most people knew right away that I wasn't from here. I figured it was the hair."

Penn's smile lit up at that word, and he brushed aside a strand of the silver locks from my shoulder. Then it was quickly replaced by the mask he wore so well. "Yes, the hair definitely does it. But it's how you carry yourself. The way you wear your clothes. The lilt to your speech. The innocence in your eyes. It's all there, and it says you aren't in control. You have no power. Which means you aren't one of us."

"That...makes sense," I admitted reluctantly. It turned

my stomach to think that everything about me gave away that I wasn't from here. "But *Page Six* thought I was a New York elite."

"What was different about that?" he demanded, latching on to my point. Ever the professor. "It wasn't your hair or your dress or your shoes."

"The confidence. The fact that I felt like I belonged there and wanted everyone to know it."

"Yes, and no. You *did* belong there. And that's all the difference."

"I don't—"

"You have to belong, Natalie. Not pretend to belong. Think about the people you know from here. Think about how they flit through life as if it were made for them, as if they owned it and nothing could stop them. You have to take that, bottle it up, and wear it like you did at Trinity. And then you have to wear it everywhere like perfume."

Easier said than done.

But he had a point.

Katherine walked through life confident that, even though her father had lost all of her money, she would land on her feet. Because there was never a time when she had not landed on her feet. Even Lark, who hardly lived in this world anymore, still had that walk like she knew her place. Lewis's sisters, Charlotte and Etta, devoured every room that they entered. No doors were barred. People listened, and they jumped and only ever asked how high.

Even Penn—no, *especially* Penn could command a room with one look of those sexy blue eyes. A quirk of his lips. A slip of his hands into his pockets. He commanded *me* like that, and I realized as I thought back that he always had. He'd known that he had me on that first look on the balcony in Paris seven years ago. *That* was Upper East Side confidence.

"You get it. You see it." He nodded.

I flushed at his approval. I found I liked it.

"Now, observe tonight. Gain that confidence and belonging and own it. Then, the real work will begin," he said as he guided me to our table.

CHAPTER 9

NATALIE

"*L*adies and gentlemen, thank you so much for attending this charity dinner to benefit the children's art foundation. Due to unforeseen personal circumstances, we had to reschedule our guest speaker last minute. And I am pleased to introduce Mayor Leslie Kensington."

Penn stilled next to me. I could feel the tension coming off of him in waves. His relationship with his mother was fraught at best. She wanted him to take over the family business and pick up where his father had left off since Court refused to do anything but drink and party. Leslie had been nothing but horrible to us when she found out we were first seeing each other. And though I'd had one positive interaction with her at Katherine's wedding last month, I wasn't looking forward to seeing her again. Especially not on her son's arm.

"Did you know?" I whispered.

He shook his head once. "This complicates things."

"Should we leave?"

He gritted his teeth. "It'll be worse if we do. I didn't want you to deal with this yet. Guess you're getting a second lesson."

I didn't ask for him to clarify. It probably wasn't going to be pleasant. Penn and I were just getting off the ground again. I was seeing past the bet. He was still struggling with the fact that I'd had a relationship with Lewis. Having his nosy and opinionated mother in the middle of that was probably the last thing he wanted. And I couldn't disagree.

We finished our dinner and then listened to his mother in her element. She was an excellent speaker. It was clear why she had been elected time and time again. She had this fire that I frequently saw in her son when he was speaking about philosophy. Not that his mother would ever equate the two.

"We're going to have to stop to say something to her," Penn said when her speech had concluded.

"Okay. Are you going to be all right?" I asked him as we stood.

He placed his hand on the small of my back, guiding me through the tables toward his mother at the front of the room, as if he were going to his own execution. "I can handle my mother. For your lesson around this, it's best to get that mask in place now. No concern for me. No concern for anything. You belong here. You own this room. Nothing she says to you *or* me can affect you in the least."

"Do you think she's going to be rude in front of other people?" I asked in disbelief.

"Mask," he instructed. "Now."

I schooled my features into a semblance of what I'd

seen Katherine do. Not blank like Penn's, but almost bored, the world at my feet, silver spoon in my mouth. I straightened my spine and felt a stillness take over my limbs even though I was still walking.

"Better," Penn conceded on a sigh. "Terrifying. My mother won't say anything purposely inflammatory, but you never know. It's better to be on guard."

We stepped around a crowd congratulating the mayor on the speech and offering larger donations to the organizer. Leslie's eyes lifted from the short, balding man who she was speaking to. They widened a fraction in surprise when she saw her son. It wasn't much, but even I noticed that she hadn't expected him to be here either. I hoped that was a good thing for us.

"Penn," Leslie said with a politician's smile. One who was as likely to shake hands and kiss babies as stab you in the back. "I didn't know that you would be here, darling."

She didn't embrace him or reach out or show joy at his presence. Penn's life must have had so little love. My heart ached. Not that I allowed it to show on my face. This new Natalie didn't feel those sorts of things. At least, not in public.

"Mother," he said crisply. He gestured to me. "You remember Natalie."

Leslie barely glanced at me. "Ah, yes, of course. How could I forget?"

Penn tensed as if he were about to defend me even though he had been the one who said not to give any reaction.

"We met at the Percy–Van Pelt wedding. You're friends with Jane and a bestselling author, correct?"

"That's right," I agreed easily. I knew that she remembered how we'd first met. When she'd thrown me out of her Hamptons mansion and stopped me from working as a vacation home watcher ever again. "Pleasure to see you again."

"Likewise. Are you who I have to thank for getting my son back out into society?"

Penn's grip on me tightened until it was nearly painful. There were so few things that riled Penn up this much.

"Someone has to keep him from becoming a recluse," I said.

"Now, if we could only get that philosophy nonsense out of his head, we'd all be better off," she said with a laugh as if she hadn't just insulted his entire profession.

I opened my mouth, ready to tell the mayor exactly what I thought about her son's philosophy nonsense, but Penn cut in, as if he could see that I hadn't quite mastered my temper, "It seems nonsense was bred into my head, Mother." He said with a lazy smile, "Must have always been there. Did I get that from you or Dad?"

"Mayor Kensington!" a voice cut in before the mayor could respond. Which was probably good.

I didn't want to hear what might have come out of his mother's mouth. She truly did not understand her son at all.

"We'll leave you to it," Penn said before taking me by the elbow and leaving his mother to deal with her constituency.

We were a safe distance away from the mayor before either of us spoke.

"Maybe we should go?" I offered.

Penn closed his eyes for a few seconds and then shook his head. When his eyes met mine again, I could still see the anger and turmoil trapped in their orbs. I knew that he suffered deeply from complications with his mother even if he never talked about it.

"Are you sure?"

"Yes, I'm sure. I won't let her ruin this. Believe it or not, I'm actually enjoying myself."

I gasped mockingly. "Penn Kensington enjoying himself at a boring charity function? Are you ill?"

He grinned at me wickedly. "All I needed was your company it seems. It's much more pleasant to be here with you than alone. And teaching is my profession."

"And you are excellent at it. I think I handled your mother pretty well."

"Yes. Until the end when I thought you were going to bite her head off."

I gave him my best Upper East Side look. "Me?" I asked incredulously. "In polite society?"

He snorted and then gestured toward the auction tables. "Come on, my little minx. You catch on a little too well."

I followed him further away from his mother and the problems she brought to the table. I'd been so mad at Penn for so long that it was strangely relaxing not to second-guess him. We made a shockingly good team. He'd been right. All of this was better with him. I let the last year slide off of my shoulders and delighted in his company.

"What do you think the most outrageous item is?" I asked Penn as we journeyed sedately down the line. Passing a signed first edition of a classic novel, an annual entrance fee to a gentlemen's club in the city, and a yacht.

"I have no idea. I'd guess something to do with a private jet. That usually wins out."

"You are correct," a man said behind us. "The use of my private jet to a destination of the winner's choice for a week."

I realized that I recognized the man as Camden's father, Carlyle Percy. And next to him was his wife, Elizabeth Cunningham. Our eyes met, and she smiled, clearly pleased to see me.

"Hello, sir," Penn said, extending his hand to Carlyle. "That's very generous."

"Least I can do. It's good to see you, Penn." They shook hard. "And this is…"

"Natalie Bishop," Penn said effortlessly.

I held my hand out, and Carlyle kissed the top. "Pleased to meet you, Miss Bishop."

"This is the girl I was telling you about, darling," Elizabeth said. She leaned into her husband's arm, but her Upper East Side mask was as efficient as ever. "The one who had her picture on *Page Six* in that latest design I'd worked on."

"Right. Of course," Carlyle said in a way that made it seem as if he had no idea what she was talking about.

Then he immediately jumped into a conversation with Penn about business. I'd never heard Penn discuss his family business before. And for some reason, I thought he hadn't been apprised of the conditions of his father's company, which was now being run by a new CEO and the board of directors. But I'd been wrong.

Maybe it was the Upper East Side mask that fit into place, but the business talk seemed to come to him as easily as the philosophy lectures. I knew that he didn't want to be running the company. But I was thrown enough by the conversation that I hardly noticed when Elizabeth tried to get my attention.

"Let's leave the boys to their boring drivel," Elizabeth said, pulling me toward the table she had been standing in front of with her husband.

I glanced down at the entry and saw that it was for a one-on-one consultation and fitting with Elizabeth herself.

"Wow. What a prize," I told her.

"Yes, well, no one will actually take me up on it," she said with a wave of her hand. "It's always some woman who wants to say that she's wearing the latest."

"Of course, and who wouldn't want to?" I said quickly.

"Speaking of, I adored that feature on *Page Six*. I'd thought that dress would be perfect for you. Someone already so bold."

I shot her a knowing look. "I have no idea what you mean."

Elizabeth's lips curved upward. "I might have heard from my daughter that you're shaking things up around here."

"Am I? I thought I was just beginning to fit in."

"If you ask me," Elizabeth said carefully, "perhaps things need to be shaken up."

"That so?" My stomach twisted in anticipation. Was Elizabeth actually going to agree that Katherine needed to fall off her high horse?

"Indeed. What are your plans for Fashion Week?"

I remained perfectly still. I'd heard of New York City Fashion Week. Melanie, was obsessed with fashion and would *die* if she found out that I might get to go. But I didn't know when it was, nor did I have any plans.

"What do you have in mind?" I asked instead of the reel running through my head.

"Anyone who is anyone will be there," Elizabeth said. *Katherine.*

"I'll have a ticket to you for my event and dress you for the gala."

Her eyes were sly and cunning, saying way more than the offer sounded. By taking my side, she was going to piss off Katherine. And I was going to be in a guaranteed spot to see it go down.

"That would be wonderful," I said with a smile.

"What would be great?" Penn asked, appearing at my side.

"Elizabeth invited to dress me for Fashion Week."

Penn didn't miss a beat, and I was sure only I could see the pain in his expression. "Perfect. We'll see you there then." His gaze dropped down to mine. "Let's go bid on that auction you were interested in."

I nodded and then smiled at Elizabeth. "So wonderful seeing you again."

"You, too, Natalie. I'll be in touch."

"Looking forward to it."

Penn and I walked in silence past the row of auction items, out one of the side doors, and into a secluded alcove before Penn released a breath of relief.

"Fuck, you should have saved me from talking to Percy," he said, slumping back against the wall.

"You seemed to be in complete control of the business talk. I didn't even know that you were invested in your dad's company."

He rolled his eyes. "I'm not. I know enough to bullshit. And *that* is the basis of my mask, Nat. I can even bullshit Carlyle Percy about a business that I don't give two shits about. And I can make *you* believe it. Even though you know I despise that company."

"Impressive."

Penn stepped away from the wall, and then his hands came up on either side of my body, caging me into the adjacent wall. "And what were you and Mrs. Cunningham-Percy discussing?"

"Fashion Week."

"Mmm," he said, dipping his head and trailing kisses down my neck. "Don't look to your left when you lie. It makes it more obvious."

"We *were* discussing that."

"Yes, but something else. She's taken an interest in you." He pulled back to assess me. "Why?"

"I don't think that she likes Katherine," I admitted.

He pursed his lips. "Harmony hates Katherine. It makes sense that Elizabeth would feel similarly, but I thought maybe she didn't know much since Katherine was always wearing her designs."

I shrugged lightly. "I think she likes the competition."

"You're asking for Katherine's wrath."

My grin was merciless. "Bring it on."

Penn's hand slid into my hair, and then his lips were against mine. His body pressing me back into the wall. Our tongues volleying for position. My heartbeat ratcheting up in response to his demanding touch. I didn't know if it was the tension that we'd both had to hold on to all night that fueled this, but I melted in him, wanting nothing more than for him to drag my dress up my thighs and thrust his cock deep inside of me. Taking me against this wall, wild and relentless. Releasing all of the pent-up energy that came with trying to fit in. I understood, maybe for the first time, why someone who had everything could want to escape this world.

Then Penn pulled back. His forehead rested against mine. Our breathing mingled in sharp pants between us.

"We should get back to my place," Penn said.

"Oh?" I whispered, pressing my lips to his again.

"I want to be me when I'm with you," he told me earnestly. "This...this is the old me."

"Can't you be both?"

He shook his head.

"You warned me that you might say and do things that I didn't like." I unbuttoned his suit pants, sliding the zipper to the base, and then gently ran my nails against the head of his cock. "You didn't factor in that...I might like both sides of Penn Kensington."

He groaned deep in the back of his throat. As if the beast had finally slipped his leash, and suddenly, the man was both sides of his ego—philosopher and monster. Achingly logical and deliciously carnal.

He slammed me back against the wall, harder than the last time. His hands gripped the blue dress that he'd chosen for the evening, wrenching it up, up, up until it was bundled up around my stomach. His cock sprang free of its restraint, revealing the throbbing length of it and his need for me.

He grasped one of my legs and tugged it up around his waist before pushing my thong aside. His fingers slipped through the wetness that was already present from our indulgent kiss. I moaned softly at the feel of his fingers

K.A. LINDE

probing and readying my pussy. Then they disappeared with a vicious grin. His cock replaced them, and in one swift motion, he thrust into my pussy.

I closed my eyes, knocking my head into the wall to keep from crying out. This wasn't a slow, playful Penn. This wasn't New Year's Eve where we had taken our time and become reacquainted with each other's bodies. Where I'd surrendered myself to him. This was something else entirely.

Frantic, frenetic, frenzied, and forceful.

Wild, electric, and passionate.

It was a shattering and a coming together.

The two sides of his person reuniting in a way I had never thought was possible. Maybe even he had never thought that he could be both people at once. And I never wanted it to end.

Even as I came to new heights with Penn's hand tight against my mouth to keep me from screaming out. And him coming deep, deep within me. As my walls tightened around him and I milked him for every drop that he had.

When we finished, breathless and shaking from the exertion, I saw stars in his eyes and the crown that we'd plucked from the sky atop his head.

And I realized I was in so much trouble.

CHAPTER 10

NATALIE

*I*f I'd ever thought that I could handle Penn Kensington, I'd been lying to myself. Unequivocally.

We split our time between his place and my new one the next week, and I tried not to overthink it even though that was my specialty. I just wanted to enjoy it.

I hadn't given up on my desire to bring down the people who had wronged me. I just felt like Penn and I were a bit more on a level playing field. Yes, he'd put a bet on me. But I *had* slept with his best friend. Regardless of the fact that I'd thought we'd never get back together and that I was never going to forgive him, it still hurt him. So, we were equals.

And by easing back into things with him, something had shaken loose in my chest. The words had come back. I'd pulled my computer out of the place it had been collecting dust and started writing again. I had no idea what it was, but the fact that it was anything after the bullshit with Lewis and Katherine was a start.

"I like to see that," Penn said, stifling a yawn as he walked out of my bedroom in nothing but a pair of boxers.

"Totle curled up on my lap under a blanket?" I pulled the covers up just enough so he could see Totle's little head hidden in my lap.

"Ah, so that's where the little traitor went."

"I didn't want to wake you up. You were sleeping so peacefully."

"You are taking full advantage of the fact that I don't have Friday classes."

I nodded with a grin. "That I am."

"And you're writing again?"

"Something. I don't know what it is." He opened his mouth, but I jumped in before he could say anything. "And no, you can't read it."

He frowned. "I wasn't going to ask. I know you'll let me read it when you're ready." Then his eyes narrowed. "Unless you happen to be writing about me, and then I think I would like to know before it releases and hits a bestseller's list."

"Yeah, well…that was different. You were an ass."

"Ohhh," he breathed, planting a kiss on my neck. "Using the past tense. I'm not currently an ass?"

I squirmed out of his touch, disrupting Totle, who seemed completely put out by the fact that he had to move a whole foot and then buried himself under the covers again. I giggled. "You are not currently being an ass. I reserve the right to change my mind if you decide to do something stupid again."

"Fair. I also reserve that right." He reached out for his maroon Harvard sweatshirt, and I pouted. He laughed.

"Really?"

I shrugged. "You said I could take advantage of no-class Fridays."

"And you normally can, but I actually have to go into the office."

"Ugh! Stupid jobs."

He dropped down onto the couch next to me, rifling through the jeans he'd discarded in the middle of my living room last night. "I've figured out the next move for our lessons."

"Oh?" I asked, closing my laptop and facing him.

"Yeah. I've been thinking over where to go next. And I think this is it." He plucked a black card out of his wallet and held it out to me.

I warily looked at it. "What's that for?"

"It's part of the lesson."

"I don't need your credit card."

He rolled his eyes. "Take it, Natalie."

I gingerly took it from him and stared down at it. I felt immediately uncomfortable. Like I was suddenly going to be sick. I knew that I was constantly surrounded by money, but it was somehow different than holding an unlimited credit card, knowing that the person who owned it had a trust fund in the nine to ten digit range.

"The second lesson is about money. Money for us just...is. It's not something you talk about because it speaks for itself. If you have the right kind of old money and the right kind of old-money name, you're in. Otherwise, you're somehow other. It's why we look down on Hollywood money. The nouveau riche who we see as a little classless. Money shouldn't scare you. Spending it should feel effortless. And I know that it makes you uncomfortable."

It did. I'd grown up with very little, and I'd never had any of my own money until the book deal, but even then, it had been like pulling teeth to get me to spend it. I hadn't even gotten a cab in the freezing rain.

"So, the other part of this is clothes. As vain and pretentious as it is, the clothes have to match. I love your bohemian clothing. I want you to wear it when we're together, but if you go out, you're going to need to play the part. And to do that, you're going to need a new wardrobe."

My mouth went dry. "What?"

"I'd start at Bergdorf Goodman and then try Barneys."

"Penn, I can't." I tried to hand back the credit card. "I went shopping with Jane last month, and she bought me all this stuff. I ended up going back after and returning it. I couldn't stomach the prices."

He nodded. "That's a good idea. Take Jane with you. Though I have no idea why you like her." He eyed me as if I hadn't just said that I *wasn't* going to do what he'd said. "Why do you like her?"

"Did you hear me?"

"Yes, but you're going to do this, Natalie. You asked me to help you become Upper East Side. To help you survive this world. The clothes help, and you're going to go out and buy them like you've been doing this your entire life. Make the personal shoppers believe you."

I frowned and felt even sicker at the thought.

"It'll be easier with Jane. Though how she stomachs my brother…" He shuddered.

"Your brother isn't so bad either."

Penn narrowed his eyes. "That is a bald-faced lie."

"Well, he saved me from Camden. He can't be that bad."

"Natalie, everyone looks good next to Camden Percy. That doesn't suddenly make Court a saint when he's actually a demon in a sharp suit."

"You're biased."

"Yes," he growled. I knew his brother was a pressure point. "Seeing you carousing with his girlfriend nearly sent me through the roof when I first heard about it."

I put my computer on the coffee table and slid into his lap, straddling his muscular thighs. "You should stop worrying so much."

"Easier when you're on top of me," he admitted. "But this isn't going to convince me to let you off the hook."

"What about a blow job? Will that change your mind?"

He considered it for a solid second. "No. But I'll take one later after I take you out tonight."

"You're taking me out?"

"Yes, I have reservations at eight. And if you don't have a new dress in that new wardrobe, then we can't go."

I grumbled under my breath. "Fine. I'll call Jane." I reached for my phone, but Penn dragged me back down on top of him.

"I'm reconsidering that blow job."

I laughed. "Too late. You'd rather I go shopping."

He kissed me hard on the mouth. "Convince me, Nat. Convince me."

I groaned. "You'll be the death of me."

Then I convinced him...thoroughly.

*a*n hour later, I stepped into Bergdorf Goodman with Penn's black card in my wallet. I'd convinced the fuck out of him, and he'd *still* insisted I needed new clothes. Bastard.

So here I was, meeting Jane for some much-needed girl time and a whole new fucking wardrobe. The bill was going to terrify me. It was going to take every ounce of willpower not to balk at the prices and agree to the outrageous sum that was sure to be the end result of this excursion.

"Natalie!" a voice called behind me.

I turned in time to see Jane striding into Bergdorf with a pair of her signature Chanel sunglasses pushed to the top of her ash-blonde hair. She was dressed in a pair of black leggings and a soft, fuzzy pink sweater. She looked like she'd just slung it on after a run, but I knew that she didn't run. Ever.

"Jane, it's good to see you."

She embraced me, planting a kiss on each of my cheeks.

"It's been too long. I couldn't believe it when I saw your number. I thought you'd be ignoring me because of what had happened at the Percy wedding. I told you it would all blow over. And look, you're back in the city with your picture on *Page Six*." She dramatically swung her boho Louis Vuitton bag onto her shoulder. "Which we need to talk about. You came to Trinity and didn't even stop to say hi." She pouted with her bottom lip sticking out. "I mean, are you mad at me or something?"

"No," I said right away, "I'm not. I've just been dealing with all of that stuff. Needed some me time."

Jane shot me a mischievous look. "With Penn Kensington I hear. Oh look, we're both with Kensington men!"

"I suppose we are," I said faintly.

It was so…strange to think that Penn and I were together again. And we were. We spent all our time together. But there was so much left unsaid between us that I wasn't sure if we were entirely on the same page. The transition to *us* again had been almost too easy. Being with him had always been effortless. But it felt unfinished in a way. And I didn't know how to fix that. If I even could. Or if time was the only healer.

"All right. Tell me *everything* that you've done since getting back into the city."

I followed Jane through the department store. "Well, I moved into a new apartment, the thing with Penn, and I've been talking to Elizabeth Cunningham."

"I saw that stunning dress you wore to my event. Is she dressing you now?"

I nodded. "Yes. For some occasions. But she said she'd hook me up for Fashion Week."

Jane squealed, turning her wide eyes to mine. "You're coming to Fashion Week?"

"Yes, though I'm not entirely clear on what I'm going to do while I'm there."

"It's only the best week in the entire world for fashion enthusiasts. Fashion converges on Manhattan, and the most brilliant designers in the world showcase the best they have to offer." Jane's ambiguous accent lifted with her excitement. "Everyone who matters will be seated in the front row of the most exclusive shows. We're there as much to be photographed watching as the models are to wear the clothing. Both look good for the designer. And then there's the gala! Which is to die for."

"That sounds like…something I can handle," I admitted. It was nice, getting the rundown from Jane.

I didn't have to pretend with her. She had liked me for who I was from the beginning. And that was refreshing.

"You'll totally handle it. And I'll be there with you the whole time. Elizabeth has me on the seating chart for her event."

"Oh good," I said as we reached the personal shopper, Sandra, that Jane was familiar with.

"Hello, ladies. How can I help you?" Sandra asked.

Jane looked like she was about to answer for me, but I jumped in. I steeled myself for this encounter. Readied myself to act like the other Upper East Siders and not flinch from the cost of a damn thing.

"My old wardrobe is so last season," I told Sandra with a bored smile. "I need all the latest and a special cocktail dress for tonight."

"Of course," Sandra said, not missing a beat. "Right this way. Let's get you started. How many pieces are you looking to fill out this season?"

Jane raised an eyebrow at me in question.

"All of them," I replied. "Let's start fresh."

Sandra's eyes glittered. "Well then, I'm so pleased with what we just had come in. With your coloring and that hair, I know exactly where to start."

HOURS AND HOURS LATER, I had a new wardrobe. Between Sandra and Jane, I had been in impeccable hands. They knew exactly what to pair with what, when I would wear each piece, and which styles were most flattering. I hadn't even looked at the sum at the bottom before I signed my name with a flourish. The clothes would be delivered that afternoon. I hadn't even known that was an option.

Jane's eyes glittered with mischief by the time we were done. "I cannot believe he gave you his credit card."

"It's not a big deal," I said. Even though it was.

"Are you kidding? Court hasn't even given me his. We've been dating for, like, two years."

"Yeah, but you have your own money," I said with a shrug.

"True. True," Jane said.

It was weird to even be talking about this with her. If Penn was to be believed, money wasn't discussed between Upper East Siders. Maybe Jane was different with me because she knew where I'd come from. Or maybe it was her weird European roots.

"Come on," Jane said, leading me down Fifth Avenue. "While we were shopping, I called for an afternoon at the spa. If you have a sexy date with Penn, then makeovers are a hundred percent in order." She ran her fingers through the ends of my silvery-white hair. "Maybe we could dye your hair."

I pulled my hair back from her hand. "My hair?"

"Yeah. To go with your new wardrobe and boyfriend. It would all fit. A little bit more...respectable, you know?"

"The silver is kind of my signature."

"Yeah, but it does stand out," Jane reasoned. "I love it. Don't get me wrong. But it went with your old clothes and old vibe. This new Natalie could use an update, and this silver takes *any* color."

My brain screeched to a halt. The clothes, the boyfriend, the apartment. It was all too new. Too different. So, so not me. And I knew that it was a sacrifice that I needed to make to achieve what I wanted. That the ends justified the means. Still, I *couldn't* let go of my hair.

It was *me*. It was more than just a color.

Maybe people saw it and thought Hollywood model, but I couldn't give it up. It felt like the last thing that I refused to leave behind. I loved it way too much.

I shook my head. "I can't part with it."

Jane shrugged. "Just a suggestion. Could you imagine Penn's face if you showed up at his doorstep tonight as a blonde?"

Yes. He'd probably lose his mind. He loved my hair as much as I did. It was a concession I wasn't willing to give to this cause.

"He loves my hair."

"Okay, okay. I'll back off. But we are doing intense eyeliner," Jane said with a laugh.

She went off on a tangent about some French makeup

artist she knew who had insisted that winged eyeliner was a staple to any outfit. Jane could talk about people she'd met all day if I let her.

I pulled out my phone to check my messages while she chatted away. I had one from Penn that said he was regretting going into the office, which I responded to with devil horns. And then an email from my agent, asking if I could chat real quick.

I furrowed my brow and made an excuse to Jane before dialing Caroline's number. I hadn't heard from her since she told me my career was effectively over.

"Hello?" Caroline said into the phone.

"Caroline, it's Natalie. You asked if I had a moment to talk."

"Yes, Natalie. How are you?"

"I'm doing well. Thank you for asking."

"That's wonderful. I actually called with some excellent news."

"Really?" I asked in surprise.

Since when did my literary agent have good news to offer me? I'd thought my time had passed. That they wouldn't touch my Olivia Davies books, and now that everyone knew Olivia and Natalie were one in the same, they wouldn't take my literary novels either. I'd burned both bridges. Also because of fucking Lewis.

"Yes. I heard from Gillian. I guess there was a mix-up." Caroline was silent a second as if she still couldn't believe it. "I've been in this business thirty years, and this has never happened to me, but Warren wants to purchase IT's A MATTER OF OPINION. They're offering the same advance as BET ON IT."

I blinked. Then blinked again.

"They want to do *what*?" I gasped.

"They're offering seven figures for the manuscript, for publication next year."

"But…why?"

"Honestly, I have no idea. But what does it matter? This is great news."

Then I shook out of the excitement and stupor of the thought that Gillian was going to buy my literary novel and I'd finally be fine again and I'd have money to live in the city and everything would be all right. Because it wouldn't.

This wasn't about my book.

This had *nothing* to do with my book.

Lewis.

Lewis had done this.

And on one hand…I was so excited that he'd fixed his mistake. Because maybe this would mean my career wasn't over. But on the other hand, it'd mean that I was subject to his whims. It'd mean that my career was tied to him. It'd mean that he was still in control.

"No," I said softly.

"Excuse me?"

"Tell them thank you, but no."

"Natalie, I don't know if you heard me. This is a major deal."

"I can't do it."

Caroline huffed. "Let's put this discussion on hold for a few days before I give them an answer. Maybe you should think about it."

"Fine," I said. Though my answer wouldn't change. I was sure of that.

I said good-bye to Caroline and then stared at the building in front of me in shock.

Jane came to my elbow with concern on her face. "What happened?"

"After I left, Lewis blacklisted me from publishing."

"Oh, Natalie…"

"Yeah. And he just fixed it and told the company to buy my book again."

"Well, that's great," Jane said. She paused when I didn't smile or respond. "Isn't it?"

"Not if it means I'm tied to him. Not if it means he can control me."

Jane scrunched up her tiny nose. "Sounds exactly like Lewis in business."

My eyes shot to hers. "What do you mean?"

"I mean…you know?"

"I clearly don't."

"That whole controlling, possessive thing he does with you, that's how he is with all business. He's not particularly liked, but he gets shit done."

"Huh," I muttered.

I hadn't had any interest in Lewis's business dealings. I didn't understand them. And I never considered that he treated people or other businesses poorly. But of course, I hadn't seen any of it because I'd been caught up in him at the time. Now, it was pretty clear.

"Well, he's not going to control me."

"Powerful men usually get what they want."

"They do," I agreed.

A slow smile stretched on my features. Maybe someone should teach them a lesson.

CHAPTER 12

*D*ing.

My eyes shifted toward the living room in surprise as Totle went racing for the door. I slung my Rolex around my wrist and checked the time. Still a half hour before I needed to pick Natalie up for our date.

"Nat?" I called down the hall as I abandoned the knot I had been tying at my neck and let the two strands of blue fall on either side of my button-up.

"Try again," a voice called out.

My eyes rose in surprise. "Lark? What are you doing here? You do know that it's just past seven? Shouldn't you be working for the next three hours?" I joked.

"Ha-ha." She smiled, but I could see the exhaustion under her eyes.

Lark worked harder than anyone I knew, and it wasn't even campaign season yet. My mother wouldn't gear up for reelection for at least another month or two, and Lark would be there every step of the way.

"No, really, to what do I owe the pleasure?" Then I

frowned, thinking of all the reasons Lark normally showed up on my doorstep. She had a habit of sleeping over at one of the crew's places when she was going through a breakup. "Are you okay? Do I need to hurt someone? Is it Thomas?"

"No, no," she said quickly. "I'm fine. It's not about me. Not exactly. It's about the crew."

"What about the crew?"

She sighed. "You know what's going on. We haven't hung out all together in forever. I feel like I never see any of you. And that's coming from me."

"Sure. We're going through a patch."

"I was going to let it go," Lark said, "but I want to call a meeting."

I snorted. "Like when we were in high school?"

"Yes."

"Lark…"

"We're meeting at Rowe's place tomorrow night."

"You know that I love you, but I don't have any interest in seeing Lewis or Katherine. And is she even back from her honeymoon?"

"She got back this morning, and this is exactly the reason you will be there, Penn Kensington."

I shook my head in disagreement. "There's no guarantee that I won't punch Lewis in his smug face…again."

"You can control yourself for one evening. We need to talk."

"I'm not going."

Her green eyes were filled with sorrow. "If you don't show up, then you're throwing away decades of friendship. And I think you're better than that."

Then she leaned down and petted Totle once more

before disappearing back into the elevator, her message delivered.

I cursed at her disappearing back. Just what I did not want to deal with right now. Yes, I had known Lewis and Katherine practically my entire life. Yes, we had more secrets than most people and a sense of jaded loyalty that hadn't been shaken in over a decade. But we weren't kids anymore. I didn't have to deal with their bullshit, especially after what Lewis had done.

My hands clenched into tight balls. Just thinking of him made me want to put my fist through the wall. He'd taken what was mine for sport. If he'd ever had real feelings for Natalie, that file I'd found had changed everything. And I wouldn't let him hurt her. Not even for our friendship.

I tried to clear away the haze of anger that threatened to overcome me. This wasn't what I wanted to bring to this date with Natalie. She already knew my thoughts on the topic. And she wasn't ready to talk about it again yet.

"Fuck," I grumbled and then went back into my bedroom to finish getting dressed. I'd deal with the crew later.

MY CAR IDLED outside of Natalie's new apartment building, and she came rushing out in a hurry, her sleek black jacket still unbuttoned. My jaw nearly hit the ground.

"Holy shit," I groaned as a smile caught on her lips.

"Sorry I'm late. Jane insisted on makeovers after shopping."

My eyes rounded in wonder as I took her in. When I'd told her to go shopping, I hadn't really known what to expect. This whole lesson thing was a shot in the dark for me. I knew what it meant to be Upper East Side, but I'd never really had to train someone. But the clothes...I loved her in her bohemian style, but this was an all-new Natalie. Gorgeous and sophisticated. Her green dress was fitted perfectly to her figure and cut in a straight A-line. The jacket molded to her shape, clearly very in style and very expensive. Her silvery hair fell down in loose curls, and her makeup was soft, accenting her already-stunning features with a pink lipstick that made me want to kiss it off her hot mouth.

"You look incredible."

"Thank you," she said with a laugh. "I'd hope so after four hours at the spa."

I pulled the door open for her and let her shift into the backseat. I took the seat next to her and couldn't seem to stop staring. I'd known she was going to be different with new clothing, but I hadn't anticipated *this*. How well she fit. How she seemed to carry herself in a completely different way in these clothes.

And even though she looked so much more like the girls I'd grown up with, that silver hair still captivated me. Showing that she was different. She was still my Natalie.

I fingered a curly strand. "I love what you did with it."

"God, Jane wanted to dye it blonde."

I nearly choked. "She what?"

"Yeah, I told her no. That I wouldn't concede that to this mission." She fidgeted in her seat as if she was uncomfortable talking about it. Which didn't seem like Natalie at all.

"Oh yeah? Well, don't dye it. I love it."

She grinned, a swift, sly thing. "I know you do."

"Cocky?"

"Hey, I'm learning from the best."

I chuckled, eyeing the way she tried to hide some unease behind that smile. I wouldn't have seen it if I didn't know her, but I did know her. And I'd said no masks in private. What was she hiding?

"Speaking of," she said, "what lesson are we working on tonight? Since I'm all dressed up for it."

The thought died at her words. She thought this was a lesson. Because...of course she did. That was what she'd asked for. Just like a year ago when she'd asked for two months of carefree sex, and I'd given it to her. Until we both caught feelings, and that had been thrown out the window.

She wasn't ready for a relationship. She'd said that, but I'd ignored her. Hoped that these lessons would bring us together again like last time. Not that I'd force her into a relationship she wasn't ready for. But I wouldn't settle for just this either. Not with how perfect we were together.

"No lesson," I said finally.

Her nose wrinkled in confusion. "Oh? I figured the clothes and dinner went together."

I laced my fingers with hers in the back of the car. "No. The clothes were a lesson. And you look stunning in them. This...the rest of this, is just a date."

Her cheeks colored. "Oh. Well, I didn't realize..."

"I wanted to take you out. As long as that's all right with you."

She paused as if debating whether or not it was okay with her. I wasn't used to this feeling. Like I had to work for the person I was interested in. But I *was* interested in Natalie and only Natalie. A year without her had shown me that. So, I would wait. I'd be patient. I'd wait for her to be there, too.

"That sounds nice," she finally said with a hesitant smile.

"Good."

We'd get there. I knew there was so much more that she wasn't telling me. So much more that she was holding back. But how could I even blame her?

Sure, I was pissed about Lewis. But I'd fucked things up with her first. With that goddamn bet. Then Lewis had shattered her trust, too. It was amazing that she was even talking to me. Let alone going out on a date with me.

We just had to take the next steps together. Prove that we could move on from what was holding us back. The lies that had torn us apart in the first place.

CHAPTER 13

NATALIE

*T*ension settled in between my shoulder blades. There was no reason for it to be there. I'd been calling our date a date all day when talking to Jane. I was excited about it. But I just hadn't put two and two together that this was a *date*, date.

I didn't know why it even mattered. Penn and I had been seeing each other for a few weeks. We'd been staying at each other's places, gone to the charity function, and been having a lot of incredible sex.

But all of that had had the sheen of him teaching me, of these lessons. They'd kept a certain level of separation. Even if it was imaginary separation. Because there was so little that actually separated me and Penn.

Now that I knew this was a real date, no lesson at all, I felt a little unsettled. Like I should have anticipated this. Thought about what I was going to say over dinner or something.

God, I needed to shake this off. I'd never had a problem being around Penn before. Not seven years ago as we'd walked Paris together. Or in the Hamptons when we'd cohabited for a few months. Not even when I'd been dating his best friend. There had been other nerves for that, but I'd always been comfortable around him. Even when I hated him.

"Breathe," he said softly into my ear as we reached the host at the front of the restaurant.

I inhaled and then let it out slowly. I was being ridiculous. This was Penn after all. It was just that relationship stuff so soon after Lewis, even if I wanted it, made me nervous. I wasn't the Natalie he'd wanted before, and he didn't know all the deep, dark edges of me yet. The parts I wasn't ready to look at in the light. The ones that said to burn this world down. That *nothing* could make up for what they'd done.

"Ah, right this way," the host said with a smile.

"Are you okay?" Penn asked, gently taking my elbow as we followed the host to our table.

"Just a little nervous," I admitted.

He grinned. "Since when do I make you nervous?"

"Have we ever gone on a date before?"

"Hmm, maybe not. Though I think there's another reason for your nerves."

I tried to force the smile on my face. How did he see through me so easily? See to my anger about Lewis. I didn't want to ruin this date, even before I had known it was a real date. I wanted to do it even less now by telling Penn what had transpired.

Penn pulled my chair out, and I sat across from him. The restaurant was exquisite. Low lighting with flickering candles on every table. Everyone was dressed to the nines, and the room was crowded with young couples holding hands and glowing. This wasn't a first-date kind of place. This was a place where you put your name on the list six months in advance and hoped you could get a table. This was a place that guys splurged on when they were proposing.

"This is nice," I said. "Fancy for you."

He sat across from me and shrugged. "I thought it'd be a good excuse to get you to go shopping."

I rolled my eyes at him. "I would have gone without bribery."

"Hey, I know how you feel about this all."

"And yet, you brought me to a swank restaurant."

"All right, maybe this isn't a lesson, but you should be comfortable here."

I shrugged him off and opened the menu. My eyes ballooned at the prices, and I closed it again. "Are you sure you want to eat here? How long did it take you to get a reservation?"

He sent me a cocky look. "I got it yesterday. And yes, I want to eat here. Get the most expensive thing on the menu."

"Who are you, and what have you done with Penn Kensington? I would have been fine with pizza."

"Oh, I know," he said with a scoff. "No one eats as much pizza as you."

"Hey, don't diss pizza."

"As if I could. It's your favorite." His glittering blue eyes bore into mine over the menu. A perfect Manhattan playboy smile on his face. "And to answer your question, Penn Kensington realized that he can be both people with you. Weren't *you* the one to say that you liked it?"

I flushed all over again at the memory. "I did, didn't I?"

The waiter came over, and Penn swiftly ordered us an exorbitantly priced bottle of red wine. He got a steak with all the trimmings, and I forced down my apprehension about money and ordered the lobster. The sommelier appeared shortly and poured our wine.

I brought the glass to my lips and took a small sip. My eyes closed briefly at the exquisite taste, and I sighed. "That is…delicious."

His eyes widened. "Are you trying to convince me to leave early?"

"Oh no, I'm eating that lobster."

He took a sip of his own and then smiled sadly. "This was my father's favorite wine. He always had it in the house."

"You don't talk about him often."

"No. Well, not many pleasant memories. It's kind of amazing that he could even taste it after all the cocaine," he said nonchalantly. "But he did have excellent taste in alcohol. One of the few good things about him."

"I'm sorry that you never had a real relationship with him and that he died before you could work it out."

Penn shrugged it off, setting the glass down. "We wouldn't have worked it out. And anyway, him dying was the main thing that set me on a better path. In some way, it was a blessing."

"Still, not great."

"No," he said carefully. Then his eyes met mine. "Are you going to tell me why you've been jittery and fidgety since I picked you up?"

God, I'd hoped that he wouldn't ask again. That he'd let it go. "I'm not jittery."

K.A. LINDE

His foot settled over my own, which had been tapping incessantly and I hadn't even noticed.

"Talk to me." A command, not a request. His sexy alpha voice made me want to do exactly what he'd said. But damn, I did not want to ruin dinner.

"You won't like it."

"I don't have to, but if it gets it off your shoulders, that's all that matters."

"My agent called today," I said with another sigh. "She said that Warren called back, and Gillian wants to acquire my next book. They've offered to match my last advance."

Penn's lips pursed. "That's...coincidental."

"Is it?"

"Lewis?"

"Yes. I mean, she didn't say that. She probably doesn't know. But I do. I know that I yelled at him in the doorway of my apartment, and now, they've made an offer on my book. As if he thinks that he can fix his mistakes and that will fix us." I paused over the words, anger boiling in my veins. I took a gulp of the expensive wine, hardly tasting it this time. "He wants to control me."

"That's not going to happen."

"I know," I said softly. "I told her to turn it down."

"Oh, Natalie." His voice was so tender that it cut through me like glass.

"Yeah. I mean, it's one thing to have my career stolen. It's another entirely to have to throw it away on your own."

"This is just with Warren," he assured me. "You can go with another publisher. Then you won't be trapped under Lewis."

I shook my head and glanced away, blinking away the

112

tears that threatened to spill. Talking about it like this was way worse than when I'd told Jane. Penn knew how much this had destroyed me. He knew my hopes and dreams and how they were now crumpled to ash.

"Maybe. We'll see."

"That motherfucker," Penn said under his breath. "I cannot believe he's doing this to you."

"Why wouldn't he when there are no consequences to anything he does?" Fire replaced the despair in an instant. "When he never has to pay for the way he treats people?"

"I can make him pay for his actions."

I narrowed my eyes. "Please don't do anything stupid. I can handle this myself."

"You wanted lessons on the Upper East Side, Natalie. Sometimes, you need to let others take care of things for you."

"No," I said sharply.

I didn't want Penn involved. Not when I didn't know what Lewis's next move was. I wanted to be one step ahead of him. That was what I'd learned from Katherine. She was always ahead of me in some way. And I planned to stay ahead of both of them. So that this looked like a small misstep in the grand scheme of things.

"Can we talk about something else? There's a reason I didn't want to tell you about it."

"Well, it was all over you. I couldn't ignore it."

"If this is our first date, then I don't want to spend the entire time talking about Lewis," I said, leaning forward. "Let's talk about something else. Your book? How is that going?"

Penn looked like he wanted to say more about Lewis, but then he effortlessly switched topics. Ever the charmer.

"I finally got a date for it. Looks like it's coming out this fall after all. Supposedly, I should be getting copies at the start of the summer."

"And is it the life-changing philosophy work you always wanted to do?"

Like my love of writing, ethical philosophy was where Penn's passion rested. He'd wanted to write a ground-breaking book about sex and morality. Especially looking at the standard view that said only relationships could equal safe and moral sex. Unsurprisingly, he argued that relationships were hardly necessary as long as it was consensual sex between adults. He said more about diseases and pregnancy, but the gist was the same. One-night stands were A-okay in moral terms and, even further, could bring about real Aristotelian happiness.

But Penn didn't answer right away. I was surprised by that. Even a year ago, he'd been adamant that this was the only route.

"I don't disagree with my central argument. I think that people can be moral and achieve happiness outside of a relationship." His eyes settled on mine as if he'd come to a deeper conclusion that he wasn't sure he wanted to share with me. "But I'll be honest and say that I can understand the standard view, too."

I nearly choked on my wine. "Since when?"

"About a year ago," he admitted.

"But you...you slept around after me."

"I did. It wasn't for moral reasons, and it brought me no real happiness. If anything, it brought me further from my intended result. Especially when it was clear that I was just trying and failing to forget you. That *you* were my happiness, and I'd lost you, like an idiot."

My mouth dropped open at his admission.

I'd known that he'd slept around to get back at Katherine. That he didn't do it out of any real pleasure. But it still hurt to find out especially since I hadn't been with anyone else while he'd been getting his dick wet with whoever walked by. It was part of the reason I'd ended up giving Lewis a chance to begin with.

But to hear that I'd changed his entire view on his own philosophical musings. To hear that *I* was now the source of that happiness he'd been searching for since his father died. I didn't...didn't even have words for that.

It made me glow from the inside out. As if butterflies had just descended into my stomach and were whacking their tiny wings all along the inside. It seemed unbelievable and wonderful. And terrifying.

That he felt that way. That I couldn't deny that I felt that way.

"And here, I can normally tell what you're thinking, but I have no clue," he said with a small laugh. "Did I speak my mind too much? I don't think how I feel about you is a secret."

"No," I whispered. "Not anymore. I wanted to think that last year was all a lie to you. Just a joke. But it wasn't, was it?"

He shook his head. "Every moment was real."

The waiter took that second to bring out our meals. I was glad for the reprieve from that conversation. It was way more intense than I'd expected. I'd thought we'd have another round of *observe the room* or *show how your clothes make you superior* or whatever Upper East Side bullshit they touted. I'd figured I might get some information on strategy. Not talk about our feelings.

My feelings were too conflicted. Too conflicted to give in to that gorgeous smile, the too-blue eyes, and the adorable dimples. The man that I was just now really getting to know. I'd been attracted to him from the start. With a body like that, who wouldn't? But it was the brain and the man beneath that mask that always intrigued me.

I'd come back to New York, thinking I could keep Penn at a distance. I hadn't anticipated falling for him again so easily. Like sand through a sieve. The more I tried to guard my heart to keep from getting hurt again, the more he broke down all the barriers I'd put up, leaving me bare.

But maybe...just maybe, he wouldn't shy away from this new side of myself I was just discovering. If I could fall for the two sides of Penn, maybe he could fall for both sides of me.

CHAPTER 14

PENN

*N*atalie had told me not to do anything stupid in regards to Lewis. And this wasn't stupid. This was very smart.

I wouldn't seek him out. But if we happened to be called to the same meeting by Lark, then it wouldn't hurt to show up and knock some sense into him. I could be perfectly rational about it. Not that he deserved it. One way or another, he was going to back the fuck off.

I stepped into the elevator for Rowe's place, only a few blocks down the street from my own. When it opened to his incredibly monochromatic living room, I was greeted by the overeager expression from one Larkin St. Vincent.

"You came," she said in obvious relief.

"I did. I don't think any of us have missed a summons before," I said.

"True. But you were so adamant."

"Well, I hadn't planned on coming. Changed my mind at the last minute."

"I'm glad you're here." She stepped aside, allowing me into Rowe's penthouse.

Rowe was seated in a white armchair, his face buried in his computer, like always. Lewis was at the bar, holding a bottle of gin and adding olives to a martini. Katherine was lounging back against the chaise as if she were some golden goddess. Her skin was sun-kissed from the weeks she had spent in the Maldives with Camden. Even her dark hair had honey streaks in it from the sun.

For a second, with all of us assembled like misfit Avengers, it felt like coming home. As if the last year hadn't occurred. As if we were back in high school or college, where our friendship was everything we needed. When we couldn't live without each other.

But the illusion was just that.

We weren't those people anymore.

We might have a shared past with secrets aplenty, but that didn't mean we had loyalty anymore. Something had been irrevocably broken between us. And a meeting with all of us together couldn't possibly change that.

Rowe glanced up then, looking up at me from under a pair of thick black glasses. He hadn't worn glasses since elementary school. "Sup."

I cracked a grin. Because despite it all, Rowe was exactly the same. "Hey, man."

"Drink, Kensington?" Lewis asked as he strode to Katherine's side and handed her the martini.

"No," I said tersely.

"Oh, how I do miss this level of service already," Katherine said. "The resort we went to took care of liter-ally everything. I don't know how I'm supposed to live otherwise." She shifted her attention to me with a twinkle in her eye. "How are you, darling?"

I fought to keep from clenching my hands into fists. I could play this game. I was the expert after all. But I simply didn't *want* to.

"Maybe we should get started." I slid my hands into my pockets and waited for Lark to begin.

She sighed heavily and then took a seat next to Rowe. "Just sit down, Penn."

"Let him brood," Katherine said with a hand wave. "It's what he's best at."

Rowe snorted. "So true."

"Mmm," Katherine said, raising her glass to Lewis. "Excellent bartender."

"Pleased to be of service." He shot her a mocking smile and then sank into the couch, kicking his feet up on the coffee table.

"Uh, no," Rowe said. He pointed at Lewis's feet.

Lewis snickered and then dropped them back down to the floor.

"Penn, sit," Lark said again, "so we can get started."

"God, Penn, listen to the woman," Katherine groaned. She shifted in her seat, wincing slightly as she slid from her hip to her backside. "We're not going to bite you. Not unless you ask us to."

I casually took a seat, and said, "Didn't get enough biting from Percy the last month?"

Katherine narrowed her eyes as she adjusted her seat again. "Let's not."

"You can give it but can't take it?"

Lewis rolled his eyes across from me. "Look who's talking."

119

K.A. LINDE

"You're perfectly aware that I take as good as I give," Katherine said with a note of pure seduction to her voice.

"Good lord," Lark groaned.

I heard her words, meant to remind me of times we had been together, but that all seemed like a lifetime ago. Why I'd ever played her games, I had no clue.

"Or did you already forget, love?" Katherine asked. She sat up and then hissed, jumping off of her ass and then slowly settling back down.

"Having issues sitting?" I asked with a shake of my head.

What exactly *had* she and Camden done during their month in the Maldives?

Lewis snickered.

"I'm fine," she bit out.

But my eyes were trained on Lewis. Anger flared in my blood.

"Have something to say?" Lewis asked. He grinned like a fool and leaned back on the couch as if he didn't have a care in the world. He was enjoying this. Enjoying my anger.

"We'll see," I said, masking my irritation behind a blank expression. He'd know it for what it was, but I hardly even cared at this point.

"Look," Lark began, "I don't like calling a meeting, but our crew has been shit for the last year. And I'm tired of feeling like I'm choosing sides whenever I hang out with any of you. Can we get everything out in the open and learn to move on?"

Everyone was silent at Lark's admission. Because none of us wanted to say no to her. We all hated it. She was the conciliatory member. The one who always brought us back together, who always managed to mediate our bull-shit. But even Lark couldn't do it this time.

"We've been through worse than this," Lark continued with a note of disgust in her voice. "Don't you all remember junior year when Hanna left? That was our lowest low. If we can get over her committing suicide, then don't you think we can stick it out through this? I knew this bet was a bad idea. I tried to tell you. And now, look at us."

"It's not the bet," Katherine said. "It's Natalie. If these idiots can agree to stop fighting over her, then we'll probably be fine."

"Natalie is not the issue," I said at the same time Lewis said, "That's not happening."

"I like Natalie," Lark said with a sigh. "She's a sweet girl, and the bet was cruel. But I think the real issue is that we took the damn bet too fucking far again. *Again*. So can you stop fighting for a minute to get us back together?"

"We're not The Beatles, Larkin dear," Katherine said, swirling her martini. "We'll be fine. Plus, after I crushed little Natalie, she's not going to be a further problem."

Lark glanced over at Katherine. "You haven't seen *Page Six* the last couple of weeks, huh?"

"What did I miss?" Katherine asked.

"Natalie is here to stay. She's becoming like…an *it* girl," Lark admitted.

Katherine actually cackled. "Well, good luck with that. I'm back now. Things will go back to the way they're supposed to be. No one will care about her when I'm done with her."

"Stay away from her," I snarled. "Both of you."

"Oh, please tell me that you're not trying to get in her

good graces again," Katherine said, bored and disappointed.

"Natalie is going to come around to me again anyway," Lewis said with such utter confidence. It was amazing to me that he was deluded enough to even say it.

"You ruined her career." I rose to my feet, glaring at him.

"And then put it back together," he said with a shrug.

"It doesn't work that way after you stalked her."

"She doesn't even believe that. It'll be fine."

Katherine gagged. "You two are seriously disgusting. *Why* her?"

Rowe cleared his throat to keep anyone else from responding. All our eyes turned to him in surprise. He hadn't said anything since the meeting started. Lark was relieved that someone else was going to jump in.

"Just wanted to let you all know that I'm dating someone new," Rowe said, looking up from his computer and meeting our gaze. "His name is Nicholas. Thought I'd let you know before I bring him to Fashion Week."

We all stared at him for a heartbeat before everyone else joined me on my feet.

"That's great," I said at once.

Katherine's eyes were enormous as she gushed all over Rowe. "A boyfriend? Oh my god, finally! I'm so excited."

"So cool, bro," Lewis said.

Lark just smiled as if she had already known. Which she probably had and it was part of the reason that we'd all been called together.

Getting details about Nicholas out of Rowe was basically impossible. He hated the spotlight, and talking about himself was a foreign concept. But it kept the heat off of everyone else, and so he endured it. Telling us how they'd met, when it had started, and how serious it was.

And somehow, something changed in the room.

Did we have problems? Yes.

Were we utterly fucked up because of that damn bet? Yes.

But here, in this moment, we were something else. Something more than just a group of fucked up, entitled, poor little rich kids. We were together again.

I might hate Katherine and Lewis for what they'd done to Natalie. I had every intention of stopping them from ever doing it again. But I also fucking loved them in some strange way. Like they were a part of me. And I was a part of them. Like family.

We were tangled up together more than I'd ever even realized.

For the first time, my loyalties felt conflicted. And I was glad I hadn't told Natalie I was coming here.

PART III
REVENGE IS A DISH

CHAPTER 15

NATALIE

"Welcome to the Cunningham Couture event," a lithe woman said at the VIP entrance to the runway show. "Let me assist you to your seat."

"Thank you," I said with a smile, handing her my invitation.

"Ah, Miss Bishop, wonderful. You're seated in the front row, next to Harmony Cunningham and Jane Devney, who are both already in attendance. Do you need help to locate your spot?"

I leaned in and saw Jane and Harmony chatting it up like old friends in the first row. My heart pounded. First row! Elizabeth had given me first row. Of course, we'd talked about setting me up with one of the few reserved spots, but I hadn't thought that it meant sitting with her daughter of all people. That was sure to make an impression.

"No, I see them," I told the woman and then entered the large room.

I was halfway to Harmony and Jane when they noticed me approaching and waved.

Jane stood and kissed each of my cheeks. "You made it. Look at our seats. Perfect, no?"

"The best seats in the house," I agreed.

Harmony pulled me into a hug next. "So good to see you again, Natalie. My mother has been raving about you since New Year's Eve."

"It's so good to see you. Your mom is so kind."

Harmony giggled. "She likes to invest in the right people. And I have to gush over your outfit. So, so cute."

I ran my hand down the black cigarette pants that I'd paired with a white blouse and a forest-green jacket. "Thank you. Jane was the one who said I should get these pants. She has incredible taste."

"Doesn't she?" Harmony said with a grin as I took a seat. "Should be almost time to go. Do you all have plans to see more runway shows or shop the boutique pop-ups?"

Jane dished out all the invites that she'd received for Fashion Week and which boutiques she had to see before they left. It felt surreal that I was even here right now. I knew I wasn't supposed to take pictures while the show was going on, but I snapped a few shots now, including one or two of the incredibly famous celebrity couple seated across the runway from me. Then I texted the whole lot of them to Melanie, who I knew would be green with envy.

My phone immediately pinged with a slew of texts from her. Most of them calling me horrible names for being there when she wasn't. Of course, I didn't point out that I had invited her to live with me, and she'd declined because of her boyfriend. She was talented enough to get into design school in the city, but she'd turned them down for him.

"This is Natalie's first Fashion Week," Jane said, pulling me from my phone.

"What?" Harmony gasped. "I can't believe it. This is my, oh, who even knows how many anymore? Hundreds, I swear. But the first year that I'm not walking in any of them."

I remembered all of Penn's lessons about how to act and look and appear to other people. Always confident. Never letting them see my nerves. Careful to keep myself under control. Haughty if everything else failed. This was my first real test of the lessons that we'd had up to this point. I knew the gala would be something else altogether. And this was more like a test run.

I shrugged one shoulder. "Yes. This is a whole new experience for me. Not my typical area of art."

"Right. You're an author," Harmony remembered.

I nodded. "Why aren't you walking this year?"

Harmony wrinkled her nose. "It was time, I think. I'm going to take up the mantle of Cunningham Couture with mother for the spring/summer 2020 line show in September. We'll start on it after this event."

"That's going to be so good for you," I said.

"The brand is expanding so rapidly. It'll be great to have another Cunningham on board."

"Thanks for your confidence," Harmony said, brushing back her sheet of blonde hair. "Oh god, what is she doing here?"

I followed her gaze and saw none other than Katherine Van Pelt striding into the now-full room. The poor woman who had told me where my seat was frantically rushed after her. As if Katherine wasn't supposed to be in here.

"Ma'am, please, all of the VIP seats were assigned weeks ago. Mrs. Cunningham put them in place herself. You are not supposed to be seated here."

Katherine whipped around and said something low to the woman. I assumed it had to be vicious because the woman blanched and then retreated to where she had been standing. She had made a big enough scene to draw attention, but when the woman walked away, everyone went back to what they had been doing.

Except my trio. We all stared at Katherine, waiting.

"She is not welcome," Harmony muttered under her breath.

"It looks like she has an invitation though," Jane pointed out.

"Maybe it was a mix-up," I offered, keeping my face neutral. A perfect blank mask taken straight out of the Upper East Side.

That was the moment that Katherine found me seated in the front row of Elizabeth Cunningham's New York Fashion Week runway show. Her eyes narrowed. Her perfect cherry-red lips pursed in disapproval. Her entire stance snapped into predator mode. And then she was walking toward me about to take me head-on.

I was ready for her. I, unlike her, had anticipated her presence. I'd prepared for what I would do and how I would act if and when I ran into her again. Because I'd be lying if I said that I hadn't been waiting for this moment since I stepped back onto the scene.

Now, she was here. And I was sitting in her place. The

only thing that would hold her back was the crowd. I had to keep from smirking at her as I stayed one step in front of her.

"Natalie," she hissed when she reached where I was seated with Harmony and Jane.

"Oh my goodness, Katherine," I said with faux excitement. I rose to my feet and wrapped my arms around her thin shoulders. "You're back from your honeymoon. Did you and Camden just have the best time? I cannot imagine how wonderful it was to have a whole month alone with him in the Maldives. Nowhere else to go. Nothing else to do." I secretively lowered my voice and winked. "Except each other, of course."

Katherine took a step back from me, as if surprised by my enthusiasm. As if I'd thrown her by not digging my claws into her back like she deserved.

Jane stood, too, with a real smile for Katherine. "Tell us everything. How was it? Look at how tan you are."

"It was...perfect," she said with the passion of a slug baking in the sun. "I am just so glad to be back now though. Get back to *my* city. And there seems to have been some error." She held up her invitation. "It looks like you're in my seat, Natalie."

I put a hand to my chest. "I'm sorry you think so. But no, when Elizabeth and I spoke after the children's art foundation charity event, she assured me that I'd be seated with Jane."

Katherine tilted her head in confusion. "The...children's art foundation event?"

"Oh yes, very important work," I said with a smile.

"*You* were at the charity function?"

131

"Of course." I fluttered my eyelashes at her for good measure.

"Look, you need to go sit somewhere else. I *always* sit in the front row. Elizabeth has been dressing me for the last two years. She assured me I'd have this seat."

"Can't do that," I said with a smile. "But maybe there's room in the general seating if you hurry."

Katherine glared at me. Her brown orbs turning almost black as she looked like she wanted to do anything to cut me down. "That…is not possible."

"Maybe next year," I said with cheer. I patted her shoulder twice and then sat next to Harmony.

I turned to Harmony as if we were best friends and ignored Katherine standing there like a fish out of water in the very place she had always considered her own element.

"So, tell me more about this design work you're planning on," I said to Harmony.

Katherine reached out and grasped my shoulder. Her voice was low. "Natalie, what the fuck are you thinking?"

I brushed her hand off of my shoulder like she was a fly. "Thinking? I don't know what you mean, Katherine. I can't help that you don't have a reserved seat. Take it up with Elizabeth, I guess."

Harmony finally looked up at Katherine with complete apathy. "Better luck next year, Katherine."

Katherine balked at us both, straightening to her considerable height. I could see the emotions roiling through. Everything she wanted to do and say. But there were too many people. Katherine liked to hide her destruction. She didn't want people to see it in the light of day. She was too perfect to do anything else. Only her friends and the line of people she'd taken down knew her true self. If she wasn't careful, someone might come along and make her pay for what she'd done.

Finally, Katherine stomped away, not admitting defeat as she railed at the person with the seating chart. But she was gone. And I'd won that round.

As soon as Katherine was out of sight, Harmony burst into laughter. "Oh. My. God. Natalie, that was *brilliant*. I have never seen anyone handle Katherine like that before."

Even Jane was giggling. "Seriously, how did you do that?"

I shrugged. "I didn't do anything," I lied. "She didn't have a seat. It wasn't *my* fault that she attacked me when she thought I'd taken her place for the show. That's delusional on her part."

"Yes. But I've seen a lot of people fold to her demands. And you actually turned your back on her. Genius," Harmony said. She grasped my hand and squeezed. "Katherine and I have a fraught history. She's a horrible person, and she did everything she could to make my life miserable for so many years. Anyone who can stand up to her like that is a friend of mine."

"I'm so sorry that she made you feel like less than you are. I've had that same experience with Katherine. And I decided I wouldn't take it any longer. Maybe you should do the same."

"You're so right. She's just so intimidating. I usually try to avoid her."

"Well, no more avoiding. If you avoid, she wins. We should stick together. And then maybe she can stop intimidating every person she thinks is in her way."

Harmony smiled broadly as the lights flickered overhead, announcing the start of the show. "I like the way you think. What are you doing after this? I have a few boutique pop-ups that I have scheduled. You should come with me. I can tell you some *crazy* things about Katherine Van Pelt."

"That sounds like a plan," I agreed.

And like *my* plan was finally beginning.

CHAPTER 16

NATALIE

*T*he applause was deafening. Everyone in the entire room was on their feet, applauding Elizabeth's latest collection of fall and winter apparel. The line of waifish models stood onstage, looking like a row of dolls on display. Elizabeth was stunning in her own right as she bowed for the crowd and took credit for the works of art before us.

Cheers died down, the models returned backstage, and soon, everyone was milling around or rushing off to their next show or meeting or boutique event. I'd learned before showing up that Fashion Week was essentially a mayhem for anyone in the industry. It was a make-it-or-break-it experience for careers.

"Come on," Harmony said, latching on to my arm. "Let's go see my mom."

I reached out for Jane. "Are you coming with?"

She shook her head. "Go ahead. I have a meeting next with Christopher Michelangelo-Cortez, who is *so* up-

and-coming. The MCZ line is out of this world. Text me later, and if I'm free, I'll meet you at a pop-up!"

I laughed because it was just so Jane. "All right. If you're busy, then I'll see you at the gala tomorrow night!"

"Of course," Jane said as if there were no other option. Then she strolled out of the room, already on her phone, probably making some other business connection.

Harmony grinned and pulled me along after her. "Okay, it's going to take a minute to get through to my mom. As you can imagine, this is, like, *her* time. And it's going to be nuts."

Harmony guided me through the crowd and to the side of the stage nearest her mother. She was speaking to a group of industry people, and Harmony just pulled out her phone to pass the time.

"Um…where's your Crew Influencer page?"

"My what?" I asked, glancing over her shoulder.

Crew was the hottest social media app around. Rowe had created it when he and the crew were in high school for a way for them to connect, and it had blown up. Facebook had tried to buy him out, but he'd declined, claiming he didn't need the money.

"Your Influencer page," Harmony gushed. She flipped her phone around, so I could see her page, which was displayed with dozens of glossy pictures of her all over the world and a running tally of comments from admirers. She currently had five-point-five million connections.

"Holy shit! Five-point-five million people follow you?" I gasped, completely losing my cool in that moment. "That's incredible."

Harmony shrugged one shoulder, but the smirk on her face said everything. "Thanks! It's basically my life. And I have no idea why you don't have one. How do you expect people to know who you are if you're not giving them access to your life? *Page Six* is great and all, but this, you can curate yourself."

"I mean, I have Crew. I just don't have an Influencer page."

"Well, we will fix that. Hand me your phone."

I reluctantly passed it to her, and she went to work, setting up a page for me. She asked if she could go through my pictures and actually seemed surprised when I said yes. Perhaps she was used to people having nudes. Or being afraid to show the ugly selfies that you didn't post online. Photography wasn't my art form, but I usually erased anything I didn't love.

About ten minutes later, she handed the phone back to me. "Okay. Here's your Influencer page. I only posted three pictures, but you'll want to update it regularly to keep your connections interested." She showed me a few features. "I'm going to follow you now. Eep! I'm so excited for you."

I stared down at the Influencer page in shock as I saw my numbers go from zero to one—Harmony. Then from one to three and three to ten and ten to twenty right before my eyes.

"Jesus, who is connecting with me already?"

Harmony shrugged. "People who like your picture and my friends and stuff. It'll be great." She glanced up. "Oh! My mom is ready."

Harmony stepped up to Elizabeth, and I was at her side. Elizabeth looked stunning in a black pantsuit and silver statement necklace.

She embraced her daughter. "Harmony dear, what did you think?"

"Brilliant as ever," Harmony said. "Probably the best yet."

Elizabeth beamed. "Thank you. And you, Natalie?"

Suddenly, all eyes were on me.

I kept my best mask on my face and smiled brightly. "No one does it better. Watching it from the front row was such an experience."

"Excellent," Elizabeth said. "And I'll see you at the gala tomorrow night?"

"Of course. I'm so thrilled to be wearing one of your pieces again."

Elizabeth grinned. "Natalie, let me introduce you to Paul. He works for *Vogue*."

And then it was a string of introductions. All these people who wanted to know who I was. Everyone thought I was important because Elizabeth had made me important. It was insane. And the spotlight made me a little dizzy. I could see for the first time why Katherine wanted this life. This insane socialite lifestyle where my world was built around free clothes, parties, and connections with other fashionable people. Where I made money off of looking good, knowing the right people, and posting it online for others to stare at. Exhausting but still exciting.

Finally, I ducked out of the crowd. Harmony was still speaking with people, and I wouldn't leave without her since I still wanted to hit those pop-ups. But I needed a minute to myself. A second to breathe.

"I wondered if you'd ever get a minute alone."

I snapped to attention like a deer caught in headlights. "Lewis, what are you doing here?"

My pulsed thumped against my neck. Fear was the first emotion. Even though I was in a room with so many other people, it felt like I was alone with him again. This was the first time I'd seen him without Penn since the breakup. And it made me uncomfortable and also sad. We'd dated not that long ago, and now, I didn't even feel okay being near him…let alone be alone with him.

"Charlotte was walking for Elizabeth," he said effortlessly.

Of course. I'd seen Charlotte on the runway today and at the Trinity soft opening in December. She was a tall, strong, and beautiful black woman who wore her natural hair on the runway. It was incredible to see. I'd been so wrapped up with Harmony and Jane that I hadn't thought about the fact that Lewis would be there to watch her.

"Oh, of course. Well, you should go find her," I said, turning to walk away.

He grasped my elbow to stop me.

I wheeled around, ready to smack that smug look off of his face. "Don't touch me."

"Natalie, please," he said. His big brown eyes were pleading. He looked heartbroken. But he'd done this to himself.

"No. We're over, Lewis. You did this."

"It was a mistake."

"Which part?" I asked, shaking out of his grip.

"All of it. I shouldn't have kept the file. I shouldn't have done any of it. I want you back. I fixed my mistake. I know that we can work this out."

"What part of my personality makes you think that I would forgive you for what you did?"

"So you can forgive Penn for fucking over your life but not me for trying to look out for you?" he demanded.

I groaned and shook my head. "I don't want to do this with you, Lewis. We're over. I don't have to justify my actions to you any longer. And you didn't *fix* your mistake. All you did was try to control me again. I'm not going to be controlled ever again," I icily told him.

"Natalie, I love you."

"No, you don't," I said simply. "Please, just leave me alone."

I tried to walk away again, but he grabbed my upper arm. Hard. Hard enough to bruise. I made a sharp noise of protest.

"Stop it, Lewis! You're hurting me."

"So, just like that? You're going back to him? Even though he's fucking toying with you? Is that why you sent him to the crew meeting? So that he could threaten me?" he growled. "I won't be threatened."

"Lewis, I have no idea what you're talking about. But if you don't let me go, I'm going to scream," I growled. Tears stung my eyes at the pain.

He blinked as if he realized what he'd done. Then he dropped my arm as if I'd burned him. "Natalie, I'm so sorry. Oh fuck, I didn't mean..."

"But you did," I gasped, holding my arm.

"I don't know what came over me."

"You didn't get your way," I spat at him. "For once, there are consequences to the shit that you pulled, and you didn't like it. Well, get fucking used to it."

I strode away from him, keeping my head tilted high,

even as it buzzed with the surprise jolt of pain and the words he'd said. At the fucking entitled bullshit.

But also...he'd thought I'd sent Penn to a crew meeting.

What crew meeting?

Harmony waved me over just as I pulled out my phone to call Penn. I ground my teeth. A call would have to wait. I still wanted to go with Harmony. I opted for a text instead.

Did you go to a crew meeting?

Penn's message came back almost instantly.

...yes.

Motherfucker.

When exactly were you going to tell me about this?

I was livid. And I had to keep it together. Because I was supposed to leave with Harmony to go to boutique pop-ups. This whole experience was good for who I was becoming and what I wanted to accomplish. I couldn't exactly walk away to go yell at Penn. But fuck, all the old suspicions wormed their way back into my heart. Just like that. A snap of my fingers, and it all flooded back.

Can I call you?

No, I'm with Harmony. We're heading to a pop-up.

Fuck, Nat. I don't want to do this through text. I could leave campus and come to you?

Don't bother. I'll swing by campus when we're done. I guess this gives you time to get your story straight.

It's not like that. At all.

I clamped down on that old familiar rage. That black pit that I'd settled into that said, *Burn it. Burn it down. Burn him down.* But I didn't want that. I didn't want to hurt him, too. It just felt like I was screwing myself already.

I'll just talk to you later.

Please don't worry about this all afternoon. It was harmless.

The crew is NEVER harmless.

Then I stuffed my phone back down into my purse and swore to ignore him until I was done hanging out with Harmony.

"Everything all right?" she asked when I finally reached her.

"Yeah. Fine."

"Things looked tense with Lewis." She arched an eyebrow as we headed out of the room.

"Oh, yeah," I said, "he's not happy about me and Penn."

Harmony giggled. "I would think not. But who can resist Penn Kensington, right?"

I wanted to grumble under my breath that I certainly had when he was acting like an asshole. But that wouldn't solve anything. I needed to talk to Penn. Not bitch about him to one of his many exes.

"Pretty much," I finally said.

"Lewis is the jealous type anyway."

"That I noticed."

"I was always surprised you two ended up together," Harmony said. "That you jumped from one to the other and back."

"It didn't exactly happen that way."

"It never does." Harmony held up her hands. "Trust me. No judgment here. Penn and I have a messed up past. I get what it's like to do stupid things for guys. The guy I was seeing before just started dating someone else. And I want to stab him and beg him back. I hate it."

"I'm sorry," I said reflexively. Though my mind was only half on this conversation. The rest of me wanted to dig into my bag and see what Penn had said. But I wouldn't. I needed to calm down before I stormed uptown and unleashed on him.

"Don't be sorry. He was kind of a jerk anyway." Harmony smiled at me. "Here's the boutique. God, I'm kicking myself for wearing heels again. So much freaking walking. They always say we can dress down, but I just never do."

I let Harmony carry on as we stepped into the first pop-up. And I tried to ignore the buzz at the bottom of my bag.

CHAPTER 17

*A*fter a few hours of looking at clothes, talking to designers, and chatting it up with all the people in the know, I bowed out of the next event with Harmony. I liked her. Surprisingly so, considering that she'd grown up here. But I could only handle so much of this world when I had this shit with Penn roiled up inside of me.

I stepped into the first cab and told him to take me to Columbia. I tilted my head back on the seat and closed my eyes. My feet ached like I couldn't believe. My head felt about the same. And as much as I was ready to get this over with, I didn't want to walk into this confrontation. Because I knew it would be something drastic.

I was glad that I'd had a few hours to cool down so that I wouldn't immediately combust on him, but it hadn't made me feel better. He didn't have to tell me everything. But his friends were our downfall. They knew how to screw us up, and he was an idiot if he didn't see that.

I'd only been on Columbia's campus once since Penn and I got back together. He'd asked me to meet him for dinner one night when he stayed late. Usually, I spent the days working on my new book. I wasn't going anywhere with it yet, but I was glad that I was writing after what had happened with the last manuscript.

The philosophy department was located almost directly off of the main quad near the library and a pretty impressive-looking church. My heels clicked across the brick-lined sidewalk as I approached the imposing building. I stepped inside and was still surprised that it looked like any other university I'd ever been on. Columbia had such a feel of reverence about it that it was hard to think it could look like home. I took the hallway to the elevator that opened up to the third floor. His office was a corner space with a plaque on the door that read *Dr. Kensington*.

I knocked once and heard a relieved sigh on the other side.

"Come in."

With a deep breath, I turned the knob and entered Penn's office. My eyes drifted around the cozy room covered against one wall with floor-to-ceiling books and books and more books. Penn's desk sat at the center with an array of monitors. His steely-blue eyes met mine across the short space, and tension crackled between us. Even though I was mad at him, I couldn't look away from that desk. From what we could do with that desk after-hours.

I stopped that train of thought and nudged the door shut behind me. That was *not* why I was here.

"You didn't answer any of my texts."

"I stopped checking them," I said, tossing my bag down onto a chair in front of his desk.

"You shouldn't shut me out."

"I was busy."

"Then let's get it out. You're mad because I saw the crew."

"Yes, I'm mad," I said carefully, bracing my hands on his desk and leaning forward. "I told you not to talk to Lewis about this. I told you that I would handle it."

"You told me not to do anything stupid."

"This was stupid!" I snapped back.

"It wasn't. Lark came to see me. She called a meeting for the crew and asked me to show up, for old times' sake. So, I did. It's not my fault Lewis and I got into it when we were together."

I narrowed my eyes. "You purposely went so that you could have it out with him."

"Yes," he agreed easily, "I did. I knew you didn't want me to say anything to him, Natalie, but he is stalking you. I wanted him to stop. He clearly is not listening."

"No, he's not listening. He was at Elizabeth's runway show and cornered me." I instinctively rubbed my arm as the memory of his grip arrested me. "He told me he saw you."

Penn's eyes focused on where I touched my arm. "Why are you holding your arm?" He slid out of his chair, all cold, lethal calm. "Did he hurt you?"

"He grabbed me. It hurt. I'll live."

"What's next? Is he going to hit you? And you're here, mad at *me* for saying something when he's doing this shit? Honestly, he got the least of what he deserved. I should have flattened him," Penn growled.

"I told you to let me handle it, and you didn't."

"Because you shouldn't have to! I can deal with Lewis."

146

"Why didn't you tell me that you were going then?" I demanded.

He sank back into his seat. "I should have told you. It was stupid."

"Then why *didn't* you?"

"You hate them. With good reason. But in some fucked up way, they're still my friends."

My nostrils flared. "They are *not* your friends! Friends don't act like this. They don't treat each other like this."

"They're the people I've always relied on. The ones I've always gone to. I've known them my entire life. We were inseparable for so long. And even when I wanted to get out of this world, I didn't want to escape them because they were all I'd ever known. It makes no sense that I should feel anything at all after their shit, but I do."

"Just because they are the only people you've ever known doesn't make them friends."

"Katherine picked me up from the airport the day my dad died," Penn said softly. "Lewis sat with me. He didn't say anything or try to make me feel better. But he was there all day. Lark called in Chinese that night and gave me all her egg rolls. Rowe came in late. He'd been away on business when the news broke. When he made it back to the city, he hugged me." I met his gaze as he poured it out. "Rowe, who hates to be touched, had initiated the hug. So, they might not look like friends. It might look like all we've ever had together is secrets and betrayal and bullshit, but there's more there. It's more like family."

I closed my eyes and stepped away. "That all makes sense. They might be your friends or even family in some sick, twisted way. But they're also monsters." I faced him again. "And they make you monstrous."

"I am not going to be that person again. Is this about the fucking bet?" he groaned. "Is it always going to be about the bet?"

"It's not the bet. It's that all of our problems start and end with the crew!"

"Yes, yes they do," he growled. "Like you fucking my best friend."

"Jesus Christ, we weren't even together. And it's not like you didn't bang half of the Upper East Side."

"Because you left me!" he said, throwing his arms out.

"Yes, I did. And it was the right thing to do after the bullshit you pulled on me, Penn. We could go around and around in circles about all of this if you wanted. But the fact is that the crew fucks everything up between us. And...and I don't want that." I huffed out a breath as the words...the truth escaped me. I wanted this. I wanted Penn.

Penn stepped around his desk and let down his defenses. "I don't want that either. I guess I'm still mad that you were with Lewis. Just like you're still mad about the bet. We're not over it. And I shouldn't be surprised. It was fucked up on all accounts."

"It terrifies me to think that you went to see them. I don't know what that could mean. Or why you'd hide it from me."

Penn threaded our fingers together. "I shouldn't have hidden it. And nothing happened. Except a whole lot of posturing between me and Lewis, Katherine sore from kinky sex with Camden, and Rowe getting a boyfriend, who you'll meet tomorrow."

I blinked. "I did *not* need that image of Katherine and Camden."

"Tell me about it. That was all of us."

"And Rowe has a boyfriend?"

"Yeah, he told us that he's bisexual. Though we'd always guessed. We had just been waiting for him to come to us. Which I honestly never thought would happen, considering it's Rowe."

"For sure." I shook my head to clear all my loose thoughts. "I hate that I jumped to conclusions about all of this. I don't want this to keep happening."

"We both have issues with trust, Natalie. It's not going to go away overnight. We have to try to keep the past where it belongs."

I leaned forward into his chest, and he wrapped his arms around me, cocooning me in his warm embrace. I should have come straight to him. It felt as if this argument had been brewing for weeks. Longer even. Maybe it had been brewing all along.

He pressed a kiss into my hair. "I don't want to do anything to hurt you."

"I know," I whispered. "I know."

His hands slipped under my jacket, sliding the material over my shoulders and then carelessly tossing it onto the chair. He tilted my head up until I was looking at him. "I *won't* hurt you."

I nodded with a hard swallow at the depth of affection I saw in his gaze.

"This isn't like before. I'm not leaving you. I'm not lying about our relationship. This is just me. I'm not perfect. I'm still working on me. And I'll probably fuck it up again, Nat, but I'm willing to try with you. For you."

I stood on my toes and pressed a firm kiss to his lips. "I might continue to jump to conclusions," I said against his mouth. "I've been hurt a lot, and it scares me. This scares me."

"As long as we go through this together, then we'll be fine." Penn slipped his hands down my arms, and I winced as he ran across the upper arm that Lewis had grabbed earlier. Penn glanced down at my arm with a crinkle in his brow. Then he got a look at my arm, and his concern flipped on a switch. "Holy fuck! Did he do this to you?"

My eyes followed where he was holding my arm out. And there, in a perfect arc on my upper arm, was a growing, mottled bruise.

"Oh my god," I whispered. "I knew it'd hurt when he grabbed me. I didn't realize that I'd *bruised.*"

Penn released my arm, and his hands balled into tight fists. His chest heaved as if he were fighting with himself from throwing that fist right into the wall since Lewis wasn't here to be the punching bag.

"You have to file a restraining order," he got out through gritted teeth.

"What? No way."

"Natalie, you have a bruise on your arm from him. What if you see him again and I'm not there? This is serious."

"I can't," I whispered, staring down at the bruise.

"Look, you can use my attorney. Even just to get a temporary one to show him that you're serious. We can assess whether you need a permanent one after we see how he reacts to a temporary order."

My eyes bulged. "Penn," I said, fear creeping into my voice.

"Please," he said. I could see he was trying to even out

his breath. To try to be calm and rational in this moment. "Please, do this, Natalie. Because if he thinks he can get to you, he will."

I paused as his words hit me. He was right. I'd been reckless, thinking that I could deal with Lewis's stalking alone. He'd proven that he wasn't capable of letting me go, of not getting his way. And I didn't want to wait to see if something else would happen.

"Okay," I said softly. "Okay. I'll talk to a lawyer."

"Thank you," he said, pressing his lips hard against mine. "Thank you for letting me take care of you. We'll go in the morning."

I nodded, my throat tight. I couldn't even believe this was happening to me. "In the meantime, I…think I'm going to need to figure out how to cover this for tomorrow night."

"Ah, the gala. Are you sure you still want to go?"

"I have to go. I already have the dress."

He cracked a smile. "What is this world doing to you?"

"Brought me you," I said, kissing him again. "Can't be all bad."

"Definitely not." He whirled me around so that my ass rested against his desk.

"My, Professor, are you having inappropriate thoughts?" I teased.

He grinned. "My sexy girlfriend is in my office after-hours. What do you think?"

"Girlfriend?" I raised my eyebrows.

His hand went to the waist of my cigarette pants and slowly undid them. "What would you call yourself?" He hooked his thumbs in them, tugging them over my hips.

"Partner? Would you prefer I stick to something more gender neutral?" He bent down and removed my aching feet from each of my heels and then slid my pants and thong off of my body. "I can use pet names if you like. Babe, baby, sweetheart, boo…bae?"

I laughed. "Not bae. Definitely not."

"But you don't object to the rest? Just girlfriend?" His pants slipped down his hips.

"Maybe…maybe girlfriend would work," I said tentatively. I'd been trying and failing to keep him at a distance. What other word really was there? I was very obviously his girlfriend.

Penn reached behind me and slid all his books and papers and pens off of the desk. Then he hoisted me up, laying me back on his now-empty desk. My eyes widened as he hovered over me.

"That's what I like to hear," he said, grabbing my legs and tugging me toward him. He leaned forward, pressing a fierce kiss onto my lips. "You're my girlfriend. *Mine*," he growled, palming his cock in his hand and spreading my legs further apart.

"Yes," I groaned. "Yes."

He entered me in one clean stroke, and my body rocked backward on the desk. I reached behind me and gripped the other side for leverage as Penn straightened to his full height. Then he seized my thighs and thrust deep into me again. And again.

My eyes rolled back as he took me right there on his desk. My…my boyfriend. Christ, he was my boyfriend.

It was almost beyond belief after all that we'd gone through. That either of us could get past what we'd endured to get to this moment.

That my heart was mended enough to fall so hard again.

So utterly and helplessly for this man. This wonderful, complicated, messed up genius of a man. I was his, and he was mine. And we'd set fire to the world. Burning up so completely that we were starting anew.

CHAPTER 18

NATALIE

I met with Penn's attorney the next morning. She was young and sympathetic to my concerns. I'd been expecting some stodgy, old man who thought that one bruise wasn't enough to get a restraining order. Or order of protection, as the lawyer called it.

But I confessed everything that had happened. Showed her the proof of his stalking and the file that he'd kept on me. We'd taken pictures of the bruise on my arm, and she said I definitely had a case. I didn't know if that made me feel better or worse.

What it really made me feel was furious. Like I was some statistic. Poor girl in a domestic violence situation. Afraid of some man because he was bigger and had more power than me. It made me want to look deeper into his background to find some way to make him hurt like I was. To expose him for the entitled dick he was. Not to stop at a restraining order that a judge might not even give me permanently if Lewis put the weight of his name behind it.

"Are you finished in there? We should get going," Penn called from the living room.

I stared down at my arm. No bruise. The makeup artist I'd hired for the event had done such a perfect job that I couldn't even see a hint of it. It made me happy and irrationally angry.

"Yes," I said, stepping out of his bathroom in the low-cut lilac dress Elizabeth had sent over this morning. It had a soft, almost-water-like texture to it with an empire waist and a high slit to reveal the nude Jimmy Choos I'd paired with it. My silver hair was pulled to one side in loose waves that draped over one of the skinny straps. "What do you think?"

"I think it needs one more thing," Penn said.

He pulled out a small red Cartier box. My eyes widened in shock.

"Um…what's that?"

"A surprise," he said coyly.

He stepped up to me and then cracked the box. My heart skyrocketed. Terror hitting me that he might propose and another *stranger* feeling…like I might want that one day.

Settled into the red cushion was a pair of circular-cut drop diamond earrings. They were the most perfectly clear diamonds I had ever seen in my life. A soft gasp escaped me.

"Penn, I can't."

He plucked the earrings out of the case. "You absolutely can. They go with your dress."

"They go with *everything*," I blurted out.

He laughed as he passed them to me. "Exactly."

I gingerly took them in my hands as if they were made

of glass and might shatter. I turned to the mirror in his living room and exchanged the cheap earrings I'd been wearing with actual, a hundred percent real Cartier diamonds. My hands shook as I finished clasping them, and then I admired them as they shone brightly in the mirror.

"They are beautiful," I breathed. "Thank you."

He took my hand, as he had that first time we met, and kissed it. Somehow, he still made me flush. "Now we're ready to go."

Penn had acquired a limo for the night to take us to the gala, which was being held at Cipriani Wall Street. The building had been built to look like Greek revival architecture with beautiful columns and intricate moldings. After we stood for pictures with the press and passed a slew of A-list celebrities and models, which I barely kept my cool with, we entered the event. Tables took up much of the space in the dimly lit room, and a stage was against one wall to honor some of the greatest fashion icons of our time.

We were seated with people that neither of us really knew and were relieved when the ceremony was over so that we could mingle. I'd promised to find Jane and Harmony, but I hadn't found them in the crowd. And after the long ceremony, I needed another drink.

Penn and I moved to the bar. As we waited in line for drinks, I pulled out my phone to text Harmony and find out where she was. Penn had his own phone out, and then he glanced up at me, then down at his phone, and then back.

"What?" I asked, putting my phone back into the

pocket of my dress. Seriously, thank god for dresses with pockets!

"Why am I getting a suggestion to like your page? Since when did you set up an Influencer page?"

"Oh yeah, yesterday. Harmony set it up. Crap, I was supposed to update it with more pictures. With everything that went down, I forgot."

Penn clicked on my page, and his eyes bugged. "How do you have fifteen thousand connections? Are you sure you set this up yesterday?"

I blinked. "What?"

He thrust the phone at me, and I stared down at my profile in shock.

"Oh my god," I said, jittery with excitement. "That's insane, right?"

"I don't even know how that's possible."

I clicked through some of the pictures and scrolled through some comments. "It looks like Harmony tagged me in a picture, and Elizabeth recommended me to her followers. Because I didn't do anything else."

Penn shook his head. "I didn't even know you wanted to do that."

"Harmony says I should curate my own content instead of relying on the newspapers and tabloids to do it for me."

Penn wrinkled his nose. "You don't want to be like Harmony."

"No," I agreed. "But this is kind of fun."

He shrugged indifferently. "All right. If you enjoy it."

"I should go find her and ask her about this. I didn't expect it to blow up like this literally overnight."

He pointed toward the corner of the room. "I saw

where she was sitting. She's over there. I'll wait if you want to go hang out."

"Are you sure?" I asked.

"You can handle yourself in a crowd just fine. We already worked on that."

"And what are we working on next?" I asked, standing on my toes to give him a quick kiss.

"Guess you'll have to wait and see."

I laughed. "Well, boyfriend, I will be right over there. Come find me with our drinks."

"All right, girlfriend, I will find you," he said, flashing a dimple.

His smile was contagious as I slipped out of his grip and headed toward Harmony. I pulled out my phone to check for myself that my Crew page had actually exploded and was just as shocked to see it on my phone as on Penn's.

"Natalie!" Harmony said, jumping out of her seat and pulling me into a hug. "That dress is stunning. I am so mad at my mom for not giving it to me."

Harmony was in a showstopping yellow number that looked fantastic with her blonde hair.

"Yours is incredible. I couldn't even imagine you in anything else."

"Aww, thanks, girl!"

"Also, check this out." I showed her that my account had exploded.

"Oh, fifteen-K! So good for a day. Let's try to get you to fifty by this weekend. Here, take a selfie with me." She pulled her phone out and snapped a picture of us. "I'll post it on my Crew page and tell everyone to share the love with you."

"You're ridiculous. Thank you!"

Harmony was busy Photoshopping the image, running it through a filter, and then adding some special tags at the bottom for maximum exposure when a group of girls walked up and gasped over our dresses.

Harmony waved her hand at them. "Don't even. This thing? It's nothing compared to yours, Fiona."

"Oh, no way, Harm," Fiona said. She brushed her sheet of light-brown hair off of her soft, pale shoulder. "Yours is way cuter. Don't you think so, Isabel?"

"Definitely," Isabel agreed instantly. "Sloane was just talking about how no one could wear canary like you, Harm."

"I wish I could pull it off," Sloane said with a grin.

"You are too sweet," Harmony said with a big smile. "You all know Natalie, right?"

"Oh, Natalie," Fiona said, "we've heard so much about you. You were front row for the Cunningham show!"

"I was," I said. "Elizabeth was so generous to offer me the spot."

"And who are you wearing?" Isabel asked, fingering the expensive fabric.

"Isn't it obvious?" Harmony asked.

"Cunningham, clearly, Isabel," Fiona said with an eye roll.

"Ohh," Sloane said. "That explains so much."

"What does it explain?" I asked.

"Nothing," Fiona said.

"You look *so* good in that lilac. With that silver hair," Isabel continued. "Maybe I should dye my hair." She fingered her nearly black tresses.

"That's why Katherine is in some off-the-rack piece,"

Sloane said as if her friends were daft. "Doesn't she normally wear Elizabeth Cunningham?"

"She does," Harmony said with a sly smile.

"I can't believe she would show up in that dress," Fiona said, giving in to their catty behavior.

"I mean, just look at her," Isabel said with a shake of her head, gesturing to Katherine standing nearby. "It's *so* sad."

My eyes found Katherine in a stunning black dress that hugged her curves. I never would have been able to tell that she was in a dress off the rack if I hadn't just tried on that same dress a couple of weeks ago. I didn't even know that was supposed to be insulting, except the girls kept going on and on about how humiliating it was. That marrying a Percy was supposed to help her taste and not degrade it.

To me, she looked like the same old Katherine. Just as beautiful. Just as much a snake. And as Camden approached, he skimmed her backside. She shuddered and stepped out of his touch. The thought of them together made me kind of sick. I swiftly looked away.

"It's good to see her knocked down a peg," Harmony said.

"I wouldn't mind watching her fall in the mud," Fiona said viciously.

Isabel and Sloane snickered, clearly in agreement.

And though I was the reason that this had happened, it made my stomach twist at the way they were talking about her. When I'd spoken with Elizabeth after the charity event, she'd agreed to give me the front row ticket that belonged to Katherine and a dress she'd held in reserve for her as well. I was literally walking in her shoes this weekend. And it felt good to see her stumble, to see her socialite status begin to fracture. It was what I'd wanted after all.

I'd wanted revenge for what she'd done. I'd wanted to take the thing that she cared about. And I had. Or at least, it had begun.

It was another thing entirely to hear people talking about Katherine so quickly after bringing me into their circle. Like vultures ready to eat away at carrion. And I was the fresh new meat.

I saw then how sad and lonely it must have been for Katherine on her pedestal. She'd put herself there. And everyone had hoped for her to fall. I was just the only one who had succeeded in making her stumble.

The girls continued to chatter about Katherine as if she weren't a matter of feet from us when my phone started buzzing in my pocket. I pulled it out and was surprised to find my sister's number displayed.

"Excuse me for a minute," I told Harmony and the rest of the group. I stepped away and answered the phone. "Melanie? Is everything okay?"

"Natalie, I'm so glad that you answered. I know you're at the Fashion Week gala. I'm so jealous, and I need pictures, but I had to call you."

"That's fine. You're okay?"

"Better than okay," Melanie gasped. "I'm engaged."

"What?"

A ringing filled my ears. *Melanie* was engaged. Only a few hours ago, I'd thought about what it would be like if Penn proposed. It had been a distant thought, but still. And now, my little sister was engaged?

She was seven years younger, and I *hated* her

161

boyfriend. Hated him with the fire of a thousand suns. They had dated basically their entire lives, and then he'd broken up with her the week before homecoming their senior year of high school so that he could take her best friend, Kennedy, instead. And Mel had still taken him back. She'd only just turned nineteen. What the hell was the rush?

"Michael proposed," Melanie gushed. "And I said yes. It was magical. I can't believe it."

"Me either."

"Please be happy for me, Nat. I know that you don't love him, but he's going to be your brother-in-law soon."

"Of course. Of course I'm happy for you," I said, dredging up enthusiasm from somewhere that I didn't recognize. "Do you have any information? A date?"

"No, no, it just happened. I had to call you. But we're going to have an engagement party in a couple of weeks, and we want you to be there. Do you think you can make it?"

"Yes, I'll be there. I'll bring Penn."

Melanie squealed. "Yes, please bring Penn. You know I love him."

I rolled my eyes. "I do remember that."

"This will be perfect. I can't wait. Okay, I have to call a bunch more people. Have fun at your gala. I love you!"

"Love you, too," I told her.

I would definitely be there for that engagement party. And figure out what Michael was thinking...and hopefully fix this disaster.

CHAPTER 19

PENN

The line at the bar was long enough to make a man want to drink.

I ordered a double when I finally got to the front because I wasn't going to wait again if this continued. I didn't remember having this problem in past years. I tipped the bartender extra for having to deal with this many people and then took my drink and Natalie's champagne far, far away.

My gaze traveled the room again, finding her still standing with Harmony. I took one step toward her when I saw the three people who had approached them. Fiona, Isabel, and Sloane. Three of Katherine's friends. Socialite types who had more money than brains. They also happened to be three of the women I'd slept with last year to try to get over Natalie and get back at Katherine. Walking over there would *not* be smart. And it would result in a lot of questions.

I was surprised that the cling-ons weren't attached to Katherine. I found the form I knew so well standing all alone. I narrowed my eyes in confusion. *Katherine*, all alone? Since when? She was always abuzz with friends and followers and people who wanted a sliver of attention. But now, those people were with…Natalie.

I frowned. Lark had said that Natalie was some new *it* girl, but I hadn't really processed that until this moment. She was in a designer dress, surrounded by all these people she hardly knew, and she had fifteen thousand followers in twenty-four hours. Maybe she really *was* this *it* girl.

It was unsettling in some way. She'd asked me to train her, and I had. Maybe I should cancel any further lessons. She was succeeding beyond what I'd imagined she would. This world didn't take well to outsiders, but I'd made her an insider. And now, she was practically kicking Katherine off of the throne she'd claimed for so long.

Katherine glanced in my direction then. Our eyes met, and we spoke across the room, as we'd done for so long, growing up.

She arched an eyebrow. Clearly saying, *"What are you looking at, Kensington?"*

I shrugged and tilted my head at the troop of girls surrounding Natalie. *"Where are you cling-ons?"*

Katherine rolled her eyes. *"As if I care."*

I snorted. She cared. Katherine always did. Then Camden appeared. His hand moved to her ass, touching her where I gathered welts had graced her backside from whatever kink he was into. She winced and then stepped out of his embrace. But I saw something else there, too.

Was that *relief*?

Was Katherine *glad* to see Camden Percy?

She didn't meet my eyes again once he was there, so I

had no way to ask. But what could have happened on that honeymoon to change how she felt about a man she had hated for years? Maybe it was best not to know.

Natalie was still engrossed with the other girls, so I slipped to the periphery of the crowd and found the person I had been looking for.

"Rowe," I said with a nod of my head at my friend.

He dipped his chin in greeting. "Penn. This is my boyfriend, Nicholas Moreno." He gestured to the man standing next to him.

Nicholas was an inch or two shorter than Rowe with curly brown hair and skin a golden brown. They wore matching tuxedos and were both practically glowing. Rowe's fair skin was pink at the introduction.

I shook hands with Nicholas. "Nice to meet you. Penn Kensington."

"It's a pleasure. I've heard so much about you."

"Oh god, I can't imagine," I said with a laugh.

"He's pretty tight-lipped but not about his friends."

"Why do I find that doubtful?" I had never heard Rowe be particularly loquacious.

"Because you know me," Rowe deadpanned.

"You two met at a tech summit?" I asked Nicholas.

He nodded. "Who knew that the famous Archibald Rowe was such a sweetheart?"

Rowe nearly choked. "Please. Infamous."

We all laughed at that.

"Well, it was nice to finally meet you," Nicholas said. "I'm trying to convince him to let me meet Katherine now."

"Ah, Ren is hanging out with Camden," I said, gesturing to the center of the room.

Nicholas wrinkled his nose. "I've heard of him, too."

"Unfortunately, we all have."

Nicholas wrapped an arm around Rowe's shoulders. "Come on. We don't have to hide in the shadows."

"I like the shadows," Rowe said, but he obliged him, giving me a quick good-bye.

I was blissfully alone for a whole minute, waiting for Natalie to get away from the crowd of mean girls, when my brother appeared at my side.

Jesus Christ, I'd thought the night was off to a good start before this.

"Hey, little brother," Court said with a shit-eating grin.

I turned my steely gaze on him. "What do you want?"

"Want? Nothing. I thought I'd say hello."

"Sure you did."

Court snickered. "I saw your girlfriend looking all hot."

"And this conversation is over," I said, taking a step away.

"Chill. Chill. It's so easy to rile you up."

"What do you *want*?" I repeated.

"I can't want to talk to you?"

"No. You slept with my ex-girlfriend. We're not on speaking terms."

"How many times do I have to say that Emily came on to me?"

I glared at him. "That doesn't make it okay."

"Now, you have a new girlfriend."

"And if you touch her, I'll kill you," I spat at him.

He sighed in exasperation. "I'm not interested in Natalie."

"I don't like her name in your mouth."

"Look, I saved her from Camden. And that was when she was fucking your best friend. I'm not the monster here."

I massaged my temple, wondering why I was even still having this conversation.

"What? Not even a thank you?"

"Thank you," I said begrudgingly. I hadn't even been dating Natalie when Camden tried to hit on her while he was high. But I was glad that Court had stopped him. Even if it made us far from even.

"So...you pissed election season is coming up?" Court asked, changing the subject.

I groaned at the thought of my mother campaigning again. It was never a good time to be a Kensington. "Yes. It's going to be awful."

"It always is. I wish she'd fucking leave us out of it for once."

"With Dad dead, she has to parade us around as her poor little children that she had to raise without him. Which is *true*, except for the part about either of them raising us."

"Yeah, and we were fucking adults when he passed, and good fucking riddance."

"Amen," I muttered.

"I kind of hope she loses, so we don't have to deal with this again."

I kept hoping that, but my mother always got what she wanted. A quality she had instilled in both of us apparently. "Wishful thinking."

"Did we just have a real conversation?" Court asked with raised eyebrows. "Did we actually agree?"

"Who knew it was our mother who would bring us together?"

"Mommy issues," Court said with a laugh.

I couldn't help it. I laughed, too. "She'd love to hear this."

"Uh…is that Natalie running over here?" Court asked.

I turned away from my brother and ignored the confusion in my stomach that said that conversation wasn't supposed to be possible. He was right. Natalie was practically jogging over to where I stood with Court.

"Looks serious," Court said and then disappeared to give us privacy.

"What's wrong?" I asked as soon as Natalie was before me.

"Melanie and Michael are engaged."

"Isn't that the jerk who broke up with her?"

"Yeah. For her best friend."

I furrowed my brow. "And they're back together? And now engaged?"

"Yes. She asked me to come to her engagement party. We have to stop this from happening."

"Breathe, Nat. Slow down. When is the engagement party?"

"I don't know. In a couple of weeks."

"And you want to go…to break them up?"

She nodded as if that made perfect sense. "Yep."

"Or you could go there to support your sister and let her make her own decisions. And her own mistakes. Just like you did. It's not like she's going to listen to you if she got back together with him."

"I know," she grumbled. "But…she *can't* marry him, Penn."

168

"No, I'm sure it would be a bad choice, but it's also not your choice."

She huffed. "Fine. *Fine*. Be logical about it."

I cracked a smile again. "That's what I'm here for."

"Well, will you go with me?"

"To your sister's engagement party?"

"Yeah," she said softly, her cheeks blooming a soft pink. "To Charleston."

This was something I'd never done before. Go home to my girlfriend's house and meet the parents. Play the nice guy. All the other girls that I'd dated were from this world. It had been a different thing entirely. With Natalie, this would be important. And I wanted to be there for her.

"You don't have to," she said hastily, as if she had over-stepped.

"No, I want to go. I'll go with you."

"You will?" she said in relief.

"Of course. It'll be an adventure."

"A better reason for you to be in Charleston," she muttered.

I agreed. The last time I'd been there, she'd turned me away.

This time…we'd be together, taking that next step in our relationship.

CHAPTER 20

I was nearly asleep on the flight to Charleston when it hit me. I sat up straight in the first-class seat that Penn had insisted on purchasing for us to return to my home. I'd thought it was a frivolous expense. He'd just ignored me.

I yanked out my laptop and connected to the wifi. I'd been waiting all week to hear back about the restraining order about Lewis. The attorney had said that I'd hear Monday at the latest. But while I'd been waiting, there had been something itching at the back of my mind. Something that I should remember but couldn't.

Apparently, I'd had to get to thirty thousand feet before I would remember.

Anselin-Maguire.

That was the business deal that Lewis had been working on when we were dating. His father had brought it up over dinner because he had to close the deal over the phone at night. There was also that weird point where he'd had to do business at a party. I'd thought it strange then but hadn't put much thought into it.

Now, I could see the red flags.

Maybe there was something here to go on.

The name didn't pull up anything in particular. Maguire was really generic and wouldn't get me anywhere. So I searched for Anselin instead. I skimmed through a few articles about the company but didn't see anything out of place.

I huffed. Maybe it was just coincidental that he'd had weird business hours. It had felt like a lead.

I kept searching through the most recent articles until we hit a bout of turbulence, and Penn woke from his slumber. I slapped the laptop closed.

"Are we almost there?" he asked.

"About to descend into Charleston."

"I didn't think we were supposed to have bad weather."

"Afternoon showers are pretty common," I told him with a smile as I stuffed my computer back into my bag. "Won't ruin anything."

He stretched out and opened the window shade to the dark sky beyond. "Why did I decide to take the last flight in? And why do airplanes make me so sleepy?"

"For most parents, when they can't get their kid to go to sleep, they drive them around the neighborhood. And now, those kids always fall asleep on long car rides. Your parents probably flew you around the neighborhood."

He rolled his eyes at me. "Hilarious."

"I thought so."

The flight attendant came over the intercom, informing everyone that we were about to land and to stow our belongings. It was a rocky landing with the storm overhead, but we landed safe and sound and found Amy waiting for us.

She squealed and rushed me. I laughed, dropping my bag, and pulled my best friend into a hug.

"I missed you like crazy," Amy said.

"Missed you, too," I said. "I'm glad to be home."

"Only because you brought your big hunk of a man home with you," Amy said, releasing me and hugging Penn. "Glad you could make it."

"As if I would miss it."

Amy snorted. "Let's get the bags."

Luckily, our suitcases appeared first, and then we loaded up Amy's Tahoe. It was a lot of car for one person. But if it worked for anyone, it worked for Amy. She chattered the entire way to my parents' house about the bedroom that she was renovating.

"Did you really have to renovate my old room, like, this week?"

She shrugged. "I didn't know you were going to come visit or that Mel would get engaged like an idiot. Do you think she's knocked up?"

I choked. "Dear god, I hadn't thought of anything worse than her marrying Michael. You succeeded. Congrats."

"Well, why else would a freshman in college get engaged?"

"Love?" Penn piped in.

"Shut it," I said at the same time Amy said, "Yeah, right."

We both burst into laughter. It was so good to have the easy banter of being with Amy. We talked on the phone, but it wasn't the same. I hadn't realized how draining it was to constantly be on when I was in the Upper East Side until I let it all roll off my shoulders. No lessons, no cameras, no expectations. I could see why Penn wanted to get away. It was exhausting.

We pulled up into the driveway of my parents' two-story yellow Charleston-style home with the colonial columns and balconies on both floors. While it looked large, I knew that looks could be deceiving. I'd spent four years of high school in this little house, but Melanie had basically grown up in it. I knew it would always feel more like home to her than me.

But there she was, waiting to greet us on the porch. She vaulted down the stairs in her heels and miniskirt and straight to my car door. I was barely out of the passenger seat when she squeezed me around the middle.

"You made it!"

I beamed like a fool. "Sure did. And I brought a friend."

Penn stepped out of the backseat. "Hey, Mel."

"Friend or *boy*friend?" Melanie teased.

"Boyfriend," Penn confirmed.

Melanie shrieked in excitement and attacked Penn. I just shook my head and grabbed my messenger bag.

"Good to see you, too." Penn patted her back twice before extracting himself. "Let me get the bags, Amy."

"Aww, a gentleman," Amy teased. She passed Penn his suitcase and then my bag. "Okay, kids. As much as I want to stay and hang, it's late, and I have to open the gallery in the morning."

"Such an adult," I joked.

"Hey, one of us needs a real job."

"What's that?" I asked, poking her in the ribs.

"I hope you're writing up there," Amy said. She tugged

me in for a hug. "Because, otherwise, I guess good dick is a decent enough reason."

I cackled and released her. "You're the best ever."

"Don't I know it. See you tomorrow for the party," Amy said. She waved at Melanie. "Congrats, Mel! Hope you're not knocked up."

Melanie's face turned bright red. "Oh my god, I'm not!"

I giggled. "I mean, you can't blame her for asking."

"Why did I even invite y'all?" Melanie grumbled before grabbing a bag and helping Penn with it up the stairs.

"Better go rescue him before my dad meets him."

Amy scrunched up her nose. "I think it's too late."

"Oh boy."

"Good luck with that."

I waved good-bye and hurried into the house to where Penn was currently introducing himself to my father. Penn had straightened to his considerable height and was currently shaking my dad's hand.

"Daddy," I said, peeking around the corner. "Oh good, you met Penn. Let's get you inside."

He made a disgruntled noise like he was about to say something about the fact that he owned a gun—it wouldn't be the first time—but I ushered everyone back inside. My father had served more than twenty years in the military and was now a local cop. He'd had a gun in his hand most of his life. And he liked to intimidate every guy who walked into our house. Poor Mel had had it worse than I ever had since our dad still hated Michael despite practically helping raise him. I knew better than to bring guys home.

My mother was standing in the living room, looking

like a straight ray of sunshine in the most outrageously wonderful hippie clothes. "Hello, and welcome!" she said. "You must be Penn. I'm Natasha, and I see you've already met my husband, James. We're thrilled that you're here."

My dad grunted behind Penn.

Penn put on the charm and hugged my mother, who beamed at the approach. "It's so good to meet you. I have heard so much about you. I'd love to see your shop."

"Oh dear, I knew that you'd be as slick as a snake. I cannot believe that you're a summer solstice baby. You have all the makings of a Sagittarius." She waved her hand. "No matter. We'll read tarot later and figure it all out."

Penn smiled at her in a bemused way. "Looking forward to that."

"Excellent. Have you ever had tarot read?"

"Mom," I groaned.

"I haven't. First time for everything," Penn said amicably.

"Natasha, don't bother him with that stuff," my dad said.

"I'll have you know, philosophy has the same roots as the mystic arts," my mom said with a sly smile. She winked at me. "He has a good aura."

I shook my head and just let it happen. I'd prepared Penn as best I could. My mother, the dreamer songbird, who ran an apothecary shop and read tea leaves and tarot and the stars and anything that predicted the future. My father, the strict religious military man, who must have married her out of love because how else could it have worked?

"It's late," Melanie said. "I'm going to go back to the

175

dorm. I just wanted to be here to say hi. You'll meet Michael tomorrow."

"Looking forward to it," Penn said.

"Are you?" I grumbled.

He shot me a look that said, *Behave*.

"Nat, please, please, please don't bring the stuff up from last year. Michael gets really uncomfortable about it all. I want this to all go smoothly."

"I won't bring it up. I'm here for you."

Melanie exhaled in relief. "Awesome. I'm going to head out then. Still have class in the a.m." She grinned at Penn. "Sorry to say that you'll get my room. It's a bit pink."

"I appreciate the hospitality," he said carefully.

I tried to hold in my laugh.

"We're tired, too. I think we should all get some sleep, so we can wake up bright and early," Natasha said. "So wonderful meeting you, Penn."

"You, too, Mrs. Bishop."

"Please, it's Natasha."

I took his hand and pulled him toward the stairs. "Come on. I'll show you where you're sleeping."

"Separate rooms," my father said from the bottom of the stairs.

"Night, Daddy," I said, rolling my eyes when I turned my back. "You'd think I was still in school."

"He has rules. I can appreciate someone with principles."

"You're too good," I said, opening the door to Melanie's room.

Penn's eyes widened in horror.

"It's more than a little pink."

"You think? Pink fucking exploded in here," Penn said.

He eyed the twin bed as if he'd never seen one before. I realized he might not have ever slept on one.

"This okay?"

"Of course," he said at once. "Why wouldn't it be?"

"Because I know you, and this isn't what you're used to."

"It's a glimpse into you. I'll be fine in here. Where will you be?" He glanced down the hallway as if he could guess which bedroom had been mine.

"Are you having inappropriate thoughts?" I asked slyly.

He pressed a chaste kiss to my lips. "Never."

"Oh, I'm sure. My room is the second door on the right. The bathroom is the first if you want to brush your teeth or shower or whatever."

"Thank you."

I reached up onto my toes and kissed him again. "I'll miss you in my bed tonight."

He groaned. "Are you trying to kill me? A man can only take so much."

"Just imagine me tonight. All alone. Thinking about you," I whispered against his ear. "Touching myself while I think about you."

His fingers dug into my skin. "Fuck, Natalie."

"Yes, please."

"I should not think about those things while in your sister's pink bedroom."

I laughed and kissed his earlobe. "Touché. I'll see you in the morning."

"Good night."

I'D BEEN DREAMING about Penn. We were on a beach,

snuggled up under the night sky with nothing but each other for comfort. It was peaceful and wonderful, and I hadn't wanted to wake up.

But my door had creaked. There was this creak that never went away, no matter how much WD-40 we sprayed on it. My eyes flew open, and I jerked my head to the side…only to find Penn shutting the creaky door behind him.

My eyebrows rose in surprise as he tiptoed across the room and then put his hand against my shoulder.

"Natalie," he whispered.

"I'm awake," I whispered.

I scooted over in bed and held the covers up. Mine was only a twin, but it would be better than not having him here at all. I rolled onto my side to give him more room, and he slipped under the sheets next to me.

"That was terrifying," he admitted.

I giggled softly. "Have you ever snuck into someone's bedroom?"

"Sure. But not when their parents were down the hall. Usually, it was more sneaking *out* because the person was dating someone else…or married."

"You were terrible."

"True," he agreed. His fingers splayed on my hip and drew lazy circles into my skin. "This sneaking is way more fun."

"*Way* more fun," I agreed, pressing a kiss to his lips.

"Did you think about me?" he begged.

I slid his hand down the front of my small sleep shorts and let him feel the wetness there.

He leaned into my shoulder. "Fuck."

Then he began to massage me. Easy circles around my

sensitive clit. Slicking a finger through my folds and then drawing the wetness up to use against my clit. His leg shifted over mine, holding it down on the bed, and then he pressed my other leg further away, securing me open for him.

I whimpered at the sweet agony of him touching me and not getting inside me. "Penn," I groaned.

"Shh," he said, swallowing my word with his mouth. "Show me how you came for yourself."

His erection pressed hard into my stomach, and I reached out with trembling fingers and wrapped my hand around him. I stroked. He stroked. Soft, urgent noises erupted from us. As quiet as we could be. And it only made it hotter. Trying not to be heard so desperately that the heat just built and built and built. Until he flicked against me one more time, and I shuddered into orgasm.

He lengthened even further in my hand as I gasped and came undone from his ministrations. He was close, too. Just from this.

I let the waves of pleasure release, and then I slid down on the bed and replaced my hand with my mouth. Penn groaned deep in the back of his throat at the heat of me on his cock. The feel of me stroking him up and down, up and down, while my tongue ran up his shaft.

I handled him with ease as he managed to get even longer. He gripped my hair in his hand, urging me deep onto his cock. Demanding me to take him fully. To relax my jaw and deep-throat him. I swallowed once and then slowly took him all in.

He tightened his grip on my hair, holding me down for a split second. Just when I thought I couldn't take it, his hips thrust slightly, and he shot hot cum down my throat. I swallowed reflexively, pulling back to suck him clean.

He lay, pressed against my childhood bed, nearly naked, looking sated. He held his arms out. "Come here."

I stepped into his embrace and sighed in bliss. He stroked his fingers through the hair he'd just been pulling vigorously.

"Should that have been as invigorating as it was?" he asked with a chuckle.

"Mmm," I murmured.

"You know you have stars on your ceiling," he said after a minute.

I nodded, staring up at the glowing constellations that I'd put up myself when we first moved in. I'd always been obsessed with them since my mother told me the stories of the stars when I was a child.

I pointed to the right of us. "Corona Borealis."

"Our crown," he said, kissing my hair.

"Always my favorite story," I told him.

His fingers continued their slow stroking as we stared up at our own night sky. "Ours is my favorite story."

CHAPTER 21

*M*ichael was a prick. And he was draining the joy out of being home.

I could tell that Penn was on a short tether. He had a temper on a good day. And he'd already walked into this situation, hating Michael. So, him acting like a piece of shit didn't help. And Penn's tolerance for entitled, poor little rich boys was pretty high, all things considered.

"I was telling Melanie that my business professor wanted me to work with him for this internship this summer. He knows my father, of course. The Baldwins are a household name here in Charleston. Surely, you've heard of my father, Thomas Baldwin," Michael said to the dull-eyed crowd in the living room.

"No," Penn said, his pointer finger resting on his temple while his elbow sank into the arm of his chair. "Can't say that I have."

"Well, no matter," Michael went on. "I think I'm going to take this internship and do a little unpaid work to get my foot in the door."

"Like you need it," I grumbled under my breath.

"Natalie," Melanie admonished.

Who knew that, after a few short months on the Upper East Side, I wouldn't be able to deal with a little... well, a lot of narcissism?

"I think we need to get out for a minute," I said, jumping to my feet.

Penn stood, too. "Excellent idea."

Michael glanced between us with disdain. "Don't want to hear about my internship?"

"Oh, we wish we could, but I remember my mom saying she needed help," I said, fighting back an eye roll.

Penn tipped his head at Michael and then veered us out of the living room.

"What a prick," he hissed into my ear as soon as we were out of earshot. "If I had to listen to another word out of his mouth, I was going to give him a real lesson on business, and it wouldn't have been pretty."

I laughed. "Right? He's the worst."

"He really is. Why is Melanie with him?"

"I don't know. They've been together forever. She doesn't see his flaws anymore. Just his sort of pretty face and the money that she's never had...the life she could have."

"She'd be better off with this life than what he's going to offer. I know many people who married people just like him, albeit with a lot more money and prestige. And now, they're either miserable or divorced. Not worth it."

"Like Katherine?" I asked.

He sighed. "Katherine made her bed. Now, she has to lie in it. Though, to be honest, she looked pretty happy to see Camden at the gala."

I stopped in my tracks. "Are you telling me that Katherine is *happy* to be married to Camden Percy?"

"I don't know," he said with a shrug. "I thought she'd be glad to be out of his clutches after a month alone. But I can read her better than anyone, and I would definitely say it was at least relief on her face."

I ground my teeth together. Fuck that. I'd thought Katherine would be nice and miserable, marrying that douche. She'd gotten what she deserved. Earned this isolation and torment. I didn't *want* her to find peace and be happy with Camden fucking Percy, who made Michael look like a fucking saint.

"Let's not talk about her," Penn said hastily.

"Fine," I muttered.

We stepped into the kitchen where my mother was standing over a book on astrology. She didn't look up until we were practically on top of her.

"Oh hello, dears. Having fun with Michael?" she asked with a knowing smile.

"Do you have any errands that would get us out of the house?" I begged.

She nodded. "Here." She passed me a slip of paper. "Can you get the cake from the grocery store? We already have everything else for the party out back. Take as long as you need."

"Thank you," I said with a sigh. "Michael is so..."

"Isn't he?" my mother said. "Blocked energy, that one. All muddied and black around the edges. He could use a chakra cleansing."

I snorted. "Good luck telling him that."

"I did try," she said.

Penn grinned. "I'm sure that went over well."

"Men are generally skeptics anyway," she said, brushing it off. "He's young. He has time. Now, go on. Get out of here. And take your father's car."

"Dad's car?" I asked in surprise. "Does he know that you're letting us drive the Chevelle?"

She winked. "What he doesn't know won't hurt him."

"Come on, Penn. Let's get out of here before my dad finds out."

I snatched the keys hanging next to the door and pulled Penn out of the house. I veered him around back to my dad's precious, restored 1960s Chevy Chevelle. It was the only thing that my straightlaced father had ever put time and energy into. And it made no sense since he was hardly the kind of man who would drive around a bright orange muscle car. But he did. One of the things I loved about him.

"What a car," Penn said in awe. "Can I drive?"

I shot him an incredulous look. "Yeah, right, Kensington." I popped the driver's door. "We don't trust city boys to handle stick shifts down here in the South."

He raised his eyebrows. "Should I make a joke about you handling my stick shift?"

"Would I have even set you up if I didn't expect you to spike the ball?" I said, dropping into the seat.

Penn sank into the passenger seat. "I liked the way you handled it last night."

"I think you still handled me," I said, warmth hitting my cheeks.

"I think you liked that even better."

My eyes were shining with excitement. "Maybe."

Then I peeled out of the driveway and hit the open road into town. We zipped through the city in my dad's car that handled better than anything else I'd ever driven. I'd only been behind the driver's seat a handful of times, and all had been with my dad's supervision. He'd probably go through the roof if he knew that my mom had sent us out in it.

"You really love this," Penn said thoughtfully.

"Who *wouldn't*?"

"But it lights you up."

"I guess it does. Maybe because he's always had this car. Through move after move after move from the military, we kept the car. The only time we didn't have it was when we were stationed in Germany. And he stressed the whole time about it not being driven enough or getting hurt by my uncle, my mom's brother."

"You're more like him than you think."

"I keep hearing that. My mom and Mel said the same thing when they convinced me to move to New York."

"They convinced you?" he asked as I pulled into the parking lot for the grocery store. "I didn't know that. I thought it was Lewis."

"Well, Lewis and Jane planted the idea. But it was really my mom and Melanie who were the ones who thought it was the right choice." I hopped out of the car and walked with him into our favorite grocery store. "They said that I was happiest when I could move around a lot. That Charleston wasn't my home and I needed to go where my heart took me."

"And that was New York."

"It's something in the water," I joked.

"Do you feel like your writing is better for it? Are you freer?"

I nodded after a pause. "Yes, and no. I feel like New

York is where I should be. My writing is so, so much better there. Like it just pours out of me from all the energy I'm absorbing from the city." I glanced over at him with a laugh. "Don't tell my mom I said that."

"Noted."

"But also…no, because I'm not really any freer. There are just new restrictions. And with Lewis stalking me and Katherine purposely trying to ruin my life, it's more constricting than ever."

He sighed. "Hopefully, we'll hear about the restraining order on Monday, and you can stop stressing. As far as Katherine is concerned, I think she has her hands full with Percy. Let's hope she stays out of it."

I stopped then at the entrance to the grocery store. "Is that what you really think?"

"What do you mean?"

"That I should just *hope* Katherine leaves me alone? After what she's done to me? She's the queen of staying two steps ahead. I don't think I want to hope that she's too distracted to realize that I'm becoming an insider in her circle."

"No, I don't. I want her to leave you alone. But we don't even know what she could try to do to you."

"Then maybe we should figure it out," I said, walking with him again. "Because I don't want a repeat of her wedding."

"All right," he said calmly. "I'll give it some thought." Then he frowned. "I'm not sure this should be a lesson."

"What?" I asked in confusion.

"How to think like Katherine Van Pelt."

"I don't *want* it to be a lesson. But if you think I need it to survive her, then teach me your ways, oh wise one."

He cracked a smile as we made our way to the bakery. I handed the order form to the baker, and he moved into the back room to collect the cake. I impatiently tapped my foot. I hated to admit it, but Penn's words made me anxious. Me joining the inner circle of the Upper East Side had negative consequences for Katherine. And I had to stay one or two steps ahead of her if I didn't want it to backfire on me.

"Oh my god, Natalie, is that you?" an alarmingly fake-tanned woman with a coifed Southern hairdo said. She beamed at me as if I should recognize her. "It is you. Wow! It's been years. You remember me from high school? Mary Beth Wilson. Well, Buchanan then." She held up her left hand and showed off the diamond ring. "Five years is right around the corner."

"Wow, Mary Beth," I said softly.

I had forgotten all about her. She'd been one of those cheerleader types who didn't spare me a glance in high school. She didn't make my life miserable or anything. She simply hadn't cared about anyone else outside of her circle. And I'd only ever really had Amy.

"Good to see you."

Mary Beth's eyes flicked to Penn and back. "And this is your...husband?"

"Boyfriend," Penn clarified, holding his hand out. "Penn Kensington. Nice to meet you."

"Well, hello," Mary Beth said, all flustered as she shook his hand. "You picked a good one, Natalie."

"Uh, thank you."

"What have you been up to these days? Busy-bee-ing? Carleton and I have two kids. A girl and a boy, Marianne and Jesse. It's exhausting, but I love the mom life."

"That's great. I moved to New York," I told her with a shrug. "No kids. Just been writing books and...stuff." I didn't know exactly how to explain what else I did.

"Don't be modest, Natalie," Penn said. "You wrote a *New York Times* bestselling novel and live on the Upper West Side."

"Wow," Mary Beth said, her eyes bulging. "Congratulations! I will have to tell Carleton about this. You know I still run the alumni club. Maybe we could post a feature in the alumni paper about your book!"

"Oh," I said, embarrassed. "I don't know."

"I'll reach out! I'll find you on Crew. We can connect."

"Miss Bishop, your cake," the man said behind the counter.

I heaved a sigh of relief and grasped the cake out of his hands. "Well, we have to go. Bye, Mary Beth. Great seeing you."

Then I hustled Penn the hell out of there. I could barely focus as I steered us back to my dad's car. I passed Penn the cake as I unlocked the car, dropping the keys once before getting it right. Then I sank into the driver's seat and covered my face.

Penn took his seat. "Well, that was interesting."

"So fucking embarrassing."

"Why? To talk about your achievements?"

"I mean, people can *know* what I do with my life, but, god, it's so, like, small town. Running into someone I knew in high school. And by knew, I mean, we never spoke more than three words the four years I was there. Now suddenly, I'm with *you*, and she's interested in talking to me."

"What do I have to do with it?"

I snorted. "Everything. She was checking you out."

"So?"

"I'm sure she was wondering what you were doing with me."

"And you care...why?"

I rolled my shoulders back and sighed. "I don't know. It's just awkward. No one cared who I was in high school. Why would she want to write an article about me?"

"Maybe everyone was so self-absorbed in high school that they didn't think of anything but themselves. You don't know her or what her motives are. And you aren't the person you were then. She should *want* to write about your accomplishments."

A laugh bubbled out of me. "God, no matter where you go, high school follows you, doesn't it?"

He frowned and glanced down. "Yeah, it does."

I tilted my head back. "Was I a total spaz?"

"I find it endearing if it helps anything."

"Well, let's try to get through this engagement party and not mention anything that just happened in there. Deal?"

"Deal."

CHAPTER 22

NATALIE

*L*uckily, the party was in full swing when we showed back up with the cake. I had to endure a nice little lecture from my dad about "stealing" his car. But it was worth it for the drive. Even if I was still off-kilter because of Mary Beth Wilson, née Buchanan. And I still couldn't figure out why it had freaked me out so much. I could deal with the likes of Katherine Van Pelt, but get all worked up over Mary Beth? Pathetic.

"You saw Mary Beth?" Amy said, bending at the waist and laughing hysterically. "How did *that* go?"

"Awful. I was a spaz, and she was checking out Penn the whole time."

"Of course she was. He's the hottest guy in, like, existence. Not my type, but you know, for people like her, he's the cream of the crop."

"Awkward."

"Def," Amy agreed.

"Am I a total weirdo for getting all worked up over some person I hardly even recognized?"

"Nah. It happens. You're in a different place in your life. It brought you back to reality to see someone like her. It'll pass."

I took another sip of the Coke I'd snagged from the cooler.

"Penn looks like he's having a really good time," Amy said with loaded sarcasm. "I've never seen him dressed down. Does he normally wear jeans and a T-shirt?"

"No," I admitted. "He's so far out of his comfort zone, it might as well be another planet."

"At least he didn't freak out on Mary Beth."

I rolled my eyes. "I'm never living that down."

"Nope. Anyway, Penn can charm, like, anyone. Half of the party probably wants to bang him, and the other half is uncertain about their masculinity around him." Amy tapped her finger to her lips. "Actually, I'd wager more than half want to bang him."

"You're the best friend a girl could ask for," I said with a nudge of my shoulder.

"Duh." Amy groaned. "Don't look now. A troop of Melanie's little college friends is approaching."

I took another sip of my Coke and wished I'd grabbed a beer even though I didn't really like it. I only recognized one of the girls, Marina. Her family owned a boating company, and her brother, Daron, was my age.

"Hey, Natalie," Marina said with a wide-grinned smile.

She was like girl next door met town sweetheart. I was certain my sister corrupted her on a regular basis.

"Good to see you, Marina."

"This is Tatum," she said, gesturing to a brunette with a pixie cut and then a curly-haired ginger, "and Christy."

"Are you really living in New York?" Christy asked.

I nodded. "Yeah, I moved there last year."

"That is so cool," Tatum said in a monotone drawl that could have been sarcasm. I wasn't sure.

"Thanks."

"Is it true that your boyfriend is the son of the mayor of New York City?" Christy asked.

I startled. "Um…yeah. Penn's mom is the mayor. How did you know?"

"Oh, it's all over the Charleston High Crew page," Marina said.

She pulled her phone out and showed it to me. I took it and saw with deep, deep regret that none other than Mary Beth had posted *all* about me in the alumni group that I hadn't known existed.

"Shit," Amy said, barely containing a laugh. "Didn't see that coming."

"Was she good at much in school other than gossip?" I asked Amy as I passed the phone back to Marina.

A few other girls had congregated around me. A crowd was forming. Great.

"Are you really a socialite?" Christy asked. "Like, you have designers dress you and you go to, like, Fashion Week events and charity functions?"

I opened my mouth and then closed it.

"Yeah, I found her Influencer page," another girl said. "She has sixty thousand followers."

"Jesus, did it increase that much over the week?" I asked.

Christy looked at me with hero worship in her eyes. "How do you do it? You were, like, a nobody in high school, and now, you're *somebody*."

"Wow, thanks," I muttered sarcastically. "Amy? Some help?"

"Nope. You got this one," she said with a snicker.

"Well, when I was working in the Hamptons, I met a group of people who lived on the Upper East Side. We became...friends. And they assimilated me into their group. I started dating Penn. And now...I guess this is part of my life."

A way, *way* dumbed-down version of reality. But as much as I could feed these gossip-hungry girls. I hadn't expected Mary Beth to tell the entire world of Charleston what I was up to. Or that it would permeate through our town so fast. Or that anyone would even care.

"Melanie told me you were living an awesome life in New York, but it's different, really *knowing*," Marina explained. "You're like a celebrity with a celebrity boyfriend."

I glanced up at Penn in the distance, hoping he would see the sea of girls desperate to know more about my life. But he was with a few of the other guys, drinking beer—which I'd never seen him do—and joking around. No saving for me.

"I'm not a celebrity," I said. "Just...I live a different life than I did here."

They kept chattering, bouncing more questions off of me, and searching through my page right in front of me. I realized then why this bothered me. Why Mary Beth had bothered me. Why it all felt so wrong.

I'd thought I was coming home to escape. Letting my world in New York slide off my shoulders. That I could slip back into my Natalie Bishop shoes here in Charleston. Be the loner girl who'd only had one friend and no one knew. The girl who liked to live in libraries and write stories and swim a lot.

But I wasn't that girl anymore. I'd brought the Upper East Side with me. It was a second skin now. And I couldn't just take it off and be *me*. The two sides of me were so perfectly overlapped that there was only one *me* anymore.

I understood now, when I hadn't fully grasped it from Penn before, that I couldn't escape the Upper East Side. He'd said he wanted to escape, but he couldn't. I'd thought that it would be so easy. But it had followed me here of all places. To the grocery store and my sister's engagement party and a crowd of preening college freshmen.

If I couldn't escape it here after only such a short period of time, how could Penn hope to leave it behind when he'd been in it his whole life?

"All right, ladies, let's give Natalie a breath of air," Michael said over the questions from Melanie's friends.

I didn't realize that the crowd had grown and grown as word spread, that half the party was hanging around me. Melanie was standing next to Marina, filling her in on all of my amazing adventures at Fashion Week.

"Back it up. Natalie needs some of her own space now." He flicked his hands to push all of her friends out of my face.

And I thought it was nice. Maybe the nicest thing that Michael had ever done for me.

Then he faced me, and I saw rage on his features.

"What the fuck do you think you're doing?" he hissed.

I straightened at his words. At the anger in them. "I wasn't doing anything."

"You think this whole party is about you?"

"No," I spat.

"Then fucking act like it, Natalie. God, this is about me and Melanie. It's our day. You don't have to come in and try to take over the spotlight just because you're some whore to a guy with money."

My jaw tightened. "You should rethink what you're about to say."

"I don't have to rethink anything," he snarled.

"Are you sure you want to do this? Because I told Melanie that I wouldn't."

"I'm sure that you're the attention whore. It's what you've always been. You think you're so cool, being the loner, but you're just desperate for people to see you. And I see you. I see you for what you really are—nothing."

I wouldn't stand here and let him talk to me like that. If the Upper East Side had to follow me around, then I'd use the Upper East Side for what it was really good for.

"Michael, I watched you break my sister's heart so that you could take her best friend to homecoming. I watched her cry all weekend while you fucked her best friend," I said, stepping toward him. "I saw how she took you back, and I see the shell of a woman she is now when she's around you. I see the abuse and harassment and debasement. So, you can stand there and tell me that I'm nothing, but those words are wasted on me. I'm not going to cry and grovel to you because your daddy has money while you're a worthless piece of shit." I blinked at him, giving him the same look I'd seen Katherine give to people she believed were beneath her. "But if you hurt my sister or try to talk to me like this again, then I'll make sure that your life is a living hell. I will ruin you. Wreck you. I will make you wish that you'd never been born. And don't doubt that I can do exactly that. You have no *idea* the resources at my disposal."

I waited. Staring him down like the flea that he was. Waiting for him to snarl back at me like I was the bad person.

But he backed up a step. Losing ground to me as he took in my words. As he saw the dead certainty in my expression.

"You can leave now," I said, waving my hand at him.

He gritted his teeth and then stormed off as if he were about to go find Melanie. But I couldn't even seem to care.

My eyes found Penn's across the backyard. He looked concerned as if he'd seen what had just happened and disapproved. But he hadn't been able to hear what was said. And I couldn't face what I'd had to do to that prick... even if he deserved it.

I just walked out the side exit around to the front of the house. My hands shook when I took a seat on the front steps.

Amy appeared a few minutes later. I'd been expecting Penn.

"Hey there, bestie," she said. "I told Penn to let me take this one."

I released a giant breath. "I hate him."

"Yeah, Michael is a real dick. But whoa, Nat, I didn't even know you had that in you to tell him off like that. I've never seen you fight dirty. Even to people who deserve it."

"I know," I whispered. "Am I becoming like them?"

"Like the people who hurt you?"

I nodded. Fear trickling into my voice. "Like Katherine

and Lewis and Penn and all the other people in New York."

"Maybe they're bringing out the fighter in you. Michael had it coming after all."

"He did," I agreed easily. "But did I have to make him crawl like a worm?"

"Personally, I enjoyed it." She sank into the seat next to me and nudged me with her shoulder. "Just remember that you have something none of those Upper East Siders were born with."

"What's that?"

"A moral code. You know when right is right and wrong is wrong. You'll know if you go overboard. You can pull yourself back. And anyway, I think Penn likes you too much to see you become a bad person."

I sighed. I didn't know how to say that I'd thrown out my moral code after Katherine and Lewis ruined my life. She knew what I'd planned for them, but she didn't know what lengths I planned to go. What I'd do to make them pay. Maybe...maybe I didn't even know. Maybe I'd find out and pull back, just like Amy had said. Maybe, in the end, it wouldn't be worth it.

But as I stared that future in the face, I couldn't imagine stopping. And I didn't know what scared me more.

CHAPTER 23

NATALIE

The rest of the party had gone off without a hitch. Melanie had been preoccupied with her friends, and Penn had been suspiciously quiet. So, I never got to talk to either of them about what had happened.

I awoke the next morning with a sinking pit in my stomach. I needed to talk to Melanie. Sure, Michael had had it coming for being a dick. But I had *promised* Mel that I wouldn't say anything. The last thing I wanted was for her to be mad at me since I was sure Michael wouldn't give the full story.

After throwing on a pair of sweats and an old Grimke University T-shirt I'd found in one of my drawers, I headed down the stairs, hoping to find Mel alone. She was lying out on the couch with the blankets pulled up to her chin. Her normally perfectly straight brown hair was pulled into a messy bun on the top of her head. She didn't have on a lick of makeup. And she was the prettiest I'd ever seen her.

"Nat," she grumbled. "You're up early."

"So are you."

She yawned dramatically. "Dad left for work at the crack of dawn, and I couldn't go back to sleep. Mom made me some tea before heading to the shop."

"Did she read for you out of it, too?" I asked, sinking into the armchair.

"Thankfully, no."

"Lucky."

She yawned again. "Are you up for good? Maybe I could snag your room."

"Sure. I just wanted to talk to you a minute about last night."

Melanie's smile brightened. "Oh, good! I wanted to talk to you, too. I wanted to thank you for being so nice to Michael. I know how you feel about him, and it meant a lot to see you two get along."

"It...did?" I asked quietly.

"Yeah. You were the highlight of the party. Such a hit with all of my friends. I mean, honestly, how do you even have sixty thousand connections?"

I shrugged. "I really don't know."

"Well, it's so cool! And everyone agrees."

"And Michael didn't say anything else to you?" I couldn't help asking.

"About what?"

"What he thought of the party?"

"Sure. He said he had a great time. I know he was so glad that you and Penn could make it."

I stared at my sister. Was I in some alternate universe? I'd been sure that Michael would run straight to Melanie and whine about how I'd treated him. It was almost too good to be true that Melanie hadn't even *noticed* our

199

confrontation. That she had been so caught up in her friends that she missed the whole thing.

Then my stomach twisted further as realization hit me. No, of course, Michael hadn't gone to Melanie. I'd put him in his place. Just like Katherine had done with so many people all over the Upper East Side. Like she had done with me. She was the reigning bitch queen, and no one ever stood up to her. No one would dare. And why was that? Because she had the power to make it worse. Far, far worse. And I had shown Michael the same thing. He'd seen that I was serious about wrecking his life if he tried to pull shit on me.

I stood from my seat in a hurry. Oh god. This was how Katherine got away with it. She put the fear of god in them, and then she walked away scot-free. Certain that no one would talk.

No wonder Melanie was oblivious. I had protected her the best way that I knew how. And it was terrifying.

"Are you all right?" Melanie asked.

"Uh, yeah. I'm fine. Go ahead upstairs. I'm going to make some coffee and wait for Penn."

"Thanks! You're the best," Melanie said, standing and pulling me in for a hug. "Hey, Nat, I was going to ask— would you be my maid of honor?"

A knot lodged in my throat. "Really? Not Marina?"

"Definitely you. I know we haven't always been close, but that's just normal sibling stuff. I'd really love to have you up there with me."

"Of course I will. I'd be honored," I told her truthfully. I might dislike her fiancé, but I loved my sister.

"I'm so excited." She yawned again. "But I need a few more hours of sleep before I can show my enthusiasm."

I laughed and watched her climb the stairs. My unease refused to abate as I ventured into my parents' kitchen, found the coffee grounds, and set the pot to percolate. About ten minutes later, Penn appeared around the corner. His dark hair was wet from the shower, and he was dressed down in khakis and a polo with an Arc'teryx jacket.

"Is that coffee?" he asked me with big puppy-dog eyes.

"I'll pour you some."

"I can get it. You go change. I have a surprise for you."

"A surprise, huh?"

He nodded. "I had an idea and talked to your mom last night."

"Oh dear lord, this can't be good."

"On the contrary, it will be excellent." He reached for the coffeepot as I passed him. But he called out to me before I left, "Dress warmly."

"Why do I have a feeling I'm going to regret this?"

He grinned and I nearly sighed at that beautiful face. "You won't."

I hurried back upstairs, sneaking into my bedroom to steal clothes while Melanie was fast asleep. I changed into layers for the cold in the bathroom. I pulled my long hair up into a high ponytail, and then I braided the pony and tied off the end. I grabbed my jacket and then came back downstairs to find Penn with a thermos of coffee in his hand, a cooler, and my mother's car keys.

"You're all prepared, huh?" I asked. "Did you move in when I wasn't looking?"

"Just schemed behind your back."

I narrowed my eyes at him. "We talked about that."

"For the greater good."

"Yeah, okay."

He pulled me in for a quick kiss. "Just trust me."

And there was that word. I could trust him. I was already trusting him with my heart. Scheming with my parents I could probably handle. Maybe.

We took my mom's car into town. I was worried that Penn would need directions to wherever we were going, but he seemed to have it handled. It was strangely refreshing to have someone else drive me around my own hometown. But the one benefit was, I knew where we were going before he told me.

"We're going out on a boat? Today?" I asked, pulling up the temperature on my phone. "It's only sixty."

"It's supposed to warm up later. And anyway, we've sailed in this weather before."

"Sailing?" I groaned. "You're going to make me do physical labor, aren't you?"

Penn rolled his eyes at me and passed over the cooler. "Come on. You're the one who grew up in a boating town."

"I only lived here four years," I protested.

"Fine. I've been on the water since I was born. I'll do most of the manual labor."

"That sounds fair," I said with a smile.

He shook his head at me and then directed me to the docks. This had always been more Melanie's scene than mine. Especially since Marina's family owned one of the largest boating companies in the harbor. So I wasn't surprised when we ended up walking under the Hartage Boating sign and toward the front desk.

Marina's brother, Daron, stepped outside. He'd been the hottest guy in any of the high schools when I was younger. He had been the star quarterback and dream-boat. He now ran the Hartage Boating with his father.

"Ah, you must be Mr. Kensington," Daron said, holding his hand out to Penn.

"Yes, Penn. You're Daron?"

"That's right."

Daron tilted his head at me. "Hey, Natalie. How's Melanie?"

"Engaged."

Something flickered in his eyes. Distaste perhaps. We'd all hung out some last summer, and I knew he wasn't particularly fond of Michael either.

"That's a shame."

Oh, I liked him. "At least I'm not the only one who thinks so."

"Well, let's get you all set up."

Daron walked us down the docks to a medium-sized sailboat. He and Penn went back and forth for a few minutes about the boat, chatting like they had known each other forever. Finally, Daron seemed satisfied that Penn knew what he was doing and left us to our day on the water.

Penn helped me on the deck and then set to work on getting the boat out on the water. He was a professional at this. His strong muscles working the line and steering us into the wind. It was intoxicating, watching him move. It almost made me forget my earlier fears.

A short while later, Penn tied everything off and set us on a smooth path through the water. He dropped down next to me, reaching for a water bottle out of the cooler. A smile touched my features as all those memories of our time together out on the water in the Hamptons hit me fresh. Sometimes, it was easy to forget how real that had all been for the both of us.

"You look hot when you do that."

He set the water bottle back down. "What?"

"Sail."

"I can't believe that you forgot everything I'd taught you."

"It was so long ago."

He wrapped an arm around my shoulders. "Hence why I thought it would be nice to make all new memories out here."

"I like that," I said, nuzzling into his embrace.

He kissed my hair, and for a while, we just sat there, enjoying the wind in our hair and the sun kissing our skin. It was peaceful after the go, go, go of New York. Charleston had its own charm.

"So, what happened with Michael?" he finally asked.

I sighed. I had known it was coming, but I'd thought that I would be able to escape it for a little while longer. "He was mad that the party was about me. That all of Mel's friends were excited by my new socialite status and celebrity boyfriend."

He arched an eyebrow at that. I shrugged.

"I tried to tell them that we weren't famous, but I guess, we look famous here."

"And how did they find out about all of that?"

I explained about Mary Beth and the alumni page that had generated my newfound celebrity status.

"I see. And so, when Michael got mad, that's when he had all the girls get away from you."

"Yes, and he was mad and said I was selfish and basi-cally...nothing. And well, I'd had this realization while

Mel's friends went postal on me. I finally realized why you always say that you can't escape the Upper East Side. Because I couldn't. Even here in Charleston. Somewhere so far away from that life, and it had followed me here. And I haven't been a part of it for very long while you were raised there your whole life." I sheepishly looked up at him. "Before, whenever you said you wanted to escape but couldn't, I used to think that you were being a bit...dramatic."

He shrugged. "I really wish that I were."

"But you actually can't escape it, can you?"

He shook his head. "No, I can't."

"It follows you. The prestige, the name, the ramifications of who you are being more important than *you*. Even the people who had known me before got swept up in my new persona. And it's like that for you all the time."

"Yes. Which is why it was so refreshing when I met you in Paris. You had no idea who I was. And I don't think that you cared."

"I didn't."

"I was an ass for leading you on through the city and leaving after, but I've thought about that night a lot. How I wished my whole life could be that anonymous. But that's not possible. And it becomes less and less so every time my mother runs for reelection, which happens to be this year. Court and I were talking about it."

My brows rose in shock. "You and your brother *talked*?"

"Yes, and it was shockingly cordial."

"Wow. That's huge, Penn."

"Oddly, I think he likes you. Like...as a person, not as a conquest. Which is another shocker for me."

"I'm so glad that you two talked. That it was productive."

"Me too, surprisingly." He blinked as if the thought of him and Court getting along was too foreign. "So, you found out the Upper East Side isn't so easy to shake after all."

"Yes. And then I kind of channeled that into Michael."

"Oh?"

I fully faced him. "I think I went full Katherine Van Pelt on him."

He cracked a smile and then burst into laughter.

"What?" I gasped.

"You're so serious right now."

"I, like, verbally assaulted him."

"Nat, he probably deserved it."

"Yeah, well, he did, but I'd promised Melanie. And then he didn't even tell. I was so confused."

Penn patted my hand. "We call this using your super-power for good."

"It felt good at the time but not after. I felt like I'd betrayed Mel's trust."

"Look, what you found out about Michael is that he's all bark and no bite. When he recognized you as an actual challenger, he ran with his tail between his legs. You protected your sister. No one was hurt. And the bad guy was put in his place. What part of that is bad?"

I frowned. I hadn't really considered it from that perspective. "I guess…none of it."

Except how it'd made me feel.

But it had been worth it, too.

Maybe doing something bad for the right reason made a difference. More a vigilante than a villain.

"I think this has been very illuminating for me as well," Penn said. He moved a stray strand of hair off of my face and lopped it behind my ear.

"Oh, I'm sure. You see how small town my life is compared to where you're from," I joked. "How cute and Southern it is here."

"I saw where you got your strength and your beautiful mind and that quick wit. I've seen the love your parents have for each other even though they come from completely different places. I see how your sister hero-worships me."

I nudged him. "She does not."

"She does. I'd never seen you outside of *my* element. It's nice to see the Natalie Bishop who has no expectations on her shoulders. The one who can navigate this world as well as mine."

"I do not navigate either very well," I told him honestly.

He pulled my lips to his. "You're very, very wrong. You move between worlds so seamlessly; sometimes, it scares me."

"Bad scary?" I asked against his lips.

He shook his head. "Never with you."

"That's good. I like seeing you dressed down and just hanging out here. No stuffy suits or Upper East Side life-style. No Hamptons. None of your friends. Just us."

He nodded and then leaned his forehead against mine. "Me too."

"We should do this more often." I closed my eyes with a sigh of relief.

"Natalie?"

"Hmm?"

"I love you."

My heart skipped a beat. Those words. The three tiny words that I'd died to hear him say. And been terrified to hear. That I'd rejected the last time we were in Charleston. Even though I'd ached to hear them.

My breath released, and I threaded our fingers together. "I love you, too."

Then he kissed me, and I forgot the boat and the waves and the whole universe. Penn Kensington loved me. He was mine.

CHAPTER 24

NATALIE

We said good-bye to Melanie and my parents the next morning. Amy promised to come visit us in the city, which I thought was secretly so that she could see Enzo, but I was okay with that, too. I wanted Amy to be happy.

Even though Penn and I had been together all weekend, I dropped my bag off at my place and then went back to Penn's to stay the night. It was much easier to celebrate being in love when we had a huge king-size bed to enjoy.

And it was worse, seeing him get up, put on a suit, and head to work. This whole work thing was for the birds. I didn't even want to think about my work. Caroline couldn't believe I was turning down seven figures because of my ex-boyfriend, but considering the restraining order I had out, I didn't think that I even could sign with Warren. Probably a conflict of interest. I'd promised her another manuscript to send out. Possibly another pen name. Though I was sick to my stomach, thinking about sending out my literary novels under any other name than my own. It made it more difficult to work on.

Still, I booted up my computer, which I'd neglected all weekend. And there was my research on the Anselin-Maguire case. I'd forgotten all about it in the bliss of the weekend. But here it was all over again.

I closed out of my manuscript and got to digging. There had to be something here. A reason that Lewis was meeting with people at random house parties and closing business deals after dinner. That wasn't normal. No matter how I'd pushed it aside in the moment.

I read through the first three pages of information on Anselin, and nothing came up. I added Anselin and Warren and searched to see if there were any matches. Another couple of pages passed by. Apparently, they did a lot of business. Or at least, there was a lot of talk about it. It was the next page that I finally stopped to read through.

It was an article about the acquisition of a large tract of land in a minority neighborhood. The newspaper celebrated the purchase by Warren and highlighted the agreement not to displace the people within the area. Instead, Warren had plans to revitalize the area while keeping the old residents in it.

It was strange how much the newspaper kissed their ass. Purchasing land in a low-income area and revitalizing it was definitely a thing to celebrate. But it also sounded a bit too much like...propaganda to me. No one did anything just for the altruistic good feels. There was a reason that Lewis had purchased the neighborhood.

I had a bad feeling about this.

Lewis had bought my building when he wanted to get me a good deal for the apartment. But it wasn't normal in

New York to keep prices low just for the fun of it. Why would he have bought that land? What did it have that interested him? If he wasn't going to do something to make more money, then I wagered he needed it for something else.

I searched out the low-income neighborhood that the article said Warren had purchased and found the apartments listed for rent were twice as much as I was paying currently. My eyes bulged. That wasn't sustainable on the Upper West. How could people afford that outside of Manhattan?

The answer was, they couldn't.

As I kept scrolling through the listings, I realized that there were hundreds of them. All from this area. All from the buildings Lewis had purchased. All of these people were now displaced.

There was nothing to prevent him from doing this. I'd taken a class in college that discussed gentrification. It was a common thing in most cities. It was even hailed as a good thing by a lot of people. Gentrification was when efforts were made to revitalize a neighborhood that was predominantly low-income. It brought new tenants, new stores, and a new life to the area. But it hurt communities as much as it helped them. What happened to the people who had to leave the communities and apartments and houses they'd lived in their entire lives? How did they survive now that everything was triple what they'd paid in the past? It wasn't fair. And it was becoming more and more common to try to force out people that others found "undesirable."

Not illegal, but shady as fuck. Especially after claiming they had no intention of harming the community.

I frowned. This wasn't concrete proof. I could get that. I could find out who had lived there, what they had been paid, how many people had left. I could look up city permits to see if new construction was planned or if new businesses were intending to move in. I was pretty sure that I could do enough work to show this. And I had to bet...if he'd done this once, then it wasn't the first time. Especially considering that Anselin-Maguire hadn't even wanted to work with Warren. Lewis's dad had made that pretty clear. They had to know what they were signing away. And the type of business the Warrens ran. Just like Jane had said.

All the threads connected.

It was all there at a glance.

I could do this.

My fingers hesitated on the keys. To what end?

Ruin him to satisfy my own revenge?

It would make me feel better, but then would I get that sick feeling in the pit of my stomach again? And if I went through with this, there was no coming back. It was one thing to try to take over Katherine's socialite status, but was this worth it?

I closed my laptop.

I needed to think on it. Get my head on straight.

My phone buzzed on the counter. A text from Jane.

Hey, are we still on for coffee this morning?

"Shit," I groaned.

I'd forgotten that I'd agreed to meet Jane. I'd gotten so wrapped up in my research that it slipped my mind.

I texted her back to let her know I was on my way and

then hastily changed into one of the Bergdorf outfits I'd left at Penn's place.

It was a beautiful day in Manhattan, so I skipped a cab and walked down Fifth Avenue past the park to Jane's favorite coffee shop, only blocks from her favorite department store. Spring was right around the corner. I could smell it in the air. And hear the chirping of the birds. The people jogging through the park. The babies being pushed in strollers.

It had all the makings of why I loved this city so much.

And made me think that maybe I should just be happy that I was in love. That Penn loved me back. And put it all behind me. Did I really need my revenge?

I chewed on my lip as I debated what to do. I *wanted* to make them pay. I didn't want them to continue to get away with hurting people. The way Katherine treated people was disgusting. And what Lewis was doing was abhorrent. Even if it *wasn't* illegal, it was still repulsive. And people deserved to know who they were dealing with. That this behemoth was kicking the little guy.

But how far would I have to dig back down into that dark place when I had only just been able to see the light again?

My thoughts stopped abruptly when my phone rang. I stared down at the number in excitement. The attorney.

"This is Natalie."

"Natalie, thank you for answering. This is Shonda from Dr. Kensington's staff," she said.

"Yes, Shonda, I'm so glad to hear from you. I've been awaiting your call."

"I'm afraid that I have...unfortunate news," she said softly.

My stomach sank. "What?"

"The judge ruled to throw out your restraining order. He said that there wasn't sufficient evidence of stalking or domestic abuse. Especially considering the length of the relationship."

My body went numb. No. No, this wasn't how the legal system was supposed to work. It was supposed to protect people.

"Natalie?" Shonda asked. "Are you there?"

"Yes, I'm here. I can't believe this."

"I know. I'm shocked. I think..."

"Yes?"

"I'm not sure that I should say. It's merely speculation based on past experience."

"Explain."

"I think the judge knows the Warrens. They...donate to his campaign."

I went as still as death. I found that black place rush up at me like a car skidding across thin ice, prepared to plummet to its depths.

My voice was just as icy when I responded, "Of *course* they do."

"I'm really so sorry. I didn't...expect this outcome. Nor do I support it. We can still appeal."

"No," I said at once. "No, that won't make a difference."

And I knew in my heart that it wouldn't.

It would make no difference.

Because once a-fucking-gain, I had to be painfully reminded of this world. That there were no consequences. Not even a slap on the wrist. Not even an order of protection for harassing and stalking and bruising me. Nothing. Lewis Warren was untouchable. He had made himself that way over time. And even the judge could take the bribe to let it pass.

No. If I was going to get what I wanted, I had to do this myself.

And now, I had the tools to do it.

"Thank you, Shonda. You've reminded me of a very important lesson."

"I did?"

"Never underestimate your enemy."

She sighed. "I'm so sorry. Let me look into the appeal, and I'll get back to you."

I let her finish and then hung up. My feet carried me down Fifth Avenue, inside the little café that made me think so much of Paris, and to the table where a frazzled Jane Devney sat.

I plopped into the seat across from her. She gushed with excitement to see me. Then her face fell at the look on my own face.

"What's wrong?"

"Jane, I need to ask a favor."

"Anything. Are you okay?"

"I will be."

"What's the favor?"

I leaned forward in the booth. "I need your contact for the *New York Times*. I have something I think she'll be very interested in."

PART IV
BEST SERVED COLD

CHAPTER 25

PENN

"*D*r. Kensington?" a voice called, peeping into my office.

I glanced up to see my teaching assistant, Chelle, standing in the doorway. "How can I help you?"

She hopped inside, closing the door behind her. "Amanda has emailed me three times about that paper she 'forgot' to turn in." She mimed quotations around the word *forgot*. "I told her that, if she sent it in by midnight, we'd accept, minus a letter grade."

"That's fine with me."

"Yes, well, she just turned it in."

I checked the clock on my iMac. "It's twenty minutes before lecture."

"Yep. It looks like she banged it out last night. What should I do?"

I breathed out through my nose in frustration. Amanda was one of the rare female students in the philosophy department. She stalked my office hours to bat her eyelashes at me in hopes that I'd give her a better grade. I was sure it had worked for her in other classes. It didn't work with me.

"You said midnight. Dock two letter grades for it being late."

She chewed her lip. "She's probably going to fail."

I nodded once. She probably would. And I hated failing students. But I'd grown up in a world where money changed grades. I wasn't prone to do it myself. No matter who their parents were or how many of them batted their pretty eyelashes at me.

"Okay then. I'll see you in lecture," Chelle said and bounced out of my office as quickly as she'd come.

I pushed aside the paper I'd been reading for a peer review I had to do for a journal. I'd been putting it off and putting it off, but it was part of the job. A tedious part.

I dragged out my phone to see if Natalie had messaged me. I knew that she was busy this morning with Harmony, so it was probably wishful thinking. Everything had been...amazing since Charleston. As if a month ago on a boat in the Atlantic, our world had shifted on its axis. And I liked it. I more than liked it.

A month of just us. No interference from my friends. No big fires. Just us living our lives and Natalie falling easily into this world. Maybe easier than I'd like, but we'd been good together. We *were* good together.

But instead of a message from Natalie, there was a string of them from Lark. And then Rowe. And even...Katherine.

"What the hell?" I murmured, confused as to why I'd be bombarded by the crew.

I clicked on Lark's messages.

OMG, have you seen the news? I can't believe what's happening to Lewis.

Penn? I'm freaking out. Did you know about this?

Gah, you must be in lecture or something. If you haven't seen it already, here's the link.

When I saw the headline to the article from the *New York Times*, I didn't even bother with Rowe's or Katherine's text messages. I just opened the article and began to read.

"Oh fuck," I gasped.

The article detailed extensive, manipulative, and potentially fraudulent behavior that the Warrens had been dealing with over the last decade. It started with a recent case that Lewis had closed, Anselin-Maguire, and a purchase of land that led to the displacement of hundreds of low-income families, many who were now homeless. Then it traced this behavior back further in time. None of it was *expressly* illegal. There was no paperwork saying that they weren't going to kick people off the properties, but they'd contacted a half-dozen people who had sold to the Warrens, who had verbal commitments that the worst would be avoided. And it was a matter of whether or not those verbal contracts would hold up. Either way, it looked like Lewis had seriously fucked up, and an investigation had been opened up into the company.

What else could be lurking under the seemingly perfect exterior?

I knew what this meant. I knew the implications of this. Even if *nothing* else was wrong. Even if Warren was in tip-top shape, doing everything by the book. This would hurt. This could shake the foundation of the company. A lengthy investigation could halt business growth. Investors could back out. Stocks would drop. They'd lose millions over this article. If the investigation found something else, they could lose the company.

Katherine's father had lost his in the same way. One investigation had shown the years of securities fraud that proved that Van Pelt was rotten to the core. We'd all known. We'd been there in high school when it all came crumbling down.

I picked up the phone without a thought and dialed Lewis's number. I might hate him for all he'd done, but...I was still compelled to contact him.

I was more surprised that he answered.

"Kensington," Lewis said crisply.

"I just heard."

"Here to gloat?" he asked in a soft voice. Not deadly like I'd expect, but beaten down. Like he'd lost some part of him that had always been there. An overconfidence.

"No. I called to check on you."

Lewis scoffed in disbelief. "I'm fine," he bit out. "Stuck at my parents'. It's a media shitstorm. They've parked their vulture asses outside my place and theirs, just waiting for the carnage."

"So...is it true?"

"You going to sell my answer to the highest bidder?"

"As if I need the money," I joked.

He laughed slightly at my comment. "Yeah, I suppose we're still too fucked up with our own secrets for you to pull that shit."

He wasn't wrong. We'd always been bound in a tangled web of history and lies and secrets.

Muffled voices cracked through on his end.

"I have to go," Lewis said. There was a pause, as if he wasn't sure what to say. "I appreciate your call."

And he meant it. I could hear it.

The line clicked off, and I stared down at it. What a fucked up world I lived in. How the hell could I sympathize with him about this and also want to slaughter him for the last year of bullshit?

I shut it out and texted Lark.

I read that article and just got off the phone with Lewis. He's stuck at home with a media circus. Pretty fucked up.

You two actually spoke?! Who knew the world needed to end to accomplish this?

Ha. Ha.

Yeah, well, it's been a rough couple of months. Anyway, the rest of the crew is meeting at Rowe's after work. Come over and see the little people.

All right. But if it devolves again, then I'm out of there.

Lark responded with a GIF of Alice in Wonderland curtsying.

I checked the time. "Fuck," I groaned. I was running behind for my lecture. I thrust my phone back in my pocket, grabbed my notes, and darted out of the room. It was a reprieve to have a full hour not to have to think about how I was going to break it to Natalie that I was seeing the crew again.

I DECIDED to just send a text as I was walking into Rowe's apartment. She wouldn't like it either way, and I could hardly blame her for that. But I'd explained what the crew meant to me. How I could hate them and care for them in my own fucked up way. That they were family. More my family than the one I'd grown up with.

One of our own had been taken down. It felt wrong not to be together for that. Like we'd been together when Katherine's father was put away. Or when her brother, David, had disappeared. Or when my father had died. Or for Lark's ex-boyfriend's bullshit.

The elevator dinged open to reveal the stark white interior of Rowe's place. I had a sense of unease. The last time I'd been here, we'd had a fucking intervention. I'd gotten into it with both Lewis and Katherine. Lark, ever the peacemaker, had wanted us to all still be friends. We were connected. I felt that even now as I stepped inside to find Rowe seated at his computer and Lark staring out the window to Central Park and Katherine sipping a martini. Lark and Rowe looked the same. It was Katherine who looked a mess. It wasn't her clothes or the makeup or the perfect dark hair. But something in her eyes. Something in her poise. Something lost. What the hell was going on with *her*? And should I even care?

There was an empty spot next to her on the couch where Lewis typically sat. It felt like a hole in the room.

"Penn," Katherine said, looking me up and down,

examining my dark blue suit coat, gray slacks, and bow tie. "How professorially of you."

I dropped my leather messenger bag onto the white chair and undid the tie at my neck, letting the material hang loose. "It's a uniform. As much as your…" I gestured to her designer dress and heels.

"I wasn't complaining," she told me with a sly smile. But it wasn't the same. It had lost its heat.

"Have you heard from him again?" Lark asked, stepping away from the window.

"No," I told her. "Anyone else?"

They all shook their heads. Rowe continued to stare blank-faced at his computer. I peeked over his shoulder to see he was reading endless articles that had come out about it after the one from the *Times*.

"Who could have leaked this information?" Lark asked with a sigh. She sank down next to Katherine.

Katherine just snorted. "Anyone."

I agreed. "Literally anyone. There were so many names listed in that article, I'm shocked it wasn't all pieced together before this. It makes me wonder how many others they'd paid off to stay quiet."

"Many," Rowe said. "They're coming out of the woodworks."

"Great," Katherine grumbled.

An anxious tension permeated the room. We didn't have to say anything to know all the ways this could go wrong. We'd all gone through things before but nothing like this. Not for one of our own.

And in some strange sense, it felt like the shine was gone on reality. For a long time, I'd seen the corruption in my world. I'd tried to stay out of it. I'd walked that fine line between the two. But somehow, we always came out on top. No matter what came our way, we always succeeded.

But I didn't know how Lewis was going to get out of this one. There were life-altering consequences to this. Far-reaching implications for the company and his family.

It was as if...we really *weren't* invincible. In a world where we always had been before.

CHAPTER 26

*T*rinity was empty.

I'd seen it in all its glory on the night of the soft opening. With Elizabeth Cunningham revealing a collection down the runway before Christmas. And then again on New Year's Eve at the giant masquerade that had started it all again with Penn.

But on a random Tuesday afternoon at the end of March, it was empty. The main lights activated to illuminate the large space and the bars that lined the room. Bottles full but no bartenders.

Yet, in my imagination, I was envisioning all the ways that I could transform it. All the ways that we could use the space to my advantage.

Jane stood at my side in Lululemon leggings and an open-back sweatshirt. Her feet in tiny silver-lined Nikes and her signature oversize sunglasses on her head. She had about a hundred pairs. Today, they were Tiffany blue.

"Well, what do you think?" she asked.

Harmony nodded on my other side. Her stylish dress

couldn't be further from Jane's purposeful athleisure. "I think it'll do."

"Me too," I agreed.

I, after all, had been the one to suggest that I host my party here at Trinity.

A few days after I'd gotten back from Charleston, a literacy charity had reached out to me about hosting a function to raise money for their cause. I was uncertain at first whether or not I could even pull something like that off. But after some consideration, I decided it was too good a cause not to.

Plus, Harmony had thought it would take my newfound socialite status to the next level. And had promptly decided to join my "team" for the event. It was a good thing, too, because I'd never planned a party in my entire life. Let alone something on this scale.

"Great," Jane said, jumping in. "I'll get together a contract by tomorrow and email it over. I'm so excited that we're doing this. It's going to be such a great event for you and the club."

"Have you decided on a theme yet?" Harmony asked.

I shook my head. "Still thinking it over. I have some ideas, but nothing seems right."

"It'll come to you," Jane said.

I sure fucking hoped so or else this was all going to be a disaster.

"You know what I think you need?" Harmony asked.

I shrugged. "What's that?"

"A trial run."

"Hmm…what do you mean?"

"I was thinking girls' night out. We invite a group of girls that we want to attend the event. Then we corral them to be part of your team. It'll look good for you and for them. You can delegate some of the responsibility and get your name out even more."

"A girls' night sounds fun," Jane agreed.

"It does sound fun."

"I remember one of the first events I ran by myself. It was so horribly overwhelming. It would be good to get everyone on board," Harmony said.

A girls' night out did sound like a good way to test the waters. It was a huge undertaking that was causing me more than a little bit of stress. So much so that I hadn't even been able to write while dealing with all of this. I wanted to pull it off as seamlessly as Katherine had pulled off her Halloween event. And every other event I'd been to since then. No one should know the difference.

"Let's do it."

"Do you want me to send invites out?" Harmony asked. She pulled out her phone and started scrolling through Crew.

"No," I said at once. "It should come from me. Put me together a list, and I'll reach out."

Jane grinned. "I love this side of you."

I blinked. "What side of me?"

"So confident and in control. Knowing exactly where you belong."

Harmony agreed, "It's kind of hot."

I flipped my silvery hair off of my shoulder and smiled. "Thanks, girls. This is so fun."

It was as much a charade as the event hosting, but I had to sell it. I wasn't confident or in control. I was just acting. Trying to walk in the footsteps of those who had been successful at this before me. Channel my inner Amy and merge it with the Upper East Side superiority.

Jane at least knew where I'd come from and how I'd been when I first entered the scene. Most other people, Harmony included, didn't remember that Natalie. Or if they'd read about her in Katherine's salacious article, it was whispered behind my back as they worshipped at my feet. And I had to decide to not care or else the whole thing would drive me crazy.

"So, girls' night out. I'll add it to the list," I said with a laugh.

"Excellent. I'm excited. I need a girl time. Maybe we can finally find me a better guy than my last douche," Harmony said. "We can't all be lucky enough to snag Kensington men."

Jane and I both shrugged at the same time. Then we giggled that we'd done it together.

Harmony started to ask about logistics for the event, and I pulled out my phone to take notes. I didn't want to miss anything. But first, I checked the text from Penn. My eyes narrowed at the words on the screen.

Heading to Rowe's to see the crew. Something's happened.

Then he linked to a news article.

A slight gasp escaped my lips as realization hit me like a cold shower.

"What?" Harmony asked with round blue eyes.

I didn't respond. I just turned the screen toward them so that they could see the *New York Times* article about Warren being under investigation. About *Lewis* being under investigation...for the exact thing that I had contacted the journalist about.

When I'd contacted the journalist, she hadn't seemed that interested. She said she'd look into it. That I shouldn't get my hopes up that it would become anything. That her boss might not even want to run it. Sometimes, that happened with powerful players...especially ones who weren't in politics.

I didn't like it. Just like I hadn't liked the lack of a restraining order. But I'd done my part. She'd said she'd contact me if she needed more information or if she got the green light.

I hadn't been contacted. I'd had no knowledge that this was going to come out. I'd hoped for it. Her boss would have been an idiot not to want to bring down the Warrens. But of course, they'd had to get real proof. The proof that I'd been sure was there. And here it was...exactly as I'd imagined.

A small, satisfied smile lit up my face.

Karma at its finest.

"Oh my god!" Harmony gasped. She took my phone out of my hand and was reading the article word for word.

But Jane had stopped reading and glanced up at me. She knew whose byline that was. She knew that it was a friend of hers. She could put the pieces together. But she didn't look upset. If anything, she looked...impressed.

"This is crazy," Jane said softly.

"Isn't it?" I agreed.

"An investigation on the whole company now."

"All for shady dealings."

"Pity," Jane said with a matching smile.

"Holy fuck!" Harmony interjected. "I mean…Lewis fucking deserved it if he was really doing this shit."

"Oh, he was," Jane said. "Everyone knows they've been doing this kind of shit and getting away with it. No one wants to work with them, but they're hamstringed because the Warrens have all the power."

"Well, yeah. I mean, he had it coming. But shit," Harmony said. "I didn't think this kind of thing *happened* to men on the Upper East Side. Not…one of us, you know?"

Harmony's look pleaded with me to understand. Because to her, I *was* one of them. I'd integrated into their circle. And she wasn't wrong. Nothing bad had ever happened to these people. That was the whole fucking point. They could commit murder and get away with it.

That time was over.

It was fucking over.

"I guess it does now," I calmly told her.

"I guess so," Harmony said, passing me my phone back. "Kind of scary. Almost like…who's next?"

Who indeed?

I MADE it back to Penn's before he did. Totle and I snuggled on the couch as I went through the list Harmony had sent over for our girls' night out. It was like fifty fucking people long. I'd thought, like, ten at most. Was this normal? Did I need fifty people I didn't know helping me with an event?

It was a headache. I'd raided Penn's liquor drawer, and I was sipping from a glass of whiskey when he appeared in the living room. My eyes trailed down him. The navy jacket and gray slacks that hugged him. The bow tie hanging around his neck, undone. The electric-blue eyes that took in my own state of undress with efficiency and need. Then to the glass in my hand.

"Long day?" he finally settled on.

"Taxing," I told him. "Who knew party-planning was so cumbersome?"

"Literally everyone." He took the drink out of my hand and took a sip. "Oh, the good stuff. I think I'll have one."

"Fill mine up," I called as he headed back to the liquor cabinet.

He chuckled and did as I'd asked, bringing his own glass over as well. He sank into the seat next to me and slung his arm across the back of the sofa. Totle crawled over me, licked his dad's face, and then settled comfortably into his lap.

"Should I be thankful or nervous that you're not immediately yelling at me about seeing the crew?" Penn asked with a dangerously sexy smirk.

"It's fine," I said on a sigh. I chewed on the end of my pen as I stared harder at the list.

"Fine? The last time, you freaked out."

"Yes. Last time, you didn't tell me. And…that was before you explained them to me in Charleston." I glanced up to meet his eyes. "Do I like it? I mean, no. I don't think it's healthy, but I'm not going to tell you not to see them. You're a big boy. You can make your own decisions."

He grinned like he was about to devour me. I laughed as he nipped at my bottom lip.

"I like coming home to you."

"Me too."

He pressed a kiss to my lips. "So, maybe you should move in."

I pulled back. "What?"

"We can get you out of your new lease. You can live here."

I opened my mouth. "Are you joking?"

"Do I look like I am?"

"No. But…I like my place. We go over there still. Totle likes it over there, too."

"That's because he likes to hump your neighbor's dog."

I snorted. "True. It just feels…soon."

"Okay," he said easily. His eyes skittered over the list in my lap. "What's this?"

"Wait. *Okay*? Just like that?"

"If you're not ready, that's okay, Nat," he said, running his finger along my jaw and pulling me in for another kiss. "I'm not pressuring you into anything."

Sometimes, I forgot how amazing he was. That we worked so well like this. "Thank you."

"You don't have to thank me. I'm going to try to get you to move in with me, and one day, you're going to say yes. But you can't say yes if I don't ask."

"Sneaky."

He winked at me and then returned to the paper. "Why is every girl that I know on the Upper East Side in a spreadsheet in your lap?"

"Oh god, you know them all? That would be so helpful. I'm planning a small girls' night out, and Harmony sent me a list of people I could invite. Whittling it down is…intense."

Penn shook his head. "You don't want to be friends with any of these people, Nat. They're all snakes."

"Pot, meet kettle."

He pointed his finger at me. "Touché. I have the ulti-mate snake friends." He snatched it out of my hand and then started listing off names. "That's probably where I'd start. You do know these are all Katherine's friends, right?"

I shrugged. "So?"

"She's going to get pissed if you don't invite her."

"Well, I guess she'll just have to get pissed, won't she?"

"All right," he said with a shrug. "Just be careful. I don't want her to try to hurt you again."

"Me either."

"The stuff with Lewis is scary enough."

"Yeah," I murmured, biting my lip.

"Did you hear the shit with his mom?"

I frowned. "What about Nina?"

"They're putting her on hiatus for her UN ambas-sadorship until they find out if she was involved in any way," Penn said with a shake of his head.

I blanched. "Oh my god."

I liked Nina. She had been the best part about dating Lewis. She was this perfect, unbelievable woman who, against all circumstances, had come out on top. She was honest and good. I hadn't thought that this could hurt her.

"Yeah, Lewis is pretty fucked up over it."

"You talked to him?"

He shrugged. "I called when I found out. He called Ren and filled us in while I was at Rowe's."

I swallowed. "I didn't think this would affect Nina."

"None of us did," he said, pulling me in close to him as I swallowed bile. "Hopefully, the investigation turns up nothing, and she can go back to work."

My stomach pitched. Lewis deserved what I'd done. Even his smarmy dad who had tried to buy me out of dating Lewis deserved this shit. But Nina? No. She was an innocent in all of this. It was an unintended consequence of this mess. And it made me feel as sick as I had that morning when I realized I'd gotten away with how I'd treated Michael. I didn't like knowing that this hurt people I cared about.

"Yeah, hopefully," I whispered. "Nina doesn't deserve to be blamed for what Lewis and Edward did."

He drew me closer. "That's how it happens sometimes. It's a snowball effect. It picks up speed until it runs down everything in its path."

It felt like an apt metaphor for my revenge. And fear hit me that I wouldn't be able to control it once it started downhill.

CHAPTER 27

*H*armony borrowed the Percy limo for the night. Since the Percys were now her step-family, she'd insisted that she was owed their swank limo. Which was how Jane and I were sipping champagne in the back with her and listening to her explain Camden's reaction when he'd found out.

"You *should* have seen his face," Harmony said with a grin. She tried to imitate Camden's face with her brows rising ever higher, her mouth open, and clear outrage and disbelief across her features.

We all broke down into hysterical laughter at the imitation.

"Stop. Stop!" I crowed. "My sides hurt."

Jane waved her hands at us both. "I can't breathe."

"It was great. He was so fucking serious, too. It was perfection."

"I cannot believe you did it," I told her.

She shrugged. "It was great to hear him say that he was

going to murder me for taking it. Anything to upset him is like a job well done."

I shook my head and then finished my glass of champagne. Harmony cracked me up. I didn't know how she had lived under Katherine's oppression all these years. Her personality vibrated out of her.

And to think that I'd been nervous all week about this club outing. But now that I was with my girls, all of that melted away. It was just like all the times Amy and I had done this in college. Except for the part where I'd had a fifty-person guest list to go through and had to hand-select a dozen girls to hang out with me. That had *never* been part of my life. Surreal to think that I'd been the loner, and I was now constantly surrounded by people who wanted exclusive invites to go to the club with me.

"You ready for this?" Jane asked with a glint in her hazel eyes as we pulled up to Club 360.

"Of course she is," Harmony said.

I nodded. I was. This was the test run for everything I'd been working toward. The life I was stealing. "Bring it on."

We stepped out of the limo and walked into the Percy hotel in Midtown. We were escorted into the elevator up to the rooftop bar that had started everything with me and Penn. It had also been the beginning of my career that was still up in flames. And Lewis, who I'd just lit on fire. It was a club for new beginnings. For taking control of the now. And I had every intention of doing so.

Club 360 was slammed with people, as if everyone knew that this was the place to be tonight. Our escort easily drew us through the crowd and showed us to our mostly full booth. There were ten girls already sitting around, drinking, and chatting with each other. With Harmony and Jane, it made a solid dozen that I had invited for the evening. Everyone went silent when we appeared and then almost immediately jumped up to greet us.

"Oh my, Natalie," Fiona said, appearing in front of the fray. "Look at how amazing you look."

"Yeah, you're so hot," Sloane agreed.

Isabel pushed her way into the bunch. "For real. Why didn't I buy that dress?"

"Because it would never look as good on you," Fiona said easily.

"Yeah, Isabel, you'd be washed out in that," Sloane agreed.

I laughed at the girls, who were basically complimentary lackeys. "Oh, stop." I brushed down the sides of the rose-gold dress I'd chosen for the occasion. "You are too nice."

And it went on like that for a while. I officially met the rest of the party. I'd apparently met a few of the girls at other parties, but I didn't remember them. I wouldn't have remembered the lackeys if it wasn't for that one strange conversation at the Fashion Week gala. But they all came from the right families, Penn had picked most of them, and it was good to be seen with them. Though it was still a little strange to think about friendships that way.

Like Danielle and Carrie, who modeled like Harmony had. And Jenniel, whose husband owned a bank. Ellie and Emma—still couldn't tell them apart—who had a cosmetics line. And Sorcha, who designed for Elle. Imogen's father was in the fashion business somehow. I knew the list by heart, but putting names with faces was going to be a challenge.

A bartender was serving our party and came over with a bottle of Patrón. "Shots?"

I blinked. "Yeah, that would be great."

She grinned wide. "I thought so. Don't you always start with tequila shots?"

"Always?" I asked in confusion.

I'd never done this before. Why would she think that?

"This is Katherine's box, right? She loves a good tequila shot with her girls."

This was *Katherine's* box? I'd sat in it with Penn and Lewis the first time I was here, but I hadn't realized there was some unwritten rule that it belonged to her.

I glanced over at Harmony, who was grinning like a fool. She had been the one to call and make the reservation. I didn't have to ask if she knew. Because of course, Harmony had known. She had likely asked for it personally and put her weight behind it, like she had with the limo. I appreciated the gesture. It wasn't something I would have even known to do.

"It used to be Katherine's box," I told the waitress. "I'm Natalie."

"Oh!" the girl said in surprise. "Sorry about that. Still want tequila?"

"Sure. Might as well."

The waitress poured out thirteen shots along with limes and salt. We each took a shot and raised it into the air. Everyone looked to me to make a toast. Amy had always been the one to do that. Oh, how everything was turned upside down.

"To new friendships," I started, tipping my head to Harmony.

"New hook-ups," she cheered.

"Lots of sex," Jane added with a wink.

"And getting fucked up!" Fiona cried.

"I'll toast to that," I said with a laugh. Licked the salt and then tossed the shot back.

The rest of the girls followed suit, drinking the potent liquid and then sucking on limes.

The girls moved back into their own small circles while others went out onto the dance floor to find man candy for the night. Harmony among them. I grabbed another drink from our personal bartender before sidling up with the lackeys. I was surprised to hear them discussing Lewis.

"Oh yeah," Sloane said, "I have a friend who works for Warren. The whole place is a mess."

"Damn," Isabel said. "It looks so bad, and he's single. Do you think that I have a chance now?"

"No," Fiona said baldly.

"Oh sorry, Natalie," Isabel said when I drew close. "I know that you dated."

"He's all yours," I said easily.

"Of course, Isabel. She's dating Penn Kensington now," Fiona said. Then she snickered. "We've all been there, right, girls? We all found out how good that was last year."

I froze in place at her words. At the close way they all watched me, as if waiting for a reaction to Fiona's words. Then it all came together. These must have been some of the girls that Penn had slept with after we broke up. I couldn't believe he hadn't had more discriminating taste.

But I knew he had done it to get back at Katherine. In some sense, wasn't I using them for the same reason?

"Oh yes, he mentioned that," I said evenly. Though I would bring it up with him later as to why he *hadn't*. How many other girls on the list had he also slept with and let me walk into the lion's den without a warning?

Fiona seemed startled by my response, but Sloane's dry voice filled the silence. "I wish *my* choices were between a Warren and a Kensington."

Jane snickered next to me. "You three are *so* fun."

But the way she'd said it, it was the most Jane way ever. I had to fight from laughing at the quip that went over their heads.

"Penn and I are happy. That's all that matters."

"It is," Isabel agreed easily.

"Though I heard Lewis is so miserable," Sloane said.

"And his poor mother," Fiona said.

Jane shrugged. "If you do bad business, there are consequences. No one is exempt. Not even a Warren."

"Ugh," Isabel groaned. "Let's talk about something else. When I hear the word *business*, I start to break out. I'm going to marry someone and never have to think about it again."

Fiona giggled. "Isn't that everyone's plan?"

Jane straightened. "I don't think it is."

"Yeah, but, like, owning a club isn't a real job," Sloane said slowly.

I placed my hand on Jane's before she could go off on them. "Jane works really hard for her club. She's amazing at it. And she enjoys it. Some of us don't mind working. And some of us don't want to. Either is fine," I said evenly.

Even though I couldn't imagine never working again and letting Penn cover everything.

"Oh god," Fiona grumbled. "Look who just showed his face."

We all turned to see who had appeared.

"Don't look. Don't look!" she cried.

"You just told us to," Isabel grumbled.

But it was too late anyway. We were all looking and found Camden Percy striding into Club 360. He'd be super-freaking hot in a gray three-piece suit if he wasn't such an unbelievable dick. No amount of good looks could make up for the hideous personality lurking darkly underneath it all.

"Why are we looking at Camden?" I asked, turning back to the lackeys.

Isabel bit her lip and looked away. Sloane's eyes widened as if in disbelief that I didn't know. But it was Fiona who was the color of a ripe tomato.

"We had an affair," she whispered.

Jane and I raised our eyebrows at the same time. This wasn't the first time that I'd heard that Camden had cheated on Katherine. I remembered a particular night at Harmony's party last year where he'd been high as fuck and looking for a good time. He would have been fine with me that night if Court hadn't saved me from his clutches.

But this was the first time someone Katherine knew was admitting it.

"When?" Jane asked, leaning forward.

"Like…the last year."

"Two," Sloane said.

Fiona glared at her. "On and off forever."

"And...it's still going on?" I asked her.

She paused and then shook her head once. "He ended it after the wedding."

I eyed her doubtfully. Why would Camden end an easy fuck-buddy relationship when he despised Katherine? He didn't seem the type to give up something convenient.

"You want us to believe it's really over?" Jane asked, on the same train of thought as me.

"Well, I saw him after he got back from his honeymoon, but he sent me home," Fiona said. Embarrassment coated her voice.

"He threw her out," Isabel clarified.

"Like...bodily," Sloane added.

"Girls," Fiona groaned.

"Huh," I said in surprise. "Did Katherine know?"

Fiona's eyes bulged. "Are you out of your mind? She would kill me." She glanced sideways. "They've always been so....you know?"

I tilted my head because, clearly, I did not.

"In love," Fiona said. She averted her gaze and frowned.

I laughed softly and then realized she was serious. Fiona thought Katherine and Camden were in love? I glanced around at the rest of her friends...even Jane. They all thought that Katherine and Camden were really together.

Oh god.

The realization hit me like a two-by-four. No one else knew that it was an arranged marriage. It was a crew secret. And I'd happened to be a part of the crew when it all came out. They'd thought I was a nobody when they first told me, and then it was too late. But to the rest of the world, this was real.

It was deeply disturbing. And an edge I hadn't known that I had.

"They're in love, and yet you slept with him for years?" I asked Fiona.

"He's a man of carnal desire," she whispered.

I nearly gagged and found my eyes dragged back toward Camden Percy. Well, Fiona wasn't the only person who had slept with Camden since he'd gotten engaged to Katherine. And I doubted she would be the last either. He'd never seemed like the one-woman type, especially since I knew that his feelings for Katherine were a charade.

"Nat," Jane whispered. She pointed back to the entrance.

It was my time to curse.

Katherine Van Pelt strode into Club 360.

CHAPTER 28

Katherine wore a skintight red dress and mile-high heels. Her dark brown hair was down in waves, and even with her face partially in shadow, it was clear she had on heavy makeup. Her steely gaze swept the dance floor, owning it, and then she walked right into Camden's arms like they had been waiting for her all along.

We all watched in various forms of shock as they started making out in public. Right there on the dance floor.

Sure, he owned the hotel. He could do whatever he wanted. But it had never seemed like Camden was one for public displays of affection.

And last I'd heard, Katherine actually despised him. Except that wasn't quite true. Penn had mentioned that Katherine had seemed relieved to see Camden. That she might even...like him. My head spun with that knowledge.

I wanted her to be miserable. I wanted her to pay. And

somehow, it had turned on its head. Just becoming this wasn't enough. Not if she was happy with that bastard. Against all odds.

I rose to my feet. "Who cares if he's here?" I said to Fiona. "You can get any guy you want. You don't need to worry about one who's already married." I held my hand out to her, and she let me help her up. "Let's dance."

The rest of the girls jumped to their feet as the beat kicked in. We crushed together, letting loose, and seemingly getting rid of all our concerns. Just a group of beautiful women living the life.

Jane danced next to me with a sly smile on her lips. "Nice job."

I threw an arm around her. "Fake it till you make it, right?"

"I think you're already there."

"Huh, I guess so. Who knew it was just an attitude change that could bring me all of this?"

"Me," Jane said with a laugh, swaying her hips side to side.

Harmony appeared a minute later and swept into our dance circle. "Oh my god, did you see that Katherine is here?"

"We saw," I told her.

"She's going to kill us," she said with a chuckle. "It's going to be great."

"There's nothing she can do about it."

Harmony gave me a dubious look. "She's Katherine Van Pelt. Where there's a will, there's a way."

I knew she was right. Katherine stayed two steps ahead. And though I'd been trying to figure out what her next move would be, I still had no idea. But there had to be something coming. Knowing her.

It took longer than I'd thought it would.

I hadn't expected Katherine to be here at all. I purposely hadn't invited her to our little soiree because I wasn't ready for this showdown. I'd wanted it on my terms. Not here when I was trying to garner favor with her friends.

But it didn't seem to matter what I'd wanted. She was here. This had been a long time coming anyway.

So, I waited as she strode toward the booth with venom on her tongue and death promised in her dark eyes.

"What the hell is going on?" Katherine demanded when she reached our booth.

She didn't look at me. Her eyes were on Harmony. And then more death glares for Fiona. Well, that answered that question. Katherine definitely knew about that.

"Hey, Katherine," I said with a smile. "We're having a girls' night out."

Her eyes dragged to me as if it was the last thing she wanted to do. "And who invited *you* to this thing?"

"Invited me?" I asked her. "I think you have it backward. I did the inviting."

Katherine looked thrown for a second, glancing at her friends and lackeys in disbelief. But then recovered even though her anger seemed to have only intensified. "Well, I'm so sorry to have to ruin things then," she said dryly.

"Oh, don't worry. You can go back to your husband. It won't ruin anything for us." I stepped into her path before she could enter the booth. "We have this space reserved for the night, and we kind of wanted this to be exclusive. You understand, yeah?"

"This is *my* booth," Katherine spat.

"Actually, it's not," Harmony said, coming up to my left. "We have the space, Katherine. Just because you normally party here doesn't mean anything."

Katherine glared at Harmony. "Cute, Harm. Would you like any of my other sloppy seconds? First, Penn, and now, you've even moved on to friendships." She pointedly glanced at me. As if we'd ever really been friends.

"This has nothing to do with you. We're just having some fun. You're the one who always wants to ruin that," Harmony snapped.

I pressed her backward. I didn't want this to get ugly. And it would devolve quickly between Katherine and Harmony. Honestly, it had always been like that with me and Katherine, too, but I didn't want to fall apart here. I needed to be strong. She couldn't have what she wanted. And she would do anything to get it.

But I'd learned a lesson with Michael back in Charleston. If you backed down from your opponent, then they'd walk all over you. I had no intention of backing down.

"It's fine, Harmony. Katherine was going to leave anyway. She knows when she's not welcome," I said crisply.

I could hear the whispers behind me. The girls who watched me stand up to Katherine Van Pelt. Maybe the first time they'd ever seen that.

"You have no idea what you're doing," she hissed at me.

"I think I do. Don't make me call security," I warned carefully.

"As if they'd do anything. My husband owns this whole place."

"Then ask him to make us move, Katherine," I dared her. "Camden at your beck and call. That's how it works, right?"

She narrowed her eyes at me. We both knew that she didn't have that kind of leverage with him. Maybe no one else right now knew, but we did. Our little secret. I watched her realize it. Watched her see that she'd lost. And I smiled.

But it was the smile that must have tipped her over.

"I'm really amazed at all you've accomplished, Natalie," Katherine said with no hint of warmth in her voice. "But I'm surprised that you and Jane are still close."

My eyes flickered to Jane's. She hadn't been at my side. In fact, she hadn't said a thing the whole conversation. But I wouldn't ask. Katherine wanted me to ask.

"Isn't that right, Janie?" Katherine asked, crooking her finger at Jane. "You must not have told her that *you* were the one who outed her pen name to me."

My body seized. No. Fuck. It couldn't have been Jane. *Why* would Jane have told Katherine?

It made no sense. But at the same time, it somehow did. So few people had known about my pen name. And I knew that Lewis and Penn hadn't told her. But Jane...Jane had known.

"Natalie," Jane said. Her usual Jane calm evaporating. "I...I didn't want to."

I stared at her in disbelief. Could I fucking trust *anyone* in this community? I would have never trusted Jane from the beginning, but she had found out by total accident that I was Olivia Davies. But she promised she wouldn't tell. I believed her. I'd been wrong. Again.

This was Katherine's step ahead. But there was no way I could have anticipated Jane's deceit. Penn had been right about her all along.

"Oh, you didn't know?" Katherine crooned softly. "Sorry to break it to you."

"You know," I said icily, "I don't think that you are. Now, you can get out of here and leave us be."

"What? Not going to go run away and cry about it?"

I laughed at her. "No, I'm not." Then I dismissively fluttered my fingers and turned my back on her. I wouldn't give her what she wanted. I wouldn't break down at this news. I wouldn't run away. I wouldn't let her have the booth just because she was evil as fuck.

Instead, I faced Jane, who looked stricken in the corner. "So, it's true?"

She nodded solemnly. "I'm so sorry. I felt so awful."

"Why? Why did you tell her?"

She just shook her head.

But I didn't have time or energy for games. "For no reason then? What was in it for you, Jane?"

Because I knew my friend. Everything came with a price. And I supposed this one was the price of our friendship.

"Percy," she whispered in despair.

Of course. "You sold me out to get money from the enemy. God, Jane, you disgust me."

"Natalie, please, look at how much you've grown since then. You're incredible! You're killing it. No one cares anymore."

"I care," I said, low and dangerous. "I care. And you

know perfectly well *why* I care, Jane. As you pretended to be my friend when it happened."

"I am your friend," she insisted.

"No, I don't think you are. You should go," I told her viciously. "We're having a girls' night. It's not meant for backstabbers."

I hated the words, even as they left my mouth.

Jane had been there for me when I came back to the city. We had developed a friendship over time. But if she was going to sell my secrets to Katherine, then I didn't want her as a friend. And it was worse because she knew more of them. She knew the contact I'd gotten from her. What I'd wanted to do that day. But maybe she'd think twice before revealing it.

"Nat…"

"Go, Jane," I growled. "Just go."

She grabbed her purse from the couch, looking wide-eyed at the group of girls she'd just been hanging out with. But no one met her gaze. They were all looking at me or at the floor or off in the distance. No one said a word as Jane walked out of the booth, off the dance floor, and out of the club.

I didn't know when Katherine had left, but she was gone when I turned back around. And I wanted to count it as a win. But in truth, I felt like I'd been hollowed out. I couldn't show how upset I was. I couldn't leave this girls' night that I'd planned. I couldn't be myself for even a second…or it might all fall apart, just like Katherine wanted.

I managed to be utterly alone in a sea of people. Was this how Katherine had always felt on her throne?

CHAPTER 29

NATALIE

I crawled into Penn's bed early the next morning. We'd been up until the wee hours of the morning, dancing and drinking. My head felt as heavy as a bowling ball, my throat was scratchy, and I was beyond drained. Who knew that being *on* could suck the life out of a person?

Penn's arm tightened around my bare shoulder as I leaned my head against his chest. "Mmm, Nat."

I kissed his neck. "I just got in," I rasped.

"I like your voice like that. Sexy."

I chuckled. "I sound like a smoker."

"But a sexy smoker," he said, dragging me tighter against him.

I sighed against him and stared off into the dark. Totle was curled up around his legs, and he nudged me with his wet nose. I reached down and petted him once. My head was still spinning from the alcohol though. Maybe lying down wasn't such a great idea.

"I think I'm still drunk."

"You smell like a bar," Penn confirmed.

"What a compliment. Just what every girl wants to hear."

He slipped an eye open. "How much did you drink?"

"No idea."

I'd lost count after Jane left.

"Did you have a good time?"

I swallowed. Felt the first pricks of tears at my eyes. The pain and loss hitting me now that I was sinking into the cushions and allowed to feel again. I pushed them down, down, down. I didn't want to cry. I *couldn't* cry. It was absurd.

And yet...my throat was tight when I responded, "Well..."

He opened both eyes at that. Worry creased his forehead. "What happened?"

I sank back on the pillow. "Katherine. Of course."

"She was there? But you didn't invite her."

"No, I didn't. She was there to see Camden. They, like, made out on the dance floor."

Penn wrinkled his nose. "Percy? You're sure?"

"A hundred percent. Fiona's been fucking him for years. I think she'd know."

"Oh yeah," he muttered.

I met his gaze. "When were you going to tell me that you'd fucked all the lackeys?"

He snorted. "The lackeys? Is that what you're calling them?"

"Isn't that what they are?"

"Yes," he agreed. "And...sorry. I mean, I didn't know if you wanted to know who it was."

"Was it all of them? All of the ones that you told me to invite?"

He shook his head. "Not...all of them."

I groaned. "Just most of them."

"Look, it's not like I'm proud of it. They were the easiest way to piss off Katherine."

"I know. I know. Aren't I using them the same way?"

He arched an eyebrow. "I don't know. Are you?"

"I don't know them. And I need help and people to come to this charity event that I'm hosting. In some way, I'm using their connections to pull this off."

"And to make Katherine mad?"

"It's an added bonus," I told him.

"And how did she feel about that? Pissed, like I'd guessed?"

"Yes," I whispered. "Harmony booked us into her booth. I didn't know it was hers. Katherine asked to have it back, and when I said no and refused to back down, she told me that Jane was the one who had told her about my pen name."

Penn sucked in a breath, and his grip tightened on my shoulder. "Nat..."

"Yeah," I said, holding back the tears again.

"I should have seen that coming."

"You've never liked Jane."

"No. It wasn't really anything to do with Jane. It was the fact that she was dating my brother. Anyone who willingly puts up with him has to be bad news. I don't really *know* Jane."

"I thought I did," I admitted. "I thought we were friends."

"You were...are."

"I don't know, Penn. Maybe it's normal to betray your friends on the Upper East Side, but that isn't normal to me. When I found out, I flipped out, and I made her leave. She said that she did it to get the Percys."

"For what?"

"She didn't say, but I'm sure it's to help with her club funding. When we first became friends when I came into the city, I know that she met Lewis through me and he gave her a contact to get some kind of backing to open."

Penn ran his fingers back through my hair. "She's business savvy. That's for sure. I wonder how much Court has invested into that club."

I shrugged. I hadn't thought about that. "Is it stupid that I want to call her? That I want to clear things up between us and make things right?"

"No, Natalie, that's not stupid. You're a good person. That's how you deal with situations like this."

"I'm not," I whispered. "I made her go, and I stayed so that Katherine wouldn't see how upset I was."

His finger moved to my chin, and he tilted my head up to look at him. "That doesn't make you a bad person. And wanting to make up with your friend, no matter what they did to you, is human. When I found out about Lewis's business dealings, I called him. Without a second thought. Despite all the bullshit we'd been through."

"Yeah. But...I can't call Jane."

"Probably not right now. Not while you're a little drunk and worked up about it."

"Ugh," I groaned, burying my head into the pillow. "I just remembered that we're having the charity event at Trinity."

"So? Jane is a professional. She won't miss the chance

to have your event there even if you're on the outs. She'll probably see it as an opportunity to make up."

I gritted my teeth and then propped myself up on my elbow to look at him. "What if I'm not ready for that?"

"You'll know when you are."

"How do you know?"

He sighed and pressed a soft kiss on my lips. The sleep was wiped from his face, and he looked oddly serious. "I understand the bounds of friendship. And what splits you up and what can keep you together."

I frowned at the phrasing of that. I knew that he had been through a lot with the crew and that was why they were so tight despite the horrors they'd inflicted on each other and others outside of their circle. But it felt like he was saying more.

"What do you mean by that?" I asked.

"What Jane did was wrong. She knows it was wrong. It's up to you two to determine whether that ends or strengthens your friendship." He paused, as if uncertain about what he was going to say next. "I've been meaning to tell you something for a while. I keep making excuses for it. For not telling you. But I think...I think I should."

"You're kind of freaking me out," I admitted.

"It's nothing about us," he insisted. "It's a part of my past that no one knows. Only the people who were there."

"The crew?" I guessed.

"Yes. Me, Katherine, Lewis, Lark, Rowe, and Addie, at the time. And a girl we knew, Hanna Stratton."

I straightened in bed at that name. "The girl who killed herself?"

Penn startled. He sat up, too. "How did you hear that?"

"Lewis told me. Well, actually, Addie told me that if I

257

didn't know about Hanna, then I didn't really know the crew. And Lewis said that you were all friends, and then, when she went to rehab, she killed herself. It was one of the reasons Lewis and Addie broke up and Addie left the group."

Penn was silent. It stretched until it was taut. As if, at any second, it would snap.

"That's what he said?" Penn finally asked.

I swallowed and nodded. "I'm guessing…that's not the whole answer?"

"Well, it's the answer we all agreed on all those years ago."

"What…what does that mean?"

Penn looked down and then back up at me. Resignation on his face. As if he'd had a ten-ton brick on his shoulder and he was finally going to lift it. "So…you weren't the first bet we ever made. For a long time, we all made them just for kicks. We bet on everything. It was childish and stupid, but it was practically intrinsic to how the crew functioned.

"Then our junior year, a new girl showed up to our school. Her name was Hanna. She was new money and had clearly been top dog at her last school in, like, Indiana or something. That clearly did not translate to the Upper East Side, as you are well aware."

"I was a loner, but yes, I know the sentiment. Nothing translates here."

"She was a fish out of water. A pariah. Katherine joked one day and said that she could make her one of the most popular girls in school. I bet her on it. She said it was too easy. So, I said I bet I could get her to sleep with me."

I frowned, reflexively backing away from this version

of Penn. The one who had hurt me so completely with such a similar bet.

"Anyway, it isn't really the bet that mattered. I won. We made Hanna one of us. I slept with her. Katherine had been right. It had all been too easy. It was wrong on so many levels." He shook his head, as if trapped in the whirlwind of that time all those years ago. "After that, we all dropped her like it was nothing. We ostracized her. It went around school that she was a whore and gave it up easy, that her young, innocent vibe was just an act, that she was a drug addict. The world is a cruel place. But we made cruel acceptable."

"That's awful," I said. "She probably felt so alone."

"Yeah. It was awful, Natalie. It's something I deeply regret. And it got worse."

"Worse? Worse than sleeping with her and bullying her?"

He frowned. "I wasn't a good person. I never claimed to be. But it was Hanna that opened my eyes. I wish I could take it back."

"So, what happened?"

"Well, she came back to me and begged to make it stop, to take her back." He couldn't even meet my eyes. The sorrow and turmoil was all over his face. "I wasn't exactly kind in my response. She went to Lewis that night. They slept together, and as you can imagine, that just made it worse."

"Christ, Penn."

"I know. Katherine got tired of the whole thing after that. She never liked when the attention was on anyone but herself. And she pretended to want to befriend her again…and then planted drugs on her."

259

My gasp was audible. "Seriously?"

"We'd all dabbled. Hanna had with us, too, when she was on the inside. But...she wasn't a drug addict. And I didn't find out about what Katherine had done with the drugs until after Hanna's parents found out and sent her to rehab."

"Oh god. Where she killed herself? "Because you'd all tortured her."

He bobbed his head. "It was a horrible day. I'm not proud of what happened. In fact, it's my deepest regret. After that, Addie couldn't take it. Not because Lewis had cheated. They did that to each other all the time. But it was part of what had driven Hanna over the edge. Addie blamed us. Rightly so. And left. But we all agreed not to speak of it again. We had a story for what had happened, and we stuck by it. Our crew shrank and tightened after that. We had too many secrets by then."

I didn't know what to say. There was nothing to say after all. This had all happened a dozen years ago or more. They'd been young and stupid.

Cruel boys and girls cementing their cruel legacy in blood.

Hanna had been the unfortunate victim in all of this. She'd paid the ultimate price for the heinous crime of wanting to belong. I knew it well enough. The way that Katherine could deceive. Lewis could charm. Penn could seduce. They were all fucked up in their own ways. Party to their own manipulations and machinations. Destruction trailing in their wake.

I felt akin to Hanna for what she'd gone through. What we'd both gone through. The humiliations we'd endured at the hands of the Upper East Side. And I felt justified in my actions. In the way I was getting back at them.

Because I'd said from the beginning of all of this that I was not the first person that they'd hurt, nor would I be the last if they kept getting away with it. I was here to teach them a lesson. Lewis was already learning it. Katherine was well on her way. The admission about the first real bet, the one that had cemented the crew into perpetuity, just proved that I was doing the right thing. I was doing this for people like Hanna. So that no one had to go through what she had gone through, what I'd gone through, again. Not ever again.

I leaned back against the bed. "Thank you for telling me the truth."

"Do you...think less of me?" he asked cautiously. "I wouldn't blame you. I think less of me for it."

"No, I don't." And I didn't. "You tried to get out after that. You wanted to be something more and something better. You learned your lesson. That's more than I can say for the rest of the crew."

He settled back down on the bed. His hand slipped under my shoulders and drew me back to him. "I've never told anyone that story. And we never talk about what happened. I feel like I've been waiting my whole life to get that off my chest."

"You should have seen a therapist."

He chuckled and kissed the top of my head. "Probably. But my mother sees it as weakness."

"That's ridiculous. *Everyone* should see a therapist. We're all so fucked up. Talking is the only way we can work through what happened. After I left the Hamptons, I went every day. Well...after I could pick myself up off

Amy's floor." I sighed. "It helped me survive but not get over it. You helped with that."

"I am sorry about the bet. And our year apart. And Lewis. And Katherine. And what happened with Jane tonight. About all of it. I wish we could turn back time and start over."

I nudged him. "If we started over, I'd never still be here. I wouldn't have been able to hack it."

"I doubt that."

I shrugged. I had major doubts. I was putting one foot in front of the other and coming out on top by sheer determination. The only thing that felt easy about the whole thing was Penn.

"Do you think you're going to make up with Jane?" he asked softly against my hair.

"You think she's part of my crew? That I should push past our betrayals and see our strength and bonds beneath it?"

"I think that she was there when no one else was. That means something. You have to decide what it means to you."

I sank deeper into his arms. Penn was right. Jane had helped orchestrate the collapse of my career by aiding and abetting Katherine. Could I forgive her for that? If I did, would she do it again?

I drifted off, still debating whether it would be worth it.

And when I woke, I decided that I couldn't risk it. Even if I wanted to.

CHAPTER 30

NATALIE

J threw the door to my apartment open and rushed inside. My feet were killing me from the walk back home and the three-story climb to my place. I kicked off the uncomfortable heels. Then I rounded the corner to find Penn pacing the living room.

"I'm sorry. I'm sorry. I know. I'm late," I told him, holding my hands up. I dropped my planner and oversize St. Vincent bag onto the table in the hall and strode toward him. "The meeting ran over."

"It's fine. I was just…"

"Pacing?" I offered for him.

"Yes." He grinned at me.

I took in the image of him standing there in chinos and a blue button-up with his sleeves rolled to his elbows. His hands in his pockets with Dermot Kennedy's album playing from his phone. His blue eyes bore into mine, and I practically sighed with relief at seeing him.

Party-planning had taken over my life. I hadn't thought one charity function would become a full-time job. I was overworked and stressed and not even getting paid to do any of this. Harmony had brought on a party-planner, Gregory, to help with day-of on-site issues so that I could actually enjoy the party. And meeting with Gregory had been a lesson in how behind I was, even with Harmony and the lackeys helping. We were a matter of weeks from the big event, and I'd never felt such relief and blind panic that someone else was going to be responsible for getting this off without a hitch.

"Are we going to be late?" I asked him. He'd been planning a surprise for me all week to get me away from this, and I didn't want to ruin it. "Do I have time to change?"

"We're not going to be late," he said. "Just put on something comfortable."

"You're in *that*, and you want me in something comfortable. You do know that comfortable means lounging around the house in sweatpants, right?"

"Track pants," he said, following me into my bedroom to watch me take my clothes off.

"Sure thing." I reached into my closet and pulled out a pair of skinny designer jeans and an Elizabeth Cunningham top that she'd given me straight off a model last week when I went to see her about a dress for my event.

"I said, comfortable," he said with a laugh.

"This is comfortable," I assured him.

"But not really...you." He peeked into my closet and half-forgotten mound of bohemian clothes that I'd pushed to the very back and not touched in months. "We said that we'd always be ourselves when we were in private."

"But we're not going to be in private," I said as I tugged on the jeans.

"What if we were?" he mused.

I slipped the shirt over my head. "I don't look okay?"

"You look great," he told me evenly. "You always do. You've just been so stressed out about this party. I don't want you to get so wrapped up in all of this that you aren't writing and you forget who you are."

"Oh, I love you," I said, leaning into him and pressing a kiss to his lips. He wrapped his arms around me. "I know who I am. Clothes don't change that."

"No, I suppose not. I know how demanding this all is. I don't want you to use it to cover up your frustrations with writing. That's your real passion, and this is just a hiccup."

I glanced up at him. "I had to turn down a seven-figure advance so that my ex-boyfriend couldn't control me. I think I'm due a little moping about my career."

"A little," he conceded. "Just until this event is over. Then you have to get back on the horse."

I winked at him. "Is that a euphemism?"

He nipped at my bottom lip. "It will be later." He smacked my ass and gestured for me to lead the way out of my apartment.

I jumped at the contact, grabbed my purse, and then left my place. I locked up behind us. "Where's Totle anyway? I thought I'd get attacked when I got home."

"Rowe is puppy-sitting."

"He's obsessed with your dog."

"He is. And Nicholas adores him."

"Rowe or Totle?" I asked cheekily as we hit the street.

"Both."

Penn hailed a cab, and we drove the dozen blocks north before I recognized the brick buildings that made up Columbia's campus.

"We're going to your work? Did you want another round on your desk?"

He lazily ran his thumb up and down my arm. "Are you offering?"

"I might be."

"I will take that into consideration." He gestured to the cab where to let us off. "This is good." He passed the guy some cash and then helped me out of the car. Our fingers laced together as we stepped onto the brick-lined path that led into the heart of campus. "This way."

My curiosity was piqued as I followed him away from the philosophy department. We passed the library, walked across the quad, and went up past the business school. The sun was sinking low on the horizon. Undergrads were hastening past us and into the library to prepare for finals. A group quizzed each other from a set of flash cards. A pair of Columbia runners passed us in short black shorts, sweat glistening on their chests. Everywhere all around us showed signs of the end of the semester and the coming of summer. The bright hope extended even to me. Because in a few short weeks, that would mean that I would have Penn all to myself.

We stopped in front of the physics building.

"Physics?" I asked.

"Come on. I'll show you."

I looked at him skeptically. I had a degree in English. I'd been a collegiate swimmer. I had never stepped foot in the physics department. I'd basically lived in the fine arts department and the pool in college.

He laughed when he saw my face. "Trust me."

I tightened my hold on his hand. I did.

We took the elevator to the top floor and then another

set of stairs to what appeared to be roof access. What the hell was on the top of the physics department?

Then we came out on the other side, and I gasped. An enormous telescope sat in the center of an observatory dome. Candles covered the floor of the dimly lit room, revealing a small picnic and a perfect view of the millions of stars overhead.

I blinked away tears as I drew my attention back to Penn. "This is...everything."

He drew my hand to his lips and kissed it. "Anything for you."

"Are we...allowed to use the telescope? I couldn't imagine that they'd let you use this equipment," I said, wide-eyed.

He nudged me. "I spent a few afternoons here with a friend in the astronomy department. I have a basic grasp of the machine. I can handle it."

I was pretty sure there were actual stars in my eyes. "That's so awesome."

"Oh god, there's my nerdy girl."

I playfully nudged him. "Hey!"

"I like it," he said, drawing me into the room and toward the blanket. "Once night has finally fallen, we can use the telescope, but for now, I think you're starving."

My stomach grumbled in response. "How do you do that?"

"It's almost like I know you."

"I suppose." I crossed my legs and sat on the gingham blanket. Candlelight flickered over Penn's sharp features as he took a seat next to me. "Penn."

He had just reached for the picnic basket but stopped and looked back at me in question.

"Thank you," I said. "Thank you for doing this. It means so much to me. You mean so much to me."

He grinned that cocky little smile that made my knees go weak and then drew my lips to his. "You're most welcome."

I wanted to launch myself at him and rip all his clothes off for the gesture, but somehow, I held myself back as he went back to the basket. He withdrew a large baguette, some grapes, a container that was full of still-warm baked Camembert, a selection of meats, and a bottle of French wine.

I tipped my head back and laughed. "Oh my god, are you re-creating our first date?"

"Was that a date?" he asked.

"It was something." I stared down at the spread that he'd prepared just like he had that one night we shared in Paris.

He'd walked right into a French restaurant and come out with a spread similar to this for us. We wandered down to the Seine and ate it on the water overlooking the Eiffel Tower. He kissed me as the lights flipped on, and it had been magical.

"Perfect," I amended. "It was perfect."

We dug into the food. Memories flooding us both from that time almost eight years ago when we'd been young and stupid. We'd fallen in love in a night and not even known that our lives would drag us back together over and over again until we were here, in this moment.

"So," I said, savoring the taste of baked Camembert on my tongue, "tell me, what's your deepest, darkest secret?"

He dragged me into another kiss. "I think you know all of mine now, love."

"Ah, such easier times when it was just that you wanted to escape your life. Poor little rich boy," I joked.

"And you?" He gestured to me. "Do you finally feel like you belong?"

It was the answer that I'd given so long ago. That I acted like I belonged, but I really didn't. *Had* that changed? In some ways, I was acting more than ever. But the truth of it was, I did belong. Just as he'd said so long ago.

"I belong with you," I told him.

"Good answer."

Our kiss deepened, lengthened, until I lost where I started and he began. It was just us, tangled together, hands and lips and tongue. And I didn't want to come up for breath. I didn't want to discover the space between us. I wanted to live in the moment forever where Penn and I were one.

CHAPTER 31

PENN

"*P*enn," Natalie groaned into my mouth.

It was an encouragement. Like screaming, *Yes, yes, yes*, at me just from my tongue against hers and my hands in her hair. Sex had always been my perfect art form, but it was something else entirely with Natalie. It made me reconsider everything that I'd ever thought in the past. Made me look at myself and see everything I'd been lacking. That I'd tried to cover up with sex. As if it could fix what was broken inside of me. But only when we were together did I feel like maybe I wasn't broken after all. Maybe I just had never really known love until her.

I lifted her arms and slid her shirt over her head, getting a peek of her nipples hardening through the lacy material of her bra. My hands slipped back down her arms, her shoulders, and to the soft contours of her chest. I hooked a finger under her bra, teasing the erect peak until she squirmed under my touch.

I loved every moan and whimper and sigh that I

extracted from her willing body. The way it moved and ached as I worked on her. This wasn't just sex. This was seduction, and it made my cock harden in my pants.

But I was in no rush. I had every intention of taking my time with her.

My fingers pinched the clasp of her bra, and her breasts fell out of their constraints. I tossed the useless material aside before pressing her back against the blanket. She pulled her arms back up and stared at me with a come-hither expression on her hooded bedroom eyes.

Mine.

The word rang through my skull over and over. She was mine. This beautiful, strong, and courageous woman was mine. We'd had our ups and downs. We'd walked through fire. But we'd come out ahead. And I was going to keep her this fucking happy for the rest of her life.

I snapped the button on her jeans and then pulled the zipper to the base. I crooked a finger under the waistband and teased the edge of her panties. A purr came from her. I knew what she wanted. I was happy to oblige as I tugged the jeans and panties over her hips and down her muscular swimmer's legs.

I worked my way back up, splaying my hands against her inner calf and opening her up wider as I moved up to her inner thigh. I stopped right before her perfect pussy, already wet and waiting for me. I ran one knuckle down the length of her, and her whole body bowed in response. She thrust upward, begging for more. For me.

My hands splayed her out further before I feasted on her pussy. My tongue alternated between flicking against her clit and gently sucking it. One hand holding her down as she writhed underneath me. Soft exclamations pouring from her mouth. Her panting hitting a feverish pitch as I claimed her with my tongue.

I released one of her legs and slid a finger into her opening. Another moan of my name escaped her, and I smiled against her pussy lips. She was close. I could feel it the way she clamped around my finger, demanding more. I inserted a second finger, and she tightened like she was trying to keep me from ever leaving. My cock hardened nearly to the point of pain as I thought about finishing this by bottoming out inside of her. But I had to hold out. I wanted her to come at least twice.

My fingers curled inward, finding that spot that I knew drove her crazy. And her hands dug into my hair, pressing my face back toward her.

"Oh fuck," she panted. "Yes, oh god, yes."

I worked her in and out, in and out, while lapping against her clit until I felt her entire body seize up and release. She arched up as the orgasm hit her and then fell back against the blanket, incoherently whimpering softly over and over.

I withdrew my fingers from her and kissed her pussy one more time. She jerked against me she was so sensitive.

"Penn," she groaned, her eyes fluttering open. Her eyes said she wanted more. "Come here."

I undid the top two buttons of my shirt and then pulled it over my head. Her eyes slid down to my six-pack. She managed to sit up on one elbow, running her other hand down my body.

"Mine," she growled. As if she had heard the chorus shouting it in my head.

"All yours."

She reached for my pants, but I was there first. I pushed her back down on the ground as I undid my belt and stripped out of my pants and boxers. Her eyes lit up at the sight of my cock jutting out. She licked her lips.

Fuck, I wanted her mouth around me. I wanted her to deep-throat it until I was shooting hot cum all over her. Putting my mark on her. But I wanted to be inside of her more. Needed to feel her come all over my cock.

I bent over her body and brought my lips down on hers. She was hungry for me, kissing me back with matched ferocity. I lined myself up against her heated core and then thrust deep. I tipped my head back at the feel of her wrapping all the way around me. Her hot, wet flesh that fit around me to perfection. Like she had been made for me.

"I love you," I breathed against her lips. "Fuck, I love you."

She smiled, pushing her hips harder against mine. "I love you, too."

The first long draw out of her was sweet, blissful torture. She breathed in deeply at the sensation, and then I slammed back into her. Harder and rougher than before. It jerked her body forward, but she only groaned in pleasure in response.

I needed more. Out, out, out and then hard and fast in. The way she tensed, waiting for that moment when I'd take her all over again, made me only anticipate it more. Made me crave that feeling.

But soon, I couldn't control the out. I was close. Closer than I wanted to be. She needed to come with me.

So, I slipped my hands under her soft body and drew her up. So that we were both sitting with her in my lap.

My hands were now on her hips and ass, controlling her body as I lifted and slammed her back down on me. So that I was spearing into her over and over again.

She opened her baby blues and stared down at me with all the love and devotion in her eyes.

"Oh fuck," I groaned. "Come with me, baby."

She nodded. "So...close."

And then I thrust once, twice more, and she unleashed on top of me. Her orgasm was a pin trigger on my own. I came with a grunt of pleasure and a wave of ecstasy that shot up into her. Her arms wrapped tight around my neck, and I held her against me like a lifeline.

We sat, pressed together, both panting and breathless for a minute. Then I gently released her back against the blanket and crashed down next to her. Our chests rose and fell together. Fully sated. No words even between us. Just that moment. Our breaths. As the sun disappeared and the stars finally lit up the night sky.

"Natalie," I murmured.

She rolled onto her side to look at me. Her gaze was unfocused. Her smile lazy and dream-laden. "Hi."

I chuckled and pressed a kiss to her plump lips. "Come to Paris with me this summer."

She blinked. "Paris?"

"I have a conference, and then I thought we could stay in my flat until I have to come back to teach in the fall. Do all the things we didn't get to do the first time we were there together. Find our park bench. The one where it all started. What do you say?"

"Yes," she breathed. "Did you think I'd say anything else? Of course, I want to go to Paris with you."

"Oh good, because I already bought the tickets."

She laughed and bumped my shoulder. "Good thing I said yes."

"It is because we're leaving the day after your event."

Her eyes widened. "The day *after*? You couldn't have given me two days?"

"Uh-uh," I said, pulling her flat against me. "You've been too stressed. I want to take you away and feed you macarons and walk the Seine with you and get lost in the gardens at Versailles and drink champagne straight from the vineyard. I want you to be so relaxed that novels spring from your fingertips, fully formed. Ones you love and ones you cherish, whether or not they are ones you want to publish. Or even actually do."

"Wow, Penn, I think you drive a hard bargain," she said. "This just sounds awful."

"Did I mention the sex?" I asked with a deadly smirk. "There will be lots of it."

"I suppose I can do that." She grinned like a fool. "Macarons and champagne and novels and lots of sex. Living the Parisian life."

"So, is that a yes?"

She jumped on top of me and plastered my face with kisses. "Yes, yes, yes. Yes, of course!"

I pressed my fingers up into her hair and pulled her mouth back down to mine. "I love you." I brushed my nose against hers. "Now...how about that telescope?"

Her eyes widened with delight, and then she dragged me toward the behemoth I prayed I could actually operate.

PART V
KING'S TO YOU

CHAPTER 32

NATALIE

"Natalie, honey, sugar cakes, sweetie pie," Gregory said in distress, "you need to calm your tits before I calm them for you. I have *everything* under control. Which is why you and your little butterfly hired me. We have this set. All good to go, darling. Go to the spa and relax before you get wrinkles."

I tried desperately not to roll my eyes at the party-planner, but damn, he made it difficult. "I'm fine. I'm not worried about wrinkles."

"Everyone should worry about wrinkles. What moisturizer do you use?"

"Dear god, it doesn't matter. I just want to get through my checklist." I waved the sheet of paper in his face.

He snatched it out of my hand. "Check. Check. Check. Not happening anyway. On their way. Check. Check. Check. We're good here."

He tore the paper in half and then in half again. My eyes widened in shock.

"What the hell, Gregory?"

"You are clogging up my space," he said, dramatically waving his hands.

Honestly, where the hell *had* Harmony gotten this guy?

"If you don't believe in auras, you should. Yours is all over the fucking place."

I closed my eyes and took a deep breath. My mother was following me around, even here. "I know plenty about auras. I just want to make sure that everything is ready."

"Well, you had a look around. We went through your checklist. Now, please, baby doll, go get ready for the event and try to *enjoy* it. That's why you hired me. I have it covered."

He gave me a little push toward the exit, and I sighed. Maybe he was right. How much more could I do? I'd done it all ahead of time. And he was my day-of person. Even if he was obnoxious. If there were any fires from here on out, he would handle them. I hoped.

I bit my lip and then nodded. "Okay, okay. I'm going. Call me if you need anything."

"I do this for a living, sweetheart. I've got it under control."

"All right, all right," I said and then hustled back through Trinity, staring at what I hoped would be the finished decorations for the event tonight.

I'd made the guest list and checked it twice. Everyone who was anyone was going to be there, and I just had to make my grand entrance to complete it all.

I was almost out of Trinity when I heard my name being called. I froze in place and debated whether I should just leave or not.

"Nat, please," Jane said, hurrying toward me.

I turned slowly back around and found my friend standing before me, looking like a shadow of herself. There were dark circles under her eyes. She looked like she'd lost weight, and she hadn't had any weight to lose. Her clothes hung on her small frame. And she didn't even have her customary sunglasses on her head.

"What is it, Jane?" I asked, keeping my voice neutral. I felt for her. But I hated her betrayal. A grudge-holder was who I was as a person. I didn't know how to move past that.

"I just...wanted to apologize," Jane said. "We never really got to talk after what happened at the club, and I feel awful."

"About what? That you sold me out to Katherine for Percy money or that you got caught?"

"That I hurt you." She frowned. "Everything happened so fast with Katherine. I overextended myself for the soft opening for Trinity in December. I had all this money that was supposed to show up from my overseas banks, and Court could only help me cover some of it. And then the investors backed out at the last minute. Lewis helped me with a contact of his earlier, but they wouldn't back the whole thing. Katherine found out about it. I have no idea how. And she offered to help."

"She'd give you Percy if you outed me," I finished for her. "Classic Katherine."

"I didn't want to. It was do or die for my dream."

"Funny you say that. Since what *you* did killed mine."

"I know. I'm so sorry, Natalie. I didn't know what she was even going to do with it."

"Yes, you did," I said with a chuckle. "Don't play dumb, Jane. You're as savvy as they come. You hoard secrets and gossip like it's your job. And look, it kept you in business. Congrats."

"I didn't know what else to do."

I stared back at her with indignation on my face. "What else to do? You could have told me! You could have come to me. We could have figured it out as friends. But you didn't, and you won't. You're only telling me now because you're desperate."

"Please," she whispered, reaching out for me. "You're... you're my best friend."

I withdrew my hand and frowned. "I can't do this. I thought we were friends. And, right now, I just...I don't know. Can we figure this out after the party?"

"Okay," she agreed softly. "Sure, after the party."

"I have to go get ready."

"I'll...I'll see you tonight then. And, Nat?"

"Yeah?"

"I won't say anything...about my contact."

I narrowed my eyes at her. Was that a threat? "What contact?" I asked with a blatant glare.

"Right. Sure," she said, chewing on her bottom lip. "There never was one."

I nodded and turned away from her and out into the bright light of day. My heart constricted as I walked away. I hated what had just happened. I wanted to be Jane's friend. I wanted her at my side, as she had been for so long. It felt wrong, not including her. It felt dangerous with her having the information about Lewis.

Ugh! I couldn't think about that. There was too much riding on tonight. I'd have to figure out what to do about my friendship with Jane later.

. . .

"ARE YOU READY IN THERE?" Penn called down the hallway.

I bit my lip as I stared at my reflection in the mirror. Was I ready? Maybe this was all a horrible mistake. Maybe I didn't need to do any of this. But I did. I knew that I did. To survive in this world, I had to come out on top. I had to make myself untouchable. Make it so that no one could ever hurt me again. And then, when I secured that tonight, Penn and I could ride off into the sunset for the summer in Paris.

I took another deep breath and then opened the door to the bedroom. "Ready."

"Wow," he breathed as I stepped toward him in my soft green princess dress with a lace sweetheart neck that plunged in the front.

We'd decided to do a romantic novel theme for the event to coincide with the literacy charity we'd partnered with. So, tonight was a night of Happily Ever After. The dress that Elizabeth had created for me was the biggest, most incredible thing I'd ever stepped into. Normally, we went for fitted sleek attire. But tonight was all about embracing the magical fairy tale princess of your dreams.

"You look...incredible. Oh, how I can't wait to get under all the layers of that skirt," he said with a laugh.

"And you...my Prince Charming," I joked, "sexy in a tuxedo as ever."

"I'm happy to oblige. Shall we?" he asked, offering me his arm.

I stepped toward him on Cinderella slippers and let him whisk me downstairs, into a limo, and all the way into Midtown to Trinity. The red carpet was rolled out, anticipating the affluent crowd about to descend upon it.

Penn stepped out first to a sea of camera flashes. I took

one more deep breath. Cameras rolling. And action. I took his hand and steadied myself against him for a brief moment. Then, I turned toward the cameras and began. I walked the walk and talked the talk. Answering questions about the charity and how much money I anticipated raising for the event and how pleased I was with the turnout. On and on. With a smile on my face. And pain in my mile-high heels. Playing a role that actually wasn't a role with a Kensington at my side and the world at my feet.

It was glorious. And then I stepped inside.

Even though I'd seen mock-ups of what the interior of Trinity would transform into, it was nothing compared to seeing it in reality. Gregory had really outdone himself. I'd had no reason to fear what would happen because this was a masterpiece. The club had become a seventeenth-century ballroom, resplendent, sumptuous, and palatial. Candles filled the low-lit room, chandeliers dangled from the ceiling, and cherubs adorned the walls.

Penn brought my hand to his lips. "I'm impressed. You did all of this."

My eyes were full of stars when I looked back at him. "It's better than I ever could have imagined."

A waitress appeared then and offered us champagne.

Penn took two for us and passed one to me. He held it up. "To your official debut."

I chuckled softly. "It's like being a debutante all over again."

"Except we make the rules."

I held my glass up and clinked against his. "To making our own rules then."

He grinned and then tilted his drink back. I sipped at

mine, happy to have the bubbles whizzing through my system. Tonight was incredible. And it had only just begun. The best was yet to come.

I circled the room with Penn at my side. We spoke to Harmony and the lackeys, passed Jane and Court, and thanked everyone else for showing up, speaking to the people who had gone above and beyond on their donations and generally schmoozing like I'd never done before in my life. I was actually thankful to have Penn there. He knew everyone. And though I'd spent an inordinate amount of time staring at names and faces so that I could remember each person, he helped when the name just would not come to me. We were a pair. And it worked.

Penn had gone to get us drinks when a pair of bombshells appeared before me. Seeing Charlotte and Etta at my event made me tense even though I had known they planned to be here. But after my last interaction with Charlotte at Fashion Week, I wasn't looking forward to repeating it. But neither of them looked like they were about to attack me. In fact, Etta pulled me into a hug.

"Natalie, it's so good to see you," Etta said. She'd recently shaved off her hair on one side and left the other side at a sharp bob. Her black dress made her look more like a curvy villain than a princess, but edgy had always worked for her. "We've missed having you around."

Charlie nodded. Her black hair long and pin-straight to her waist. Gold makeup accenting her dark brown skin and the gold princess dress on her tall, thin figure. "We did. I hated how our last conversation ended."

"I miss you, too," I admitted.

They might be Lewis's sisters. They might have taken

285

his side after the breakup, but I still wanted them as my friends. They were too fun.

"With everything going on in our family, we've hardly even been out," Etta said with an eye roll. "Ava hasn't even been allowed to the house." Etta hooked her finger at Charlotte. "Neither of her boyfriends either."

Charlotte glared at her sister. "I really hate you sometimes."

A smile twitched on my lips. "You two are the best."

Etta flipped her hair. "Well, obviously."

"Any news on what's going on with your mom?" I asked softly. That was the part I hated the most about the whole thing.

Charlie shook her head. "She thinks it'll drag out through the summer."

"That's awful," I whispered.

"Mom's taken to baking nonstop," Etta said. "Which is only good for me. Charlie can't handle another pound."

Charlotte rolled her eyes. "I model! It's not actually about the weight. It's my job."

"You're getting a business degree from Harvard."

"Yeah, and look at how well that's worked out for Lewis."

Both girls fell silent at the argument they must have had over and over. My stomach pinched as the aftermath of what I'd done sank in more fully. He deserved it. But… they didn't.

I frowned and was glad that Penn appeared then.

"Charlie, Etta," Penn said with a nod. He cleared this throat as he turned back to me. "There's been a, uh…development."

"What development?" I asked. Nothing could go wrong tonight! Nothing!

And then I saw the "development" as Lewis Warren strode toward us on the arm of Addison Rowe.

"Brother," Etta began, "what the fuck?"

I would have laughed if my blood wasn't boiling at his uninvited presence at my event. But at least Etta had said the thing I wanted to say.

"Don't hate him," Addie said, holding up her hands. "I invited him. He was my plus-one."

I would have burned through Rowe's twin sister with death glares if I could. She'd done this on purpose. She'd hated that Lewis and I had been together. She'd tried to break us up. Then when all had gone wrong with us and he *purposely* hadn't been invited, she'd brought him here to…what, flaunt him in front of me? I was way past Lewis Warren, but I was not past the bruises he'd left on my arm or the restraining order I'd never received. And seeing his pretty face standing there, as if everything was okay, nearly set me off.

"Look, Addie and I are…" Lewis began.

But I held my hand up. "Don't want to know."

"Nat," he groaned, "I'm sorry."

I glared harder. "Don't call me that. And I don't care."

"I just…we need to talk."

"We really don't," I warned him.

Penn stepped between us. "Now is not the time. If you want to talk, you can do it in a place *she* chooses and not as an ambush."

Lewis deflated and tightened his grip on Addie's hand. "Fine," he agreed. "Then let's figure out a time. We have a lot to discuss."

I had nothing to say to him. And I was about to tell him to go shove it when there was a ripple of a disturbance in the crowd. I turned away from Lewis, leaving that problem for later, to figure out what was going on. And that was when I saw what had caused the commotion.

The devil herself had made her appearance.

CHAPTER 33

*A*ll heads turned toward me.

Just as I'd planned, I stood out among the sea of bullshit fairy-tale attire in my signature blood red. I hadn't been able to secure a designer for the event and had been horrified to have to dip down to a B-list design team, but the guy had pulled it off. My dress was silky to their frilly, sleek to their poofy, and sensual to their dreamy.

It was me. And I wasn't going to stay away just because I was being pushed to the side. I was still Katherine Van Pelt. I was married to the heir to the Percy throne. Who needed friends or designers or a socialite status or, fuck... everything I'd had?

People feared me. That was clear in their expressions as I stepped into Trinity and proved that I would not fucking back down. That was all I needed.

A waitress offered me champagne, and I took the glass with a smile. When I turned it on the woman, I took a step back. My spine straightened in surprise.

"Melissa?"

She smirked at me. "Katherine."

Then she walked away. As if I hadn't just seen a ghost.

Melissa hadn't lived on the Upper East Side for a half-dozen years. After her modeling career had gone up in flames. I shuddered. So bizarre.

I shook off the strangeness of that interaction and moved into the crowd. I was determined to find Camden and prove that nothing could bother me. But as I passed another group of girls, I had to do a double take at the trio dancing. Kassidy, Margaret, and Kayla. They'd been inseparable when we were coordinating the debutante ball in high school. The committee had deemed them unfit after a sex scandal spread. I'd been made president and run the thing myself. What the hell were *they* doing here?

With slightly more haste, I hurried past them and took a rather large gulp of my champagne to steady me.

"Everything all right?" a girl asked, touching my elbow.

"Fine," I spat and nearly jumped when I saw who it was. "Lydia? Lydia...Hamilton?"

"That's right. Surprised you remember," she said, grinning at the woman next to her that I recognized immediately as the designer Trihn.

She hadn't accepted my invitation to design for me either.

"You're...Trihn. Dating Damon Stone."

Trihn nodded and held out her left hand. "Married actually."

My eyes flicked back to Lydia. Something didn't sit right. Lydia had gone to our prep school freshman year on scholarship. She'd been a weird, artsy type. We'd laughed her out of the school, and she'd transferred elsewhere sophomore year.

"I'm glad that you could make it. Is Damon with you?" I asked Trihn as if I knew him.

"He's busy, but I wanted to be here for my sister," Trihn said. "Me and my girls"—she gestured to two Hollywood-esque blondes behind her—"we wanted to make sure that you stayed in your place."

My eyebrows rose. "Excuse me?"

Trihn just winked at me. "Have a good time."

Lydia patted my elbow. "Enjoy the trip down memory lane."

They sauntered off, and I felt like my world was spinning. There were too many of them. My eyes traveled the room, and I saw more. Harmony, who I'd always competed with Penn for. Maria, who I'd ostracized at Harvard. Patricia, whose boyfriend I'd slept with. Kendra, Kaitlin, Haley, Autumn, Misty…on and on. Every girl that I'd ever known. Every girl that I'd ever…hurt. Tortured. Destroyed. Pushed aside in the name of my own popularity. In the name of what I stood for and who I was and what I fucking wanted. No, demanded.

They were all here. They were all looking at me.

My heart hammered in my chest. An uneasy feeling settled in my stomach. Something I'd never let myself experience. Dread. Fear. My hands sweat, and while I kept my head high, I couldn't keep the slight waver in my breathing. The hitch that gave me away.

The only one who was missing was…Hanna.

I closed my eyes and turned away from that name. I didn't think about her. Or what we'd done. Or how horrible we'd been.

No. I wouldn't. Not here.

I swallowed back the fear and went in search of the one name I *hadn't* mentioned. The bitch who had set this whole thing up. Who had orchestrated this entire event and then unleashed these people on me. As if I'd back down from that!

Then I found her. Natalie. Standing with Penn in an enormous green dress, looking like she had no cares in the world.

I took one step toward her, prepared give her a piece of my mind when I felt another hand on my arm. I whipped around, ready to unleash a torrent of vitriol on the unwitting person, but it was Lark.

I took a breath. "Hey."

She looked worried. "Katherine, check your phone."

"Why?"

"Uh…there are some…images circulating right now."

"Images?" I asked, reaching into my clutch for my phone. I opened it to find a message from Fiona. I looked at the first and thought I would be sick. "Oh."

Oh no. It was picture after picture of Fiona and Camden together. Fiona and Camden in missionary. Fiona and Camden doggy-style. Fiona giving Camden a blow job. Fiona and Camden. Fiona and Camden. Fiona and Camden.

My jaw clenched. I wanted to yell and scream at the world for this. But for some reason, I couldn't grasp it. Instead, what came out was a whimper. A pathetic, stupid whimper. My phone slipped from my hands and fell to the ground. Lark gasped and then reached for it. People were still looking at us. Staring at me and the strange noise that had come out of my mouth.

"Lark," I whispered. My throat tight.

"Come on. Let's...let's get out of here," Lark said.

"I can't," I gasped out. "I can't leave. They'll know."

"Katherine," she pleaded.

Then we heard it. Snickers. Laughter. Gasps.

Others were looking at the message. Others were looking at me. They knew that this meant Camden had been cheating on me. Still was, for all I knew. That he was humiliating me like this in front of everyone.

My eyes finally landed on Camden. We never showed up to places together. It made it more fun to find him there, waiting for me. Except, this time, he was with Fiona. In deep conversation with Fiona. His hand on her arm.

I took a few steps toward them like I was going to say something, but what could I say? Something was breaking in my chest. What the hell was this sensation? It was fucking awful. How could people live with this?

"Camden, stop!" Fiona shrieked. Her voice was like nails on a chalkboard to me. He must have responded, but all she did was get louder. "I won't be quiet. People deserve to know the truth! It's just a fucking arranged marriage! It's not like she loves you. She married you for your money!"

My cheeks heated the color of my dress. More eyes. All eyes.

Mortification hit me. And now, everyone knew the truth. Because why would I get embarrassed if it was just a lie? Oh god. Everything I'd worked to keep hidden. Everything that we'd worked for together.

Something wet landed on my cheek. Something foreign.

293

Lark was speaking to me. But I couldn't hear her over the buzzing in my head.

I touched my hand to my cheek and found tears. *Tears?* Christ!

I couldn't...

I couldn't let them see.

They couldn't know that I wasn't strong.

That I was broken.

I couldn't take it a second longer.

I rushed from the room, ignoring the tittering from the crowd and chorus of, "She had it coming," and found a private place to cry for the first time since my dad had been sent to prison. Before the walls had been closing in. And I'd learned that no one was ever going to save me but myself. There just...was no way out of this one. I'd dug my grave. I might as well lie in it.

CHAPTER 34

PENN

*W*e'd all heard. We'd heard everything.

Natalie frowned down at her phone.

"Delete those," I told her. "I can't believe Fiona sent them."

I found Lark across the room, following after Katherine.

"Fuck," I grumbled. I couldn't just let her go. I couldn't let Katherine break down in front of everyone and not care. It was like when I'd called Lewis the day I found out about the investigation. Katherine was fucked up, but she was still my friend. "Stay here. I'll be right back."

"Where are you going?" Natalie asked.

"I'm going to go check on Katherine."

"Shouldn't her husband do that?"

Yes, the bastard should. But he was still dealing with Fiona. And I wasn't going to just let her walk off.

"I won't be long." I kissed the top of her head. "Enjoy the party. I'll be back."

"Penn, really?" she asked.

"It's the crew," I said with a shrug, as if it was an explanation.

She sighed. "All right."

I knew this event was important to her. I wanted to be there for her, but Katherine was a mess. I'd never seen her like that before. I couldn't imagine why she would be freaking out about this thing with Fiona. She'd known that Camden was sleeping around. She had been sleeping around, too, after all. Not that anyone had known it was arranged until now. Embarrassing, sure, but not enough to break Katherine. It had to be something much deeper.

I walked down the hallway that I'd seen Lark hurry into a minute earlier and found her standing in front of an emergency exit. "Did she leave?"

Lark shook her head. "She stepped outside and told me to fuck off."

"You?" I asked in surprise.

She shrugged. "She's a total wreck. I wish that I were around more to see what the hell was going on with her. But I've been so busy with the campaign and Sam…"

"Sam?" I raised an eyebrow. "*The* Sam? The guy from campaign?"

"Oh, shut up, Penn."

"I didn't know he was back in New York."

"He is. But we're not…" She bit her lip. "We're not getting back together or anything."

"Sure, you're not."

"*That* is not why you're here!"

"You're right. But we should talk about *the* Sam later."

Lark snorted.

"Think she'll let me talk to her?"

She nodded. "You above anyone else."

"Yeah," I muttered. That was how it had always been.

I pushed open the emergency exit and was surprised that it didn't ding or anything. Must have been turned off. The exit was nothing more than a metal fire escape. Katherine leaned forward against the balcony, barefoot. Her heels dangled in one hand as she stared off into the alleyway. It wasn't the beautiful view from the windows of Trinity. This was New York City as it really was without all the glitz and glamour. Just like Katherine right now. Stripped down and bare to her core.

"Hey," I muttered.

She didn't turn around, just sniffled. "What are you doing here?"

"Checking on you."

"Shouldn't you be with your girlfriend?"

"Not when I saw you crying in there. When was the last time you cried, Ren?"

"Doesn't matter."

Goose bumps rose on her arms as a breeze blew through the street. I removed my jacket and slung it around her shoulders.

"Why are you being nice to me?" she asked half-desperately. She tilted her face and stared up at me as I leaned my hip into the railing next to her.

"Because you're my friend, and you'd do it for me."

She snorted. "I would do anything for you. It's hardly a comparison."

"Seems fitting to me." I crossed my arms over my chest. "Talk to me, Ren. What's going on?"

"I can't." She trembled, and there was something manic in her eyes. As if, if she expressed whatever she was holding in, then it might explode out of her. Never to return again.

"You knew Camden was cheating with Fiona."

She huffed. "Obviously."

"You don't normally care what anyone thinks about you. The pictures were embarrassing, but they shouldn't have hurt you."

"They shouldn't have," she agreed easily.

"And yet, you're out here, crying."

"Yes," she whispered. She glanced down and then back up into my baby blues. "I'm going to sound insane."

"It's eating you up, whatever it is?"

"Camden," she breathed. "It's Camden."

My eyes darkened. "What did he do? Does this have to do with the welts? Is he hurting you?"

"No," she said once despairingly. She reached out and touched my hand. "I...I'm in love with him."

My eyes widened to the size of saucers. "You...what?" I shook my head. "With Camden Percy? The same Percy douche bag we've known our whole lives?"

She bit her lip and faced the railing, sniffling again. "It's awful. I know. It's just horrible. The worst thing I could have done. But something just...happened. I don't know how to explain it, Penn. I wish I didn't. It would make everything so much easier."

She could not have shocked me more. I stood rooted in place, trying to blink away the reality of her words.

"Stop looking like that," she gasped. "I can barely stand it. I don't want to see you thinking about it, too."

"So...that's why you're upset about Fiona."

She nodded.

"And why the arranged-marriage part stings now.

Because it started out that way...but it's not that anymore."

She dipped her head again. Sniffled again. Scrubbed the tears from her cheeks.

"Wow, Ren," I whispered. "I mean, you couldn't have chosen worse, but at least it's somebody."

She choked on her laughter and then pushed me. "Shut up, Kensington."

"It's not the end of the world."

"It is. I can't go back in there. Not after running. Everyone laughing at me. Camden still talking to Fiona. The pictures, the marriage, and all the fucking girls who are here that I hurt."

I narrowed my eyes. "What girls?"

"Like *everyone* I have ever hurt is here today. I'm sure that's a product of your little girlfriend. And you thought *I* couldn't choose worse."

"You think Natalie invited people here to get to you?"

Katherine snorted. "Oh, I know she did. It's something I would have done in her place." She narrowed her eyes and muttered, "Bitch," under her breath.

"You think she..."

"What the hell do you think she's been doing since January, Penn? Taking the spotlight, stealing my designers, my clothes, my friends. And now this? She's fucking won. She has it all. Even you. Even Camden," she spat. "You had to have seen it happening, or are you just blind to her?"

And then it all hit me. What had been happening. I'd seen it. I'd seen it all happening. But I hadn't *seen* it. Not really. Not for what it was.

"Katherine," I said softly, "I didn't know."

She sniffled again and then threw herself into my chest. Her sobs racked her chest, and I gently put my hands around her shoulders. She had been holding this in for so long. And she wasn't a good person. What she'd done to Natalie was atrocious on so many levels. And I knew Natalie didn't forgive her for it. I hadn't forgiven her for it. But this...this was something else entirely. A new level of deceit. Right under my nose.

The door to the fire escape opened, and I turned to say something to Lark but was shocked instead to see Camden Percy standing there.

His eyes took in the scene in one sweep. He sighed. "I should have guessed."

Katherine jerked away from me so hard that I stumbled back a step and had to catch on to the railing.

Her eyes were wide when she looked at Percy. "Camden."

"And here I thought, we were over this."

"Over this?" she whispered and then glanced at me. "Oh god, Camden, no. We aren't...it's not...I didn't."

Camden held up his hand. "Bravo, Katherine. You've succeeded in getting back into his arms. You orchestrated this whole thing just to get back to him. It never stops with you, does it?"

"Camden," she said frantically, reaching forward.

He took a step back in disgust.

"It wasn't like that, man," I said at once.

Camden glared at me. "Keep your fucking mouth shut, Kensington."

"Cam," Katherine whispered, "I promise..."

"And your promises mean nothing." He looked her up

and down like she was scum on the bottom of his shoe. "Maybe I'll take Fiona up on that offer after all."

"No, no, no," she breathed.

She reached for him again, but he stepped back.

"Find your own way home," Camden said and then strode away.

Katherine stared after him in shock. Her hand hung out in midair. One arm of my jacket was slipping off of her shoulder, and she didn't even seem to notice. She was suspended in that moment. Having lost the one thing she had just told me she inexplicably loved.

CHAPTER 35

NATALIE

*C*amden Percy came out of the back hallway like his clothes were on fire. My eyes widened in shock. I hadn't even noticed him go down there where Katherine, Penn, and Lark were having their little powwow. Now, he was *running* to get away from it.

What the fuck? What had happened that made him run away?

My heart jerked in my chest. Whatever it had been…it couldn't be good.

I excused myself from the conversation I was having. I wasn't going to wait around and find out what the hell Camden had just seen. I trusted Katherine about as far as I could throw her. And while I didn't think that Penn would do anything, I could see Katherine trying to get back at Camden. Fuck.

I hastened my steps and nearly ran directly into Penn. Katherine was behind him, speaking urgently to Lark.

"What the hell happened?" I gasped. "Camden tore out of here like he'd seen a ghost or something."

Penn frowned. "Let's talk about it later."

"Why is she wearing your jacket?" I asked instead.

"She was cold," he said calmly. "Come on. Let's go back to the party. Katherine is going to go home."

I narrowed my eyes at the pair of them. "What exactly were you doing that made Camden tear out of here?"

Katherine finally looked up at me. Her eyes were red-rimmed, and her makeup was messy. Her liquid dress was now wrinkled. She looked beaten down. She looked like she'd lost everything. Just like I'd wanted. So, why wasn't I celebrating at the sight?

"He didn't like seeing Penn and me together," she said with hate in her dark eyes. "You might be familiar with the emotion—if you have any left."

"Katherine," Penn pleaded. "Don't do this right now. Just go home."

"Come on. We should leave," Lark cajoled.

But Katherine barreled on. "She can stand there like a fucking innocent fairy princess after ruining my life, and I should just walk away?" She shook her head. "I don't think so."

"*I* ruined your life?" I asked with a raised eyebrow. "Looks like everyone was tired of putting up with your shit."

"It would look like that. That's exactly what you want-ed." Katherine stepped closer to me. "It's amazing. I never thought the mirror would show me with fake Hollywood silver hair, but it seems to be so."

I snorted. "I can't help it if Karma is a bitch."

"If she is, then your ass is next."

"Katherine. Natalie. Could we not?" Penn asked.

"There are a lot of people here. You don't want to cause a scene. This is an important night."

"You're *still* defending her?" Katherine asked. "Just ask her, Penn. Ask her about the shit that she's pulled. About stealing Elizabeth Cunningham and my designer clothes and my ticket to Fashion Week. About how she stole my friends and my status and turned everyone against me."

"I didn't have to turn anyone against you. Everyone already hated you," I snapped.

"Natalie," Penn growled.

"Oh god," Lark whispered.

"It's true," I said, stepping into Katherine's personal space. "You ruin lives and play god. You pick and choose who is in and who is out. You treat everyone as if they're beneath you. You destroy their lives without a second thought, and no one has ever held you accountable. No one has stood up to you and put *you* in your place. Welcome to a taste of your own medicine."

Katherine laughed softly. "Fine, Natalie. Take my throne. Let me just tell you it's cold, hard, and lonely up there on that pedestal. So, fucking take it. I can't even deal with you anymore. You won. Is that what you wanted to hear? Does it make you feel good?" She looked me up and down, and when I didn't respond, she sighed. "I didn't think so."

Then she brushed past me, passed Penn back his jacket, and strode out of the club with Lark on her tail. Somehow, Katherine still got the last word. Even when she was the broken one leaving in disgrace.

Penn was aghast. "Natalie, what were you thinking?"

"What was *I* thinking?" I asked. "Katherine has done nothing but torment me since I came to New York."

"Yes, and while part of that is my fault, it doesn't mean that you have to kick her when she's down."

"Why not? She does it to everyone else," I reminded him.

He blinked as if something was finally settling into place and he didn't want to see it. "Did you do it all on purpose?"

"All what?"

"*This*, Natalie," he bit out. "Did you take Elizabeth from Katherine along with her socialite status and her friends? Did you invite people she's hurt to this party? Did you do it all to hurt her?"

"I, uh..." I muttered, seeing his anger boil up that he usually kept on a short leash. "Yes. I mean, I couldn't let her get away with hurting me. You *knew* that, Penn. You knew that I wanted her to pay for what she'd done to me."

"So, you hurt *her* instead?" He gritted his teeth. "And I knew that you wanted to survive here, Natalie. I didn't know you were going to *ruin her life*."

"She deserved it," I snapped before I thought better of it.

"Jesus Christ," he growled low. "I saw what was happening. I saw your growing popularity and your new friends and all the time party-planning. I saw it, but I didn't open my eyes at all. I swear, it says something about what my own sense of normal is that I didn't realize how fucking far you had fallen."

"Penn," I muttered.

But he didn't stop. "You're charming. Everyone likes you. Honestly, even Katherine liked you when she first met you until she realized you were a threat. I just thought that, once you got in with the right crowd, you'd rise quickly. That you needed to stay away from the crew and find your own people here. Man, was I wrong."

"You weren't wrong," I gasped. I could see him slipping. See the edges fraying. And his judgment falling into question. It terrified me. "That did happen all on its own."

"Is there anything else I should know? Trust me. I know this world. My eyes are open now. There's *always* something else," he said, mirroring the words he'd said to me about Lewis over Christmas.

I opened my mouth. A lie formed on my tongue. But then I killed it. I couldn't lie to him. Not with it all out there in the open. Not when he was barely controlling his anger. If he found out later, it would be the end of us. The end of everything. I could see it clearly.

I shuddered. "Lewis."

Penn narrowed his eyes. "What about Lewis?"

"After your attorney couldn't get the restraining order, I, uh…used one of Jane's contacts to tip them off about his business dealings."

His eyes rounded. "How did you even know about that?"

"I just…remembered some stuff from when we were dating and put the pieces together."

"And you thought the *New York Times* should know?" he asked, his voice rising.

I glanced around to see who was looking at us, but that only seemed to set him off more.

"This is unbelievable, Natalie. I told you to let me handle Lewis. Not to go do something you'd absolutely regret later."

"You weren't handling Lewis," I reminded him. "The restraining order was never going through. He had the judge in his pocket. There was nothing keeping him away from me unless I stopped him and showed him there were actual consequences to his actions." I sighed and bit my lip. "I never anticipated the stuff with Nina. I never wanted to hurt her."

"That's the thing about this world. We never look at the real consequences of our actions," he said sharply. "I thought you of all people would have realized that one."

"Penn," I whispered.

But he just turned his face away from me. As if he couldn't bear to look at me.

My heart constricted. I stepped forward as if I could find the words to explain. All the words that I'd been telling myself for months. That they needed to pay. That they'd earned their punishment. That they'd destroyed my life and had no consequences. That, if no one else would put them in their place, then I sure would.

But all the arguments died on my lips. Penn was siding with them. With the crew. As he always had.

Finally, his eyes slid back to mine. I was sure I didn't want to hear what he would say next.

That minute, the lights switched off.

And everyone screamed.

CHAPTER 36

NATALIE

"What the hell?" I muttered in the chaos.

Penn reached out and gripped my arm. "Are you okay?"

"Yes, but what's going on?"

"I don't know. But we should find out."

People were pulling out cell phones all over the room and shining the flashlight feature around the darkened interior. A second later, the floodlights flickered on overhead. The panic diminished a fraction, but we were all still looking around, wondering what the fuck had happened.

Penn pulled me toward the staged area where we'd been planning to hand the charity an enormous check for the evening. It seemed as good as any place to try to get some crowd control. And hopefully find out what was going on.

But when we got in there, my mouth dropped open. Jane Devney stood with her hands behind her back. A police officer was slapping a pair of handcuffs on her wrists. I started forward, but Penn stopped me. And that was when I saw that it wasn't just Jane, it was Court, too.

"You're making a huge mistake," Court snapped at the officer.

"You have the right to remain silent," the officer began.

"That's not his forte," Penn said, but his tone was one of dismay.

Jane, however, didn't say anything. She was just blankly staring forward. She was cooperating, but she lost something in that moment. The spark that had always made her *Jane*.

The cops were pushing people back from the area and trying to keep the perimeter clear. "Please, scoot back. The party is over. Trinity is closed."

I stepped forward, and Penn couldn't even stop me then. "What do you mean, it's closed?"

"Please step back. We have to shut down and secure this location. Everyone, please head to the door. The party is over," he repeated, using his team to push people away from Jane and Court.

"That's my brother," Penn said, stepping in. "What's going on?"

"Nothing I can say at the time. You'll have to come down to the station," the cop grumbled. "Please, stay out of the way."

"Yes, sir," Penn said.

I couldn't even believe this was happening. Jane and Court arrested? Trinity shut down? What the hell had caused this?

That was when something clicked into place. Jane had been frantic this morning when I saw her. Talking about money and Court helping her. She'd seemed crazed about it even. She'd never talked like that before. Jane had a ton of money. That didn't make sense. And yet, somehow, it did.

"Oh god," I whispered.

"What?"

"This morning, Jane was talking about this. She was saying that Court had given her money to help keep the club open. That she'd sold my secret to Katherine for Percy money to make up for it because she was having trouble with her overseas banks." I blinked. "She doesn't have any money. They're closing the club. Court's involved."

Penn's eyes were stuck on mine. Then he took a step back. "And how long have you known this?"

"What?" I asked in confusion. "This morning? Well, I just put it all together right now."

"And you expect me to believe that you didn't call the police on Jane? That you didn't think it would be payback to Jane for betraying you to Katherine?"

My eyes bugged out. "Are you joking? I would never do that!"

"Wouldn't you? How do I know? Look what you did to Katherine and Lewis."

"Penn, why would I admit to doing that to them and then lie about this?"

"I don't know. Because you're so far gone that you can't see out the other side."

My jaw dropped. "I was planning to talk to Jane after the party tonight to try to mend our friendship. I wasn't going to *call the police* on her!"

He shook his head. "I don't know about that, Nat. I just...don't know what to believe."

"Believe me, I don't want to hurt Jane."

"I want to believe you. But...with everything else..." He trailed off, letting me fill in what he was saying.

But I didn't know how to change his mind. I didn't know how to tell him how ludicrous this was. Jane had been party to what had ruined my life. She had put the gun in Katherine's hand, but it was Katherine who had pulled the trigger. I was mad at Jane. I held grudges. That was for sure. It was part of who I was. But I didn't want to see her get arrested. That was way too far for me.

"Penn, please," I whispered.

"You're just like her now," Penn said sharply. "As bad as Katherine. We said that we'd stay ourselves. That I'd help you, but we'd still be ourselves. Now, I see how wrong I was."

"I'm not," I said with a gasp. "I'm not like her."

"I have to figure out what's going on with Court. I need to call my mother and head to the police station to sort this out," he said in the cold, detached voice he used for everyone else.

"I'll...I'll come with you," I whispered.

"I think you should...stay here. You have to clean up the party and fix the stuff with the charity. It'll be better for you to stay."

"But you shouldn't deal with the stuff with Court alone," I pleaded.

"Actually, I think alone is what I need right now."

I stilled as he looked down into my pleading eyes. "What?"

"I just need some time to think about this." He slid his hands into his pockets. "Some space."

"Space..."

"Yes. Space. Like I should go to Paris alone tomorrow."

My eyes doubled in size. "Penn…"

"We can figure this out when I get back."

I stepped forward, tears welling in my eyes. My voice came out choked. "After your conference or…at the end of the summer?"

He looked at his brother, standing in handcuffs, and then back to me. "I haven't decided."

I opened my mouth to respond. To say anything. To fix this horrible, horrible mess that was a puddle at my feet. But there was nothing to say. Nothing that could change his mind as he stepped away from me and walked to his brother's side. As he slipped out of the room to head to the police station.

And left me standing alone in the ruins of my party.

And the ruins of my life.

CHAPTER 37

I'd stayed up late into the night, waiting to find out what had happened with Jane and Court. I'd texted Penn, but his response had been brief.

Please don't make this harder than it already is.

As if I could make it harder. It was torture. We were in limbo. Possibly ended. He was getting on a plane tomorrow to fly thousands of miles away from me, and I didn't know where we stood or what would happen.

The sun had already risen the next morning when the charges hit the news. Jane was being charged with grand larceny. Her name wasn't even Jane Devney. It was Janine Lehmann. She was a dual German-French citizen who had changed her name and stolen more money than god from banks all over the world. All with the force of her personality and her supposed contacts.

I'd been deceived by the ultimate deceiver. I couldn't believe it. I'd witnessed it all. The large amounts of cash.

The frantic desperation to get her club off the ground. How she knew basically everyone. The name-drops and excessive spending and the way she had come out of nowhere to belong.

But it was Court who was paying the price. The news was saying that he was an accessory to the crime and was potentially being charged with aiding and abetting. I wondered how far that would hold up with Kensington money when his mother was the mayor. Wouldn't be pretty either way.

I slouched back against my couch and covered my eyes. What a disaster. The party. Jane. Penn. All of it. It had all gone down in flames.

Still, I waited for Penn to reach out. For something to change. I waited up until the minute we were supposed to leave for Paris. Sitting in a first-class seat and sipping champagne as we soared off into the sunset.

But it never happened.

Penn never reached out.

He'd left. And I was here without him.

I bought the first ticket to Charleston without a second thought. Grabbed the bag I'd packed for Paris and took a cab to LaGuardia. I touched down back home in a matter of hours. I hadn't called or texted Amy or my family. I didn't know what to say, and I didn't trust myself not to break down. I held back the panic with sheer will. Someone else needed to tell me that this would be all right before I unraveled completely.

I landed on Amy's doorstep and banged on the door. But when it swung inward, I took a step back in shock. "Enzo?"

His eyebrows rose in surprise, and his thick French

accent rang out. "Natalie, what a surprise." He called out into the apartment, "Amy, darling, Natalie is here."

"Natalie?" Amy yelled back. "Natalie who?"

I laughed, but it sounded strained and choked, even to me. "Me, silly."

Amy appeared then in nothing but a paint-splattered white button-up that must belong to Enzo. "Holy shit! Look at you. What are you doing here?" She wrapped me in a hug. "Why didn't you call?"

"I...Penn..." And then I couldn't hold it back any longer. I was here with my best friend. There was nothing I could do, nothing I could hide from her. The tears hit like a tidal wave.

Amy shushed me and drew me into her apartment. Enzo reached for my suitcase, depositing it inside, as Amy sat me down on the couch. A half-finished pizza sat on the coffee table. A Marvel movie was on in the background. It was all so nice and normal, and it made it hurt so much worse. So, so much worse because I hadn't even known that Enzo had moved in.

"Nat," Amy said, brushing my hair back, "tell me what happened. Are you okay?"

"Penn went to Paris without me. And Enzo moved in?" I gasped out.

"Yeah...that's, uh, why I renovated the guest bedroom."

"You didn't tell me."

"You've been kind of busy," Amy said with a shrug.

I stared at her in horror. All of this shit in my life, and I'd even neglected the one person who was always there for me. Fuck. Maybe Penn was right. Maybe I'd really fucked this up.

"I'm sorry."

315

"Hey, don't apologize. I don't care. It's me. We'll always be friends."

Enzo appeared a minute later and held out a container of chocolate icing. It was like he really understood us.

"Now, tell me about Penn. He's in Paris?"

I downed a giant dollop of frosting, and then it all spilled out. Every excruciating detail from the very beginning. Every horrible thing I'd done from convincing Penn to teach me how to belong to taking down Katherine and everything in between. Even Jane and Court even though I'd had nothing to do with that nightmare.

Spilling it to Amy was a balm. It was finally getting it off of my chest to someone who had seen me at my lowest at Christmas and knew why I'd decided to do it. And now, how it had all worked and then backfired completely.

"Well, sounds like you got what you wanted," Amy said, rubbing my back as the tears finally dried up.

"Careful what you wish for," I murmured.

"Yes. Sounds like you were a real bitch," she said with a laugh.

"Thanks."

"Anytime."

"I guess I was. But they were horrible to me, Ames. They ruined everything."

"I know," Amy said. "But everything you just told me, that doesn't even sound like you. It sounds like a stranger. The person who could kick Michael down to his size without blinking. And he deserved it, but that doesn't mean you had to do it. Any of it."

"Yeah," I whispered. "I didn't want to lose Penn over it."

"Good news: you haven't lost him yet."

"Yet." The word sounded horrible on my tongue.

"You know what you need?" she asked.

I shook my head.

"A cleansing."

I choked on a chuckle. "Seriously?"

"Let's end this cycle the way you started it. Close the circle, as your mom would say."

"You're right. You're so right." I wiped the tears from my cheeks. Leave it to Amy to have the answer. "Let's do it."

Amy grinned. "What do we need?"

A FEW HOURS LATER, Amy parked her Tahoe just off of Folly Beach. We'd called in Melanie since I knew that Michael's family had a beach house. I might not like him, but I would use his resources for something this important.

"You are *so* like Mom right now," Melanie said, popping open the back door.

"Yep," I agreed easily.

I walked around to the trunk, and Amy appeared at my side. I hefted the shovel over my shoulder.

"Kick-ass if you ask me," Amy said. She grabbed the two bags and passed one of them to Melanie. "Here you go."

"Are you sure we should be doing this?" Melanie asked.

"Stay here if you want," I said and then started walking toward the beach.

"Like I'm going to do that," she muttered, chasing after us. "But, like...how is this going to help you get Penn back?"

I stopped just before the sand. My heart contracted

painfully at her words. Get him back. Like he was already gone. Out of reach. Never to return. I closed my eyes. He couldn't be. That wasn't possible. He'd handed me my crown and said he'd never let me go. We could...we could fix this.

"It's not about getting Penn back," I said finally.

"Because he isn't gone," Amy interjected with a pointed look at Melanie.

"This is about me. It's about coming back to myself. Being who I'm meant to be, not who I became. Releasing it all and starting over."

"But you were so cool. Why would you want to change that?" Melanie asked.

My eyes caught hers. "Sometimes, it's not worth it."

Melanie dipped her head in understanding. "I'm on board. I just wanted to make sure you were doing it for the right reasons." She smirked at me. "Plus, who am I to say no to a bonfire on the beach?"

Amy and I shook our heads at her. My little sister was so innocent and naive, and sometimes, she really surprised me.

"You know, Michael ended up telling me what happened with you guys at the party," Melanie said as I kicked my sandals off and walked out onto the open beach.

I chewed on my lip. "Uh, he did?"

"Yeah, it explains why you were asking me those weird questions the next morning."

"Mel, I'm sorry. It's part of the reason I really need this cleansing."

"Well, I just...wanted to say thanks," she muttered, grabbing my hand. "I didn't realize how bad it had been before. You know with him...after Kennedy. But it's been so much better since the party. I think that has something to do with what you said."

"Using my superpower for good," I said. The memory of Penn saying that while we were sailing flashing through my mind.

"You might have done some bad in this new Natalie form," Melanie said. "But you did some good too. I think we should find a balance."

I reached out and took Amy's hand in mine too. Balance. Yes, that was what we needed.

Then, we traipsed together out to the shoreline.

We'd waited until it was well past dark so that no one would be out on the beach. School wasn't out yet, so it wasn't as packed as it would be come June, but I didn't want to take any chances. When I'd done this in the Hamptons, I'd known it would be an empty beach. Or I'd thought so until Penn Kensington walked out and changed my life.

I smiled at the memory. I'd hated him so much that day. For leaving me behind in Paris. For being the son of the owner of the home I planned to stay in. For not remembering me...and then for his memories when he did. So much had changed since then. And I couldn't go back.

We walked until our feet hit the wet sand, and Amy dropped her bag. "All right. Let's do this."

I plunged the shovel into the sand, felt it give under my weight, and then moved it out of the way. My shoulders loosened with the first move. It was intoxicating, this movement. The physical exertion of actually doing something yourself. Something with a real end result. It steadied my mind. Kept me in the present. The burn in my back, the chafe of my hands, the weight of the sand. It was rhythmic and really did bring me full circle to that last time I'd done just this.

When the hole was deep enough, I dropped the shovel into the sand with a sigh and held my hand out to Melanie. "Let's do this thing."

"Are you really sure you want to burn this? It gave you so much."

I nodded and took my book out of her hands. It *had* given me so much. It was the beginning, and this was the end. No more deception and manipulation. No more games. No more Olivia Davies or the fake person I'd let myself become out of her. Just me.

"I'm sure."

The first rip of the pages coming out of BET ON IT made me cringe. But once I started tearing them out page by page, it became easier. All three hundred eighty-seven pages in a heap in the middle of the sand. The shredded remnants of what my life had once been. The closure to that fateful night when I'd asked the moon to take the dozens of rejection letters and make it something else. It had. It had made me something else.

Amy pulled out the bottle of Jack Daniel's. I hadn't gone out of my way to get the good stuff. I wasn't staying in Kensingtons' Hamptons mansion. This was just me.

I took the first swig straight from the bottle. I managed to swallow without sputtering but coughed on the second gulp. I passed the bottle down. Amy didn't wait before tipping it back like a pro. She daintily wiped her lips and then handed it to Melanie. I thought she might hesitate or get out of it. But it must be attributed to her college party life that she took the bottle without complaint and drank deep. She did sputter at the taste, but it was with a smile. She was here. She was in. We were all too deep to stop now.

One more pull from the bottle, and then I set it aside. I was smarter this time and actually brought lighter fuel with us, so we wouldn't have to waste the whiskey. I splashed it all over the pages, moved it out of the way of the pit, and reached for the matches.

I raised my hands in the air, smiling at how right this felt. How right I felt with the universe. "I give this to you, moon. Another ritual burning. The end of it all. Close the circle. Cleanse me completely and let me start anew."

I struck the match and dropped it into the pit. It ignited, the flames growing as the pages burned, the edges curling and turning to ash. I laughed. It'd escaped me without warning. Then, I laughed again.

Amy joined in, and soon, Melanie followed. We danced around our little bonfire as my book literally went up in flames. As we enjoyed this moment together on the beach outside of Charleston and gave my troubles to the universe. Let it burn right out of me.

As the flames began to die down, I reached for my T-shirt and shorts. I let them drop into the sand and then dashed to the oceanfront. I heard my best friend and my sister racing behind me in the sand. The first splash was freezing. The ocean hadn't heated enough for this, but I didn't even care. I dived under, tasting the salt and sandy grime of the ocean, and reappeared to see Amy and Mel jumping in, too.

They swam out to me, joking and reveling in the moment. They weren't immune to the cleansing. To the power that we possessed that night. To the ways we communed and burned and washed it all away.

I already felt lighter, floating on my back until my teeth chattered. So much lighter. In that moment, I let it all go. The Upper East Side. My revenge. My grudges. I let it all wash away from me.

And when it was gone, it was just me again. Just Natalie.

CHAPTER 38

NATALIE

The next morning, my mom woke me up at the crack of dawn with the vacuum cleaner.

I covered my ears and groaned. "Mom, what are you *doing?*"

"Oh, Natalie!" she said as if she hadn't known I was lying there.

I narrowed my eyes at her. "You knew I was sleeping."

"Well, now that you're up, you want to help me?"

I laughed at her ludicrousness and decided, *What the hell?* "Fine. What do you need help with?"

"Excellent, honey. So glad to have you home. Meet me in the attic."

After a quick shower, I yawned dramatically and climbed the stairs to the attic, which was a complete clusterfuck.

My mother brightened at my appearance—the tie-dyed shirt and bell-bottoms. "Oh, Natalie, you're so yellow again." She mimed my aura. "There's my bohemian girl."

I grinned at her and crossed my arms at all the clutter. "So...what are you doing up here, and why aren't you at the shop?"

"I hired someone to help with it!" my mother announced. "He's taking over today because there's too much to do here."

"You called in sick because I'm home, huh?"

My mom hip-checked me with a wink. "Saw you coming a week ago."

I shook my head at her. Sometimes, I never could tell what she was going to say.

"Now, it looks like we need to keep you nice and busy. You talk while we sort through all these boxes and determine what we keep and love and what is going to go to a new home." New Age talk for the garbage. "So...Penn?"

That was how I spent the next three days, helping my mom go through what felt like endless boxes of junk in the attic. I was beginning to think that she was a real hoarder. I was throwing out way more than her because some of it I'd never seen in my life. Other times, it was like reliving all of our military travels one box after the other. One labeled San Antonio, two labeled Germany, one for Indiana. The home movies that we couldn't watch were added to a pile to figure out how to put on the computer. Baby clothes were stashed away for my and Mel's future children. The best childhood drawings were kept. The rest tossed. My old writing was a definite keep.

And the whole time, I talked. My mom listened. We didn't solve anything. But the work was cathartic, and so was the time with my mom.

On the third day, when we'd finally reached a midway

point that meant we could get to the farther back boxes, I stumbled on one labeled Natalie College. I ripped into it.

I wasn't surprised to find swimming trophies and medals, old school notebooks, and notes that Amy and I had passed back and forth. I laughed at a stack of pictures that we'd taken with a disposable camera that included mostly the sides of our faces, blurry images, and general nonsense. I put that box aside and rifled through the one underneath it.

My hand stilled on a picture of Amy and me in Paris together the summer after high school graduation. It had been taken only days before I met Penn, tipping my world off its axis forever.

I carefully placed that in the Keep pile, and when I glanced back inside, my gaze snagged on a bit of shiny metal half-hidden underneath a baseball cap. I moved the hat aside. My breath caught, and I gingerly reached inside and pulled out the love lock.

Tears welled in my eyes as I held the precious thing in my hand. A little lock with the letters *P & N* on it. Penn had given it to me that night in Paris. A tribute to my romantic sentiments, as I'd been so sad to hear that the city had removed all the locks from the bridges. He'd wanted us to have our own.

I'd come home and promptly thrown it into my stuff. Too angry with him to keep it, too in love with him to get rid of it. Oh, young love.

This was a relic. A remnant of the girl I'd been when I first met him. Young, innocent, eager and desperate for someone to really *see* me. Penn had been it. He still was it. He'd *always* been it. The guy I measured everyone against.

The one perfect night, ruined by the worst possible morning.

But that was all gone. Replaced by the last year and a half of time together. Every smile and kiss and laugh. Every writing session and Totle snuggle. Every time he'd just looked into my eyes and known. Like I had known. All along. Even if we'd both made mistakes along the way. And tried to wreck it all.

And now, he was there again. In Paris, without me.

I clutched the lock in my hand and decided then, *No*. No, this wasn't going to happen. I wasn't going to stay here another minute and wait for him to make a decision. Agonize over whether he was going to come back from his conference or at the end of the summer. Wonder if he could forgive what I'd done.

My eyes slid to my mother, and she just smiled. "Did you figure it out?"

"I'm such an idiot."

"You're young. You'll grow out of trying to be anything else."

I kissed her cheek. "Thank you, Mom."

"I love you. Now, go get him."

I raced down the stairs and into my room. I found the open suitcase I'd brought from New York with me. The mound of designer clothing that Penn had insisted would help me fit in. He'd been right.

I dumped it all out on the floor.

Then I found the few outfits that I'd left here in Charleston before moving to the city. The bohemian clothing that had always been my staple. Whether or not I fit in had never mattered to me.

I liked flowy shirts, flare jeans, and moccasins. I

326

wanted embroidery and tie-dye and excessive patterns in my life. I wanted it all.

I hastily threw it all into the suitcase. I snatched my untouched computer bag off of the table, bought the first plane ticket to Paris, and vowed to make this right.

CHAPTER 39

PENN

"*P*enn, your work on the Aristotelian ramifications in sexual partnerships is so fascinating," Dr. Angelica Duval said as we stepped out of the final panel for the afternoon and back toward the lobby.

"Thank you. I enjoyed your latest article as well. I was glad to see *The Journal of Philosophy* taking such a progressive stance," I told her.

She smiled up at me. The same smile she'd been wearing the whole conference. The one that said she was the prettiest woman in the discipline and she was used to being flirted with. That we had similar interests and right now would be a good time to ask her out.

But I didn't. I kept walking. Into the noisy bar full of relatively nerdy philosophy professors, drinking too much and discussing theory at volumes unnecessary for the space. That was just how these things went.

A pair of colleagues came to say hello to us and invited us to dinner the next day. We both agreed easily, and they shot me a knowing look before they left. Perhaps everyone here thought that Angelica and I would be involved by the end of this thing. Or that we already were. It couldn't be that I thought she was an excellent scholar and enjoyed her work.

Then again, I was the person who wrote about sex professionally. What did I expect them to think?

I rubbed my temple and thought about the scotch waiting for me in my room.

"Are you okay?" Angelica asked, touching my sleeve.

I hastily removed my arm. "Fine."

"You know...I've never done this before." She took a step closer to me. "Do you want to get out of here? Go get a drink?"

I stared down at her small pink lips, the chocolate-brown eyes, and rosy cheeks. The look of desire painted on her face more than the makeup. It'd be so easy. If the entire idea didn't make me nauseated.

"Actually, I'm seeing someone," I said, putting more distance between us.

Space from Natalie didn't mean this space. Time to figure out what was going on with Natalie didn't mean acting like an idiot. I didn't want a damn thing from this woman in front of me, except her company on philosophy panels. What she was asking for, she would never get.

"Oh," she chirped, straightening. "I didn't know. With your research, I thought—I mean, just...forget I said anything."

Color rose in her cheeks, and then she awkwardly stepped back and disappeared into the crowd. Well, I couldn't have handled that worse. That scotch was sounding more and more pleasant.

I headed to the front desk first to pick up a package that had been delivered for me. I'd received a text earlier that day, but I hadn't had time to leave the conference center to collect it.

The man behind the VIP counter lifted his head at my approach. "Ah, Dr. Kensington," he said, holding up his hand. "Let me get your package." He retrieved a padded envelope. "Here we are."

I took it out of his hand and looked at the innocuous envelope. "Do you know who sent it?"

"I wasn't here when it was delivered, but I was told that a woman dropped it off earlier this morning."

"Huh," I said with a shrug. "And no clue as to the contents?"

"Are you concerned? Should I have it tested?" the man asked in alarm. As if anthrax were inside it.

"No, no, it's fine. I was just curious. I wasn't expecting anything."

"Well, let me know if you need anything else."

"Thank you," I said before carrying the package upstairs to my suite.

I dropped it off on a counter and was surprised to hear the *clunk* it'd made when it hit the wood. Well, now, I was even more curious.

But first, scotch.

It had been a long day. One panel discussion of a chapter of my book. One panel where I was the discussant for three rather dry papers and thankfully Angelica's. And three other panels that I'd been cajoled into attending. It had been four too many for one day.

A headache was forming at my temples. I knew it had more to do with trying to escape the fact that I'd left

Natalie behind in New York than the panels. I'd been tempted to text her every day since I arrived, but what would I say? *Sorry for abandoning you in the city without a word?*

And then the longer I put it off, the harder it seemed to be to find the words. Maybe the words weren't right in a text anyway. It was a conversation we needed to have in person. If I hadn't had this conference, I would have already booked a flight home. Jet lag be damned.

I took a long sip of the scotch and sighed with relief. I'd been wanting that all day. It had been a long while since I'd been this desperate to day drink. It was amazing how watching your life fall into shambles could do that to a person.

I sank into the leather chair and stared out the open window overlooking the Seine and Notre Dame on the island beyond. What was left of it. I felt for the cathedral. Like my insides had also been burned through and I needed to once again be rebuilt to my former glory.

My fingers reflexively reached for the envelope. I set down the scotch and tore open the top flap. When I turned it upside down, a metal lock fell into my hand, and a small note fluttered into my lap.

I flipped the gold lock over and looked at it in shock. A small smile playing on my lips. It was the love lock that I'd given Natalie all those years ago. The *P & N* I'd scrawled elegantly in Sharpie on the front.

I'd been such a con artist at the time. Doing anything to earn her trust and devotion. I enjoyed it as much for the manipulation as her pure joy in it. She didn't know what I was doing, and looking back, maybe I didn't either. I saw something different in her then. I didn't need the full night to walk the city with her to get in her pants. But I had done it anyway because I couldn't get enough of her. Here was the evidence of the young love that had struck me before I even knew its real purpose.

My fingers curled around the metal, holding it tight in my palm. If this was here, that meant...Natalie was here.

My heart thumped in my chest as I retrieved the forgotten note.

> *It all started on a park bench in Paris.*
> *Meet me?*
> *—Nat*

She'd flown all the way to Paris? And just left a note and the lock?

I downed the rest of my scotch and grabbed my jacket before I gave it more thought. If she was here, then I wasn't going to make her wait. She'd likely already been there for hours, considering the package had been delivered earlier that morning.

As I strode out of the lobby and into the bright light of day, I had no idea what I was going to say. What she'd done...was every bit as awful as I'd blamed her for. I'd been just as bad. And I'd helped her get there.

But that didn't mean I was ready to forgive her or move on from it. I needed to see her though. Needed to know what she was thinking by flying out here. Did she think that she could change my mind about it all if she spent the money and surprised me? I'd told her we could talk after Paris. I didn't yet know if her arriving here early was a good or a bad thing.

I'd have to decide that when I saw her. Decide what to do about it all.

I hopped into the first available cab and gave them directions to the Tuileries Garden in front of the Louvre. This had all started after we ran out of the Palais Garnier and down near the waterfront. I was amazed she still remembered which one it was. But perhaps that night was branded on her memory as much as it was mine.

After paying the taxi, I walked through the garden, which was still alive with tourists exploring the grounds. When we'd come here, it had been one or two in the morning, and we'd had the place to ourselves. I navigated around the crowds and came up the back way to our park bench. I didn't want her to see me first.

Then she came into view. All orange-patterned wide-leg pants tucked up underneath her as she sat cross-legged on the park bench. Her shirt was a flowy white gauzy material that I'd seen her wear dozens of times when we lived together in the Hamptons. Her silvery-white hair was piled high on the top of her head. An over-size bun flopping off to the right without a care in the world. In her lap was her computer as she typed furiously into an open document.

It was like stepping back in time. And seeing the bohemian vision who had put a spell on me straight out of the Atlantic. The goddess who knew herself and didn't care an ounce what anyone else thought of who she was.

I'd stalled when I saw her.

But then I took her in...really took her in.

I smiled.

And moved toward the Natalie I'd first fallen in love with.

CHAPTER 40

NATALIE

*M*aybe he wasn't coming.

I hadn't really considered that when I put this plan in place. He could be furious with me and wouldn't appreciate that I'd flown all the way here and wrecked his plans. I chewed on the end of my pen and stared down at my open document. This was stressing me the fuck out. I'd been so confident when I got on that plane.

I tossed the pen onto my open notebook next to me and went back to typing on my computer, working on the new book. I couldn't do anything about whether or not Penn would show. I couldn't make him spring up out of nothing. The only thing I could control was this right here. And I was going to keep writing until he showed. Or didn't.

"That is quite an outfit," a voice said behind me.

I jumped out of my seat, barely catching my computer before it crashed into the grass. "Penn."

He didn't give me any of his telltale signs that he was

amused. Or even…that he was glad to see me. I'd probably fucked up. Oh well, too late now. I was too relieved to see him to do anything but smile at his beautiful face.

"Natalie," he said calmly, slipping his hands into his pockets. "What are you doing here?"

"I was wrong," I gasped out. I set the computer down on the bench and faced him. "I was so very wrong about everything. And you were right all along. I just didn't realize it all until Enzo."

He looked at me quizzically. "Enzo?"

I shook my head. This wasn't coming out right. I'd made all of these plans on the flight over, and now, my sleepy brain was trying to ruin this. "I flew home to Charleston after you left. I went to see Amy, and Enzo had moved in. That's why she'd renovated the guest bedroom. They were living together, and I didn't even know. I'm her best friend, and she hadn't even told me that they were living together or anything. She said I was busy. I wasn't busy. I was too fucking self-centered to see what I was doing to my life. To look past my need for revenge to what was really happening all around me. The damage I was causing to even my oldest friendship.

"So, I took a step back and saw how out of touch I'd been really. Then, well, Amy, Mel, and I had another cleansing to close the circle. I don't even know if that makes sense to you." I warily peeked up at him.

"You burned more things and went skinny-dipping?"

"Technically, yes," I said with a grin. "We burned my book. Tore out all the pages and gave them up in offering as a ritual burning to cleanse what had happened between my first ritual burning and the last. Then I let the water wash it all away. It was about me. About me coming back to myself." I gestured to my bohemian clothing. "You know, the real me."

"I see. You think a ritual burning and new clothes change who you've become."

"No. It's not that at all. It's that the person I was when I did those things, the black hole that I had fallen into, it's gone. The things I did to Katherine and Lewis and the mountains I climbed to take them down…I don't want to be that person anymore. I don't want to be a person you turn away from. A person who you think could have my closest friend in New York arrested. What happened to Jane was horrible, but I didn't do it."

"I know," he said.

"You do?"

He nodded. "When I went to see Court, she told me that you didn't know. That she hopes that you can forgive her. That she never wanted to hurt you."

"Good," I whispered. My stomach twisted at the words.

I had been worried about Jane. I couldn't believe what she had done to get to the place that she was at. Especially because I'd had such kinship with her. I could have *been* her under different circumstances. So desperate to belong that I broke the law. I was thankful that I'd never gotten that far. Gone to that place.

"How is Court?"

"Pissed off. But my mother is confident that all charges will be dropped. He was glad that I was there."

"I bet he was. I'm glad you two are getting along."

Penn shrugged as if waiting for me to say more.

"So, I guess I wanted you to know that I never wanted to hurt you. I know there are consequences to my actions that I couldn't have foreseen. And you're one of them. Or maybe I did know," I said softly, "and that's why I never told you everything that I was doing.

"Then…then I found the love lock in all of my things. I was helping my mom clean out the attic. And I realized how much of an idiot I was. Like, for forever. I blamed you for leaving me that day. I blamed you for everything. But I should have accepted it and moved on like a normal person. My grudges…they've always been a part of me. I don't trust easily, and my forgiveness is even harder to achieve. I want to try to let it go. Because the minute that I held that lock, I knew how much I was in love with you that night. Stupid young love that made no sense, and yet it was written all over that impossible lock. I kept it because I was so mad at you and so in love with you. And I realized those emotions were all tangled up with how I felt about you. How I still feel about you. We've made mistakes. We've hurt each other." I fingered the crown necklace lying against my chest. "But our love has bridged nearly a decade. And it's still burning just as hot. I can do better. We can do better. I want this so bad, Penn. Just you. Just us. And I'm not going to leave Paris until we've talked this out."

He tilted his head to the side at my long rant. "Are you done?"

I deflated at his words. "I don't know. Are you still mad? Because I can keep going."

"I'm not mad," he said gently.

I bit my lip. "No?"

"I was never mad."

My look was incredulous. "You flew across the world to get away from me, but you…weren't mad?"

"Okay, fine. I was a little mad. But mostly disappointed."

"Oh, ouch," I whispered.

Finally, a small smile broke through his features. "But I knew you were different the moment I saw you sitting there in that hippie clothing, writing furiously on your computer."

"You...you did?"

He nodded.

"And you just...let me rant and rave at you for the last ten minutes anyway?"

He grinned fully. "I had to be sure."

"Penn, I'm so sorry," I breathed.

He held up his hand. "Look, I take partial responsibility for this whole thing. I created you after all. I made you what you are. Let loose that monster within and brought you into the spotlight on the Upper East Side. It was my fault."

"No, no, no, it was my fault," I insisted. "I asked you to help. Begged you to help me survive them."

"I know, but I saw that you were messed up after what Katherine and Lewis did. I could have refused. I could have forced you to talk to me about it more. Gotten therapy or something. But I was so desperate to be with you that I didn't care how I got you. I should have cared."

I sighed at his words. We'd both been desperate, just for different things. And by the time we'd both wanted each other, it was too late.

"Either way," he continued, "I shouldn't have run away. That wasn't fair to you."

"You had every right to walk away after what I did," I told him. "Even if I hated it."

"No, I had no right. I told you that I'd be at your side, that I'd never leave, and then I left. I told you from the beginning that you would see a side of me that you might not like. But I didn't account for what it could all do for you. That's not fair to you. I don't want either of us to run away every time something goes wrong."

"I know, but...I needed the time anyway. So, you were right after all."

"Just because you came out on the other side of it all on your own doesn't mean that I want you to think that I'm going to fly across the world to get away from you. I don't want to be that person. I don't want to be my father," he said crisply. "Make you second-guess who I am and what you mean to me."

My heart fluttered at the words. He wasn't gone. I just needed to reach out and take him.

"I know what you mean to me," I said, taking a step toward him, "what you've always meant to me, but I've been too stubborn to admit it."

"And what is that?" he asked, meeting me for the next step.

"Everything. You mean everything to me."

His eyes searched mine. Our blues clashing in the space. My heart racing, hoping against all hope that we could fix this between us.

"Hmm," he said, glancing away from me. "You know that I was at this conference all week, debating philosophical theory and presenting papers."

I swallowed. "Yes. You've told me what philosophy conferences are like."

"There's this colleague of mine from Stanford who writes very forward-thinking papers. She is incredibly well respected and favorably published in some of the best journals. Her dissertation became a seminal book in the field."

I waited. Wondering where this was going. Stuck on the one word that didn't seem to fit. *She*. There weren't many female philosophy professors.

"Many of my colleagues think that she's incredibly attractive."

I held my breath at his words.

"Many think that we're already attached."

My stomach rolled.

"In fact, earlier this afternoon, before I received your package, she asked me out for drinks."

"Oh," I peeped. "I see."

He tilted my chin up to look at him. "I don't think that you do. The thought of her made my stomach turn. I felt physically sick at the idea of us going to get drinks. All I could think was that that *wasn't me* anymore. That the only woman in my life that I care about is *you*. And you weren't here. And I'd seriously fucked it all up. And how I needed to make this all right."

Tears welled in my eyes at his words. "I love you so much."

He withdrew the lock from his pants pocket and slid it into my hand. "I love you, too."

I threw my arms around his neck and buried my head into his chest. I couldn't stop the tears from falling as relief hit me like a flood. It definitely didn't help that I hadn't slept in almost a full day. But this was just…beyond what I could have hoped for from him.

"I'm so sorry," I blubbered.

"Shh," he whispered, stroking my hair. "We'll work it out together. Just like we should have."

I nodded and squeezed him tighter. "I couldn't lose you."

"You weren't in danger of losing me, love."

"It felt like it."

"I know. I'm sorry."

"Oh, shut up. Don't be sorry. This is my fault."

"We've both been idiots."

I pulled back and wiped at my eyes. "We have. I should have chosen you all those years ago and never let you slip out of my life."

"Then choose me now," he said, dragging my lips hard against his.

"I choose you," I breathed.

"Marry me," he breathed back.

I jerked back in surprise and laughed. "One day, Penn Kensington. One day, I will."

"How about now?" he teased.

"Right now?" I said, going along with his joke. "I don't think we have a ceremony waiting for us."

"Natalie, I don't want to live another second in a world where you think I don't want this," he told me evenly. "Unless you don't want this."

"I want this," I assured him.

"Then marry me."

I stopped laughing and really looked at him. "Wait... you're serious?"

He arched an eyebrow. "Yes."

"But we...we just had this huge argument and...you don't mean it. And I mean...there's no ring. Or...or anything," I whispered, suddenly on uncertain ground.

"Who said there was no ring?"

Then he removed a small blue box from the inside of his jacket pocket. My hands flew to my mouth as he got down on one knee right there in front of the Louvre, in our park, by our bench, where it'd all started. He opened the box to reveal a perfectly haloed circle-cut diamond on a simple band.

"Natalie, eight years ago, this all started on a park bench in Paris. Will you make me the happiest man alive and start our next journey together here, too?"

"Oh my god," I gasped as tears flooded my vision again. "Yes!"

He slipped the diamond on my finger and then picked me up into his arms and twirled me in a circle as Paris blurred all around us.

CHAPTER 41

NATALIE

*T*hree days later, I stood in a garden in front of the Eiffel Tower, dressed in white. My feet were bare. My hair was free, blowing easily in the breeze off the Seine. I held a bouquet of wildflowers that I'd picked up from a local market along the way. The crown necklace at my throat. And Penn waited for me at the end of the small walk in a gray suit.

My heart beat a rhythmic drum inside my chest. Excitement and disbelief. Three days didn't seem like long enough to arrange all of this, but we'd done it. Officially, our elopement wasn't legally binding until we signed paperwork back home, but all that really mattered to me was the here and now. Symbolic or legal didn't matter because, soon, I would be *his*.

I didn't falter as I continued the remaining feet to stand before Penn and the officiant.

Penn's eyes lit up, and he seemed unable to help himself. He pulled me close and briefly kissed my lips. "You look beautiful."

"Thank you," I breathed with a smile.

I'd found the flowy bohemian dress tucked away inside the very first bridal shop I looked into. When it had fit—the straps perfectly molding to me, the soft lace wrapping around my waist like a cinch, and the material falling like a curtain to my feet—I had known it had been waiting for me all along.

Like fate.

Like us.

I reached forward and clasped hands with Penn as the officiant began the ceremony. I barely heard the words. My attention was trained on Penn. The look in his beautiful blue eyes as they stared down at me with all the love in his heart. Matching the expression I knew was on my face. I didn't see the crowd gathering on the public walkways to witness our little ceremony. Or hear the sounds of the city as our wedding melody.

Just me and Penn. Making a commitment and uniting our love. Binding us together from that moment on. A promise to have a love that endured beyond death.

"Vows aren't just words but represent the commitment you make with each other in marriage for all the years to come," the officiant said.

I swallowed and nodded. Penn grinned back.

"Do you, Natalie, take Penn to be your lawfully wedded husband, to have and to hold, from this day forward, for better or for worse, for richer or for poorer, in sickness and in health, to love and to cherish, till death do you part?"

"I do," I breathed.

"And do you, Penn, take Natalie…" the officiant began as tears sprang to my eyes, unbidden.

When the officiant finished, Penn confidently said, "I do."

"Now, for the rings," he said.

Penn retrieved the rings from his pocket and passed me his. I held it tightly as my hands shook. This was it. This was when it was so real. Holding his wedding band and making this promise between us.

"Now, Natalie, place the ring on Penn's finger and repeat after me," the officiant said.

I gulped and then moved forward, slipping the ring onto Penn's finger. I looked up at him in amazement at how easily the silver band fit him. How it looked like it had always been meant to be there.

"This ring is a token of my love," I said, repeating the officiant's vows. My eyes were stuck on Penn's blue ones. "I marry you with this ring, with all that I have and all that I am."

Penn's smile was wide as he slid my ring on my finger, where I planned to keep it for the rest of my life. "This ring is a token of my love," he repeated. "I marry you with this ring, with all that I have and all that I am."

"Having witnessed your vows, it's my honor to now pronounce you husband and wife. You may kiss the bride."

Penn reached across the divide and scooped me into his arms, pressing our lips together and sealing our union. I melded my body against him, feeling the secure weight of him. This was all I wanted. And I was somehow here against all odds. I'd feared that we were broken, but it turned out that we had come out even stronger on the other side. And I could feel every ounce of that in this one perfect kiss. Just like our first in front of the Eiffel Tower all those years ago.

A cheer rose up from our unwitting crowd. We laughed and broke free, smiling brightly at each other.

"I wasn't expecting a crowd," I admitted.

"That's our life."

I stood on my tiptoes and pressed another kiss to his lips. "As long as I'm with you, that's all that matters."

"You're mine."

"I am. And you're mine."

He winked at me and then shook hands with the officiant. "Thank you for your time on such short notice."

"Of course. Congratulations!" the officiant said. "Enjoy your honeymoon in Paris."

"We will," Penn said and then swept me up in his arms and carried me to the photographer who took picture after picture of us.

After another hour of pictures, we thanked the photographer as well and headed back to Penn's flat.

The last three nights, we'd spent in Penn's hotel room, as planned, before moving everything to his flat. He wanted our first night here to be as husband and wife. And I was jittery and excited to spend the night in his bed where I'd had my first time. In fact, that thought alone felt so surreal.

"Here we are," Penn said, turning the key and pushing the door open.

I stepped forward, but he stopped me.

"You can't deprive me of this."

He swept me up into his arms and carried me across the threshold.

"Oh my god, I love you."

He didn't put me down when we got inside. Instead, he kicked the door shut behind him and walked me straight back to the master suite. "I love you, too....wife."

I circled my arms around his neck and fiddled with his hair. My cheeks were rosy pink from his words and also because I was unbelievably happy. "Wife," I whispered.

"Oh, yes," he said, stepping into the room and laying me back against the center of the enormous bed. "My wife. Shall I call you Mrs. Kensington?"

I blushed even deeper. "Oh definitely, husband."

"Mmm," he muttered, taking the flowers from my hand and tossing them to the side. "Say it again."

"Husband," I breathed.

He assessed me. "How fond *are* you of that dress?"

"Why?"

"Because I'm considering shredding it to get to you."

I chuckled. "You don't think you're getting this off that quickly, do you?"

"Yes."

I stepped off the bed. "You owe me a dance."

"Do I?"

"Yes, and cake, I think, too."

"How about macarons and champagne?"

"Even better."

Penn disappeared for a few minutes and returned with a box of macarons and a bottle of Cristal. Music filtered in through the speakers, and I laughed.

"Ray LaMontagne's 'You Are the Best Thing,'" I said. "Good choice."

"He's a longtime favorite," Penn said, popping the champagne and pouring each of us a glass. "Plus, he was what we listened to that first night. Felt fitting."

"It's perfect."

He held his glass up, and I raised mine to his.

"To us, my love. For being lucky enough to find the love of our lives and stubborn enough to refuse to let go."

I chuckled at his words and nodded. "To us."

I sipped the champagne, stole a passion fruit macaron, and then moved into Penn's arms as the soft lyrics swept us away. Penn twirled me once in place as it came to a close and then dipped me with all the skill of someone who'd had too many ballroom dance lessons as part of his etiquette training.

Our lips met, and the song bled away into oblivion. His fingers found the bow at the back of my dress and slowly pulled it loose. The straps slipped off of my shoulders next. The long, billowy material caught on my hips once before being tugged down, down, down. Landing in a heap on the floor of the flat.

I reached for his jacket, tugging it off. Then his shirt. The dozen little buttons came out of their holes before he shrugged the material off of his muscular shoulders, letting it follow the jacket. His belt was next. A hiss sound escaped as he tugged it free of the loops. My fingers snapped the button and then the zipper, and then they made a pile with the rest of his clothes.

Until he stood in boxers and I stood in nothing but a white lace thong with the word *Mrs.* in jewels against my hip bone.

He grinned. "Oh, I like this."

He walked me backward toward the bed as he fingered the lacy material. The back of my knees hit the bed, and then he was sliding the thong over my hips and removing his boxers. He followed me like a predator as I crawled backward on the bed.

This time, I didn't mind being his prey.

"I like having firsts with you," he said, bringing our lips together again.

"You can have all the rest of my firsts."

"First and last," he said as he pushed forward into me.

My eyes slid closed, and I arched my back at the sweet feel of him. He was right. He had been my first. And god, I wanted him to be my last. Just like this. My husband. And me, his wife.

His arms came down on either side of me, caging me in, as he began to move. Our chests were pressed together. My legs holding him for dear life. My eyes fluttered open to stare up into his blue orbs that I'd made a vow to only hours earlier. He pressed one more kiss to my lips and picked up his pace.

There was no quick, heated intensity to our coupling. It was pure passionate desire. The knowledge of each other's body coming easily to us. The sex more than sex. It was making love in the most intimate of ways. Two hearts joining with the two heated bodies. Making a promise with actions as much as words. Completing the agreement we had just made to love one another forever.

And as we came apart, our bodies responded in kind. Reaching new heights. New depths. A new reality. This was more than we'd ever experienced. More than I had ever even known existed.

We lay back, panting and sated. The force of our consummation rippling between us and out into the universe and beyond.

Our fingers laced together. A silent declaration.

"I didn't know it could be like that," I whispered.

He tugged me closer. "I never knew any of it before you."

"This feels like a dream."

"Then I hope we never wake up."

I grinned. "I don't think even I could dream up something as amazing as you."

He laughed. "Probably not."

I scoffed at his cockiness. "It's lucky that I love you."

"It is," he agreed. "Come. Let's clean you up."

"Why? Aren't you going to just get me dirty again?"

He shot me a devilish smirk. "Absolutely."

I pressed my hand to his chest to keep him still for a moment before he dragged me off for what was clearly a barely veiled eagerness for shower sex. "What are we going to do when we leave here?"

"Do we have to decide today?"

"No," I said softly. "But…"

"Shh," he said, running his fingers through my hair. "Our future is simple. We trust in each other, and the rest will sort itself out."

"I wish we could stay here forever. *Can* we stay here forever?"

"Alas, no. I have work in the city," he reminded me. "But you know as well as I do that we can't escape who we are just by leaving the city."

I sighed. "You're right. Hiding out here won't solve everything."

"No. Trying to escape the Upper East Side is pointless. We have to trust each other and find a middle ground."

"*Is* there a middle ground?"

He nodded. "We don't have to be celebrities, Natalie.

We can just be us. No expectations. If anyone has a problem with that, then they don't matter. Okay?"

"It's never worked in the past," I reminded him.

He smirked and grasped my chin, pulling me in for a hot kiss. "This time, we're not running, and we're not playing the game. I don't want to rule Manhattan. And you don't need to be a star socialite. You can be Natalie, and I will be Penn. The rest we can figure out as we go."

"What about the crew?"

"I think you knocked them all down a peg or two, Nat. I have a feeling things will be different when we get back." His hand slid back into my hair. "Lewis and Katherine are tired of fighting. Rowe and Lark just want their friends back. We don't have to be the way we were before. We can be something new. No more secrets. No more lies. No more till-death loyalty."

"You mean…a truce," I muttered. But it made sense. That was exactly what I wanted. What I'd done and who I'd been was exhausting. It wasn't even me. And maybe I wasn't exactly the person I'd been before it all, but I wasn't going to go back to trying to be the new queen bee either. "A truce sounds nice."

"We'll work it out together."

"Together," I agreed and then kissed him one more time, giving in to that heated gaze.

I knew it wouldn't all be settled tomorrow or even the next day. The Upper East Side still waited. But I didn't fear it anymore. Nor did I have the raging desire to burn it down. In some way, it had become a part of me. A part of who I was as a person.

Just as much as Penn was. And together, I knew that we could not only survive it, but also come to find our own place in it. The in-between place that we'd both spent our entire lives looking for.

For him to be his own person. For me to finally belong.

And for us to have it all.

EPILOGUE

NATALIE—FOUR YEARS LATER

"Okay, okay," I grumbled, holding the bottle of Jefferson's Ocean above my head as I stepped into the living room of the Kensingtons' Hamptons mansion. "I have the requisite liquor. You can all chill the eff out now."

Penn snorted. He leaned against the door to the kitchen with his hands in his pockets, looking every bit the undeniable charmer I'd fallen for in that same position so many years earlier. "Like we still need to drink straight out of the bottle. I think we have enough glasses to pour it."

"But that's not tradition," Katherine drawled from her seat on the couch.

"Right. That's not tradition," I agreed.

It was bizarre as fuck to agree with Katherine. Even still, four years after our big blowup at the charity event.

When Penn and I had returned from our honeymoon in Paris, we'd been cajoled into a reception hosted by his mother. I was wary about the rest of the crew's attendance, but to be honest, it was the excuse I needed to talk to Katherine. It wasn't pleasant. In fact, it was downright nasty. But we'd called a shaky truce. One that held much better four years later than it'd ever had when we agreed to it.

"Gang up on me, why don't you?" Penn muttered.

Addie giggled and slipped into Lewis's lap. "That's kind of what we're here for."

Lewis wrapped his arms around Addie. "You should know that by now, man."

With Lewis, it had equally been worse and better than dealing with Katherine. He apologized for the stalking and what had happened leading to the denied restraining order. For there ever having been a reason for me to try to get one in the first place. But he blew a gasket when he found out that I'd been the one to turn him in for the investigation.

Still, I'd gotten it all out in the open. And thankfully, the worst had blown over with the company by the time we got back to the States. His mother had gone back to work as the UN ambassador, and Lewis had been allowed to stay at the company. But he decided it wasn't his passion, and with Addie's help, he found out what exactly that was. None of us had expected him to purchase a minor league baseball team and build the program up to unprecedented success.

I took the first drink of the bourbon and passed it to Katherine, who drank deeply.

"Phew," she said with a shake of her head. "That is the stuff."

She passed it to Rowe, who practically rolled his eyes

from behind his computer and passed it on to Penn. "Do you even know me at all?"

Katherine rolled her eyes. Lark just laughed as she entered the room and grabbed another chair. I'd grown to love Lark. She was no-nonsense. She'd found her own middle ground. And a guy who was perfect for her.

Which was more than I could say for Katherine. Somehow, she and Camden were still married. Though no one was sure if it was happily married or not. And we'd all decided it was none of our business.

"What?" Katherine grumbled, still holding the bottle out.

"Obviously, Rowe doesn't drink after people," Lark said.

"He drinks after Nicholas," Addie pointed out in a way only his twin could.

"That's my husband," Rowe said with a shrug.

"And where is your beau tonight?" Addie asked.

"Crew only," Katherine said emphatically.

"Then what about Natalie?" Addie added like she did every year.

Katherine's grin was wicked as she shrugged. "I guess Natalie is crew."

It wasn't the first time she'd said it or the first time that we'd had this conversation, but it still surprised me to hear it.

We weren't all close. Crew didn't hang out like they used to. But they didn't have to because Penn had been right. There was this in-between ground. Where he could be friends with them and not have them be his *only* friends. Our world had expanded.

We had dinners with his colleagues from work and

discussed philosophy theory I had no clue about. They'd thrown a party for him when his book finally released. And I'd put together another one after he got tenure.

I'd gone out on tour for my first literary novel publication and gotten a close-knit group of author friends who all lived in the city. We met up for girls' nights that didn't include backstabbing anyone. Sometimes, we didn't even get out of our sweats or brush our hair or even shower. But we'd have writing marathons. And their husbands *got it*, which meant Penn fit right in with their sighs about late-night writing sessions and thinking the characters were real.

I didn't think he could complain. The name on the book said *Natalie Kensington*. It was he who constantly brought me new inspiration. And he who always made this life worth living.

But even while we had this whole new, beautiful world, we still had the Upper East Side. And we still had the crew.

"Who wants to toast this year?" Lark asked as she sipped the bourbon and passed it to Addie.

"I do," Penn said, stepping forward.

Lewis downed a large quantity of the bourbon before passing it to me.

"Four years ago, we put our differences aside," Penn said. "We agreed to come to the Hamptons on Labor Day weekend to finally discuss what happened with Hanna and commemorate her life. Her death was horrible. Our part in it was worse. I'd give anything to go back and fix what we ruined. But we don't get a do-over. We can only go forward. So I'm glad that we're here again to pay our respects to Hanna Stratton. We can't make amends. But we can honor her memory."

Everyone reached for the drinks that they'd already gotten before I found our traditional bourbon. We raised our glasses to Hanna, as we had the last four years, a silent moment for the person that they'd hurt. To all the people we'd all hurt. And the life that we'd led to be those people.

We drank deep. Letting the past go. Moving on, but not forgetting.

It was a moment of bonding that was good for the entire party. We had our own lives now, but it was important to remember, so we didn't end up back in that same place.

When I'd washed up on the Hamptons, I'd never guessed that I could fall into this amazing, terrifying group. I'd palpably felt the bond between them. And this distant yearning had grown inside me. They had something— money, status, power—but it was more than that. They had the unshakable knowledge that they would always be there for each other. Their own type of family unit.

I hadn't understood it, even as I'd dived headfirst into it. I'd never had anything like it. Just me and Amy, which I'd always thought was enough. And somehow ... in my deception, I'd finally been accepted. At the moment when I was certain that it wasn't for me.

As we did every year, we found our way into the heated pool. They complained about Penn's music. Joked about Katherine being a bitch. Tried to coax Rowe out of his shell. We stayed up late into the night, reminiscing about our past and making all new memories.

And when everyone finally gave up to go to bed, Penn

took my hand and guided me down to the beach. The wind picked up as we approached the Atlantic. But we ignored it to stare up at the stars blanketing the night sky.

"There," I said, finding the crown and pointing out our constellation.

"Here." Penn fingered the crown around my neck, just like I had known he would.

Standing here with Penn each year felt like a new beginning.

A reaffirming that we'd done the right thing by eloping.

I was crew.

I was a Kensington.

I was just me.

The End

Love Natalie & Penn?
Get ready for a new second chance stand alone romance
with Lark and Sam in…

THE
LYING SEASON

Six years ago, Sam and I were on top of the world. We
won the campaign. Our dreams were in sight. Most
importantly, we had each other.

Then he lied.
And it all fell apart.

Now, he's back in New York City.
Working on the mayor's reelection with me.
And it all feels so familiar.

Except for his fiancé waiting in the wings.

And I should know better.

Coming January 28th!
Preorder everywhere now!

ACKNOWLEDGMENTS

Thank you to everyone who helped make the Cruel series possible. It was quite an adventure bringing their story to life and incorporating so much inspiration from the classic novels that I love. I hope you enjoyed Penn & Natalie's journey, and if so, would leave a review!

I can't wait to bring you the next wild adventure on the Upper East Side with *The Lying Season*, a sexy second chance stand alone romance!

ABOUT THE AUTHOR

K.A. Linde is the *USA Today* bestselling author of the Avoiding Series, Wrights, and more than thirty other novels. She has a Masters degree in political science from the University of Georgia, was the head campaign worker for the 2012 presidential campaign at the University of North Carolina at Chapel Hill, and served as the head coach of the Duke University dance team.

She loves reading fantasy novels, binge-watching Supernatural, traveling to far off destination, baking insane desserts, and dancing in her spare time.

She currently lives in Lubbock, Texas, with her husband and two super-adorable puppies.

www.kalinde.com

For exclusive content, free books, and giveaways every month.
www.kalinde.com/subscribe